Take Me with You

By K.A. Linde

Cover Designer: Najla Qamber Design

Editor and Interior Designer: Jovana Shirley, Unforeseen Editing, www.unforeseenediting.com

Visit my website at http://www.kalinde.com

ISBN: 978-0996053037

Other Titles by **K.A. Linde**

Avoiding Series

Record Series

Take Me Series

Contents

1 GRANT

I'd never given much thought to falling in love.

For someone like me, it'd seemed like an impossibility. Why dwell on something that would never happen? I'd had no interest in chicks for more than what they could give me in one night. *Fuck 'em and then show 'em the door.*

There were always clinger groupies, who would claim to love me. But they loved what I could offer them—sex, a one-night stand, a story to tell their friends about how they'd slept with a rocker, with Grant McDermott.

I was a name.

A symbol.

Nothing more.

My eyes slid over to the blonde sleeping in my bed. I brushed a strand of hair out of her mouth and pressed a kiss to her lips.

That was before Ari.

"Grant?" she whispered in her sleep.

My name on her lips was better than a thousand one-night stands.

I'd almost lost her to a whole lot of stupidity. Some groupie slut, Kristin, had come on to me at the ski lodge where my band, ContraBand, was playing the Poconos music festival. And by *come on to me*, I meant she had stripped down naked in my room and ambushed me, thinking I'd fuck her desperate ass. Ari had walked in, and all hell had broken loose.

After a month of miscommunication over Christmas break, we'd reconnected on the shore at my uncle's beachside pizza place, Duffie's.

The past two weeks, we'd been pretending that nothing had happened, but I knew something was brewing behind her big blue eyes.

"Yeah, Princess?" I said, sliding my body against hers. My hand ran over the dip in her waist and down to the curve of her tight ass. I tugged her closer to me, rocking her against my dick.

"Mmm," she groaned. Her eyes fluttered open. "Again?" Her voice held groggy disbelief.

Ari really hadn't believed me when I said my appetite was insatiable. I could fuck her all day long, and it wouldn't be enough. I'd still want more. Sex had been my escape for too long for me to ignore the pull now that the same person was frequenting my bed.

"Again," I agreed.

I rolled her onto her back and kissed my way down her front—between her breasts, over her soft stomach that often made her self-conscious from my attention, to her hip bones that peeked out from her cotton underwear, and down between her legs. My breath came out hot and urgent as I blew on her through the material. She whimpered and writhed in my grasp.

"Grant...Grant." Her words were a moan, an encouragement.

My fingers hooked under the elastic and pulled them off. She stiffened beneath me and pushed herself up to the top of the bed. I reached for her, but she shook her head.

"I have class." Ari looked at the comforter, the desk, my cherry red guitar—anywhere but at me.

"Not for an hour."

"I need to shower and change."

"I can take you," I insisted.

"Don't worry about it." She slid off the bed and shrugged on her jeans. "Don't you have to work at the recording studio today?"

I'd gotten a job working at a studio in Trenton when I wanted to show Ari that I was serious about something other than playing in a band. Her dad was the CEO of a bank in Boston, and I'd never seen money like that before. I couldn't give her that, but I wanted to.

"Yeah. Later."

I wanted to throw her down on the bed and fuck her until she stopped suggesting ways to keep us apart. But I couldn't finesse my way into that—at least not with Ari. She would call me on my bullshit.

"Okay. Well, I'll see you after work then," she said, sidestepping the issue.

She threw her cardigan back on, tossed my old man's dog tags over her head that I'd given to her last semester when I asked her to be my girlfriend, gave me a peck on the lips, and then dashed out of the room.

I crashed back into bed and stared up at the blank ceiling. I didn't fucking understand what had just happened. I had my fucking girlfriend back. We were fucking together all the fucking time.

Yet I felt like the pussy getting ditched after a one-night stand.

I roughly slammed my hands down on the steering wheel of my BMW. *What the hell was wrong with me?*

I couldn't believe I'd run out of Grant's bedroom like a crazy person. I *wanted* to sleep with him. I *wanted* to be with him. But I had been acting like a total idiot, and if he hadn't already noticed, then he certainly had after that spectacular performance.

Unlike most people my age, I actually knew who I was, and I'd never pretended to be anyone but myself in a relationship. Not everyone liked that I wasn't afraid to speak my mind, and I didn't need someone else for my own personal validation.

Then, Grant McDermott had walked into my life.

He loved everything about me that intimidated other guys. He'd push back when I tried to pull away. He fought for me and sacrificed for me and…loved me.

And lately, all I could think about were the million logical reasons that we would never work, like the fact that ContraBand had been selling an insane number of copies of their new single, "Life Raft"—a song Grant had written for me last semester. They weren't hitting the *Billboard* charts, but I saw fame on the horizon even if Grant acted as if he didn't. As much as that excited me, it also terrified me. I couldn't think about losing him.

Not to mention, there was the scary fact that his dad was about to get out of prison where he had resided for the last thirteen years after murdering Grant's mom in front of him.

On top of that, we'd never really *talked* about what had happened over Christmas break when we were apart. We'd both swept it all under the rug, assuming it was fine now since we'd slept together, but there was still so much we needed to address, so we could move forward and trust each other. Our month apart had been a reality check that things weren't always going to be perfect between us, and after we'd gotten back together, it was easier to ignore that than to face it head-on.

Plus, I still hadn't even told him about Henry, the guy who worked for my father. My parents had tried setting me up with him, and he had kissed me while I was drunk one night in Boston. It had only happened because I thought that Grant had slept with some groupie slut on New Year's. But still…he didn't know about it, and this would never work out if we couldn't be honest.

I shuddered. The last person I wanted to think about was Henry.

Parking at the apartment that I shared with my three crazy roommates—Cheyenne, Gabi, and Shelby—I bounded up the stairs and went inside. Since Grant and I had gotten back together three weeks ago, I hadn't been home this early in the morning. I usually kept a change of clothes at his place and would leave for campus from there. Staring at my roommates' surprised faces after I'd barreled through the door, I could see they thought three weeks seemed more like a year.

"What are you doing home?" Cheyenne asked. She flipped her crazy red hair over one shoulder and cocked an eyebrow. "Shouldn't you be in the throes of passion or whatever?"

I rolled my eyes and kept walking toward my room. "What? Just because I'm home early one morning, I haven't been in the throes of passion? Jeez, I don't see you and Vin together every morning."

"Whoa! Chill. Vin and I aren't even dating."

"That's because he's a douche bag." I pushed open the door to my room and leaned against the doorframe, waiting to see Cheyenne's response.

Cheyenne shrugged. "Well, yeah."

"Would the both of you shut it?" Shelby asked. "This feels like last semester all over again with you two bickering like an old married couple."

"We do not!" I said defensively.

"She doesn't like to give us the goods," Cheyenne complained.

Shelby looked at Gabi for backup, but she had her nose buried in her laptop while dripping milk from her cereal onto the table.

"Gab?"

"Oh. Huh?" Gabi asked.

"Never mind," Shelby said.

"You guys can't sit there and act like you don't want to know what's going on with them." Cheyenne threw her hand out at me.

"Actually, since she's never home, I assume that the sex is pretty amazing," Gabi said, looking at her computer screen.

"I never thought she'd be the one to go from proud holder of her V-card to sexpot living at her boyfriend's house in a matter of a couple of weeks."

I huffed at Cheyenne's comment. "I'm still standing *right* here."

I hadn't even considered what my roommates might be saying about me while I was away. I knew that I'd made a drastic change in my life by agreeing to date Grant, but I'd thought they would be happy for me. Maybe they were, and this was their backward way of showing it.

"Anyway, I have to get ready for class."

I disappeared into my room and changed into a purple V-neck sweater and jeans. Instead of taking the time to straighten my hair, I pulled it up into a tight ponytail at the nape of my neck. After applying some mascara and baby-pink lip gloss, I made a hasty retreat.

"You know," Cheyenne said when I walked back into the living room.

"No, I don't."

"You'd think you'd be in a better mood with how often you're getting laid."

I slung my backpack over my shoulder. "I probably would be if you stopped badgering me about it."

"Yeah, Cheyenne. If she wanted to tell you how big Grant's dick was, she probably would have already," Shelby cut in.

"Grant would probably show you before I'd tell you," I said, crossing my arms over my chest.

"Noted," Cheyenne said with a wink.

"Cheyenne!" Shelby cried. "You're not going to ask Grant to show you his dick."

"You're right. That doesn't sound like me at all." Sarcasm dripped out of every word.

Laughter bubbled up out of me. I couldn't help it. I'd been on edge all morning, and now, I was clearly losing my mind. I was sure that it all had something to do with my crazy course load and the issues with Grant. I wished I knew why Grant and I couldn't work out our problems. When we had gotten back together on the beach, I'd thought the worst was over, but I had a feeling that the worst was yet to come.

3 GRANT

"Dude, I got that track from last week," Corey called out.

His hair was spiked up into a fauxhawk with a backward trucker hat resting about halfway back on his head. He wore black shades at all times, even in the studio, and alternated between different colored deep V-neck T-shirts underneath loose plaid button-ups.

I'd been working for Corey for almost two months now, and I still didn't know what to make of him. The guy was a genius in the studio, but his social skills were limited to which obscure band he was into that week.

"Can I listen to it?"

Corey shrugged. "Yeah, man."

He fiddled with the controls as I walked into the sound room and crashed back into one of the plush leather armchairs. A few seconds later, "Life Raft" filtered in through the speakers. I sat forward in the chair as the guitar riff picked up, and I belted out the first verse.

It was...*perfect*.

Our shit demo that thousands of people had listened to was nothing compared to this version. A real studio made a hell of a lot of difference. That fucking meant I'd get *the talk* from Miller again today at rehearsal.

I hadn't told Ari yet, but Hollis—the Pacific Entertainment manager for the popular rock band, The Drift—had called Miller to try to recruit us. This was despite the fact that I'd managed to piss off Hollis after storming off stage on New Year's Eve before proceeding to get into a fistfight with Donovan Jenkins, the lead singer of The Drift.

Apparently, the success of "Life Raft" had jolted ContraBand into the spotlight, but part of me didn't want it to be a reality. I fucking liked waking up to my beautiful blonde every morning, going to the studio, and playing local gigs. But the guys weren't content with playing at The Ivy League, a local Princeton bar, and I knew they weren't fucking going anywhere without me.

"This is the fucking shit. Can you send it to me?"

Corey nodded. "I had extra time."

He popped a disc out of the network of computers, dropped it into a case, and passed it over to me. It had a black cover with the band name, *ContraBand*, slashed across the front in lime green. The words *Life Raft EP* were scrawled underneath.

"EP?"

"I couldn't get 'Hemorrhage' out of my head, so I put together the other tracks you were working on."

"Fuck, man. Thanks." I reached my hand out and shook Corey's.

"Sure thing. Just get me tickets to Madison Square Garden when you guys make it."

I laughed. *Madison Square Garden. Yeah, right.* "Will do."

Once I reached my blue truck, I stuck the CD into the player and listened to our music on the drive home. Corey deserved a fucking medal for this shit. Every song was flawless, so clear and crisp.

It was exactly what I'd needed after Ari's mad dash out of my apartment this morning. Work had kept me from thinking about her, but "Life Raft" was her song. I couldn't keep my mind off of her with those lyrics pouring through the speakers.

I'd never been in a relationship before, so this was all new to me, but chicks didn't run away from me. I knew we had issues we still had to deal with from before Christmas break, but something with her wasn't right, and she was going to fucking tell me what the problem was.

"Hey, dipshit," I said when I walked through the garage door at my place.

I smacked Vin on the back of his head and veered toward the sound system.

"Fucker!" Vin shot back. "Where the fuck have you been all damn day?"

"At work. Where the fuck do you think I've been?"

"Following around your piece of ass like a whipped motherfucker."

"What did you say about Ari?" I growled, taking two steps toward Vin.

Miller intervened, "Can we go two days without you two at each other's throats?"

Vin glared at Miller and crashed back into the couch. He still hadn't gotten over the fact that Miller had hooked up with my cousin, Sydney, at the ski lodge the weekend we'd performed at the Poconos music festival. Vin had taken Syd's virginity in high school and acted as if he had some claim over her. The truth was, she was even more of a slut than I had been before Ari, and that was fucking saying something.

McAvoy walked into the room a minute later, surveyed what was going on, and then reached for a joint. "I'm probably going to need this, aren't I?"

I ignored them and inserted the EP into our stereo. "Just listen to this."

The music blasted through our sound system. McAvoy slowly put the joint back behind his ear, Vin leaned forward in his seat, and Miller's jaw dropped open.

"Is that us?" Miller asked.

"No. I gave someone else the rights to our songs."

"We sound fucking killer!" Vin cheered.

"Corey put together an entire EP for us."

We spent the next twenty minutes of practice listening to the recordings. We had put them together to ensure we'd look more professional if Pacific lost interest.

Except Pacific hadn't lost interest—as much as I wanted them to.

"Hey, have you heard from Pacific lately?" I fucking hated saying Hollis's name. The guy was an asshole who had preyed on my relationship with Ari. He would have to figure out his place with us before I'd even consider signing with them.

"Hollis sent me the final deets about The Drift tour. He wants us to meet him at the NYC kickoff," Miller said.

"He wants us to fucking hang out with Donovan and his shit bandmates?" I stood and stopped the track that was playing.

"Bro," Miller said, "be glad that he wants to see us at all after what went down with Donovan."

"The motherfucker deserved it for what he did to Ari."

Signing with Hollis was one thing, but the thought of being around Donovan Jenkins made my blood boil. That asshole had kissed Ari and insinuated that he'd fucked her. It was one thing to want us broken up, but it was another to actually act on it.

"Where is Ari anyway?" Miller asked.

That was a good fucking question. Normally, we'd already be a half hour into rehearsal and working on perfecting the new song I'd dropped on Miller last week. Ari hadn't missed a rehearsal since we got back together. She might be lost in a mountain of chemistry homework on the weathered couch, but she would still be *here*.

I was used to singing "Life Raft" to my life raft.

So, where the hell was she?

Incoming call: Grant McDermott

I bit my lip and then silenced my phone. I couldn't talk to him right now, not here. I'd thought I would have been done with this already and then on my way to band rehearsal like normal. Everything had run over, and I didn't want to tell Grant that I'd come here.

I glanced around the examination room and then swallowed hard. I couldn't keep my feet from tapping anxiously on the linoleum tiles as I waited for the doctor to come back. I couldn't believe I was even here right now.

Incoming call: Grant McDermott

God, can't you give me a minute, Grant? I deliberately ended the call that time. Maybe he would get the picture.

Knock, knock.

The door cracked open. "Aribel," the doctor said.

"Hi," I said softly.

The doctor closed the door behind her and took a seat on the rolling stool next to the computer. "Well, you're not pregnant."

I sagged forward in the seat. That was so good to hear. I hadn't missed a period or anything, but even with condoms, accidents could happen.

"The rest of the tests will come in later this week. A nurse will give you a call to let you know the results. Here's your prescription." The doctor handed over a piece of paper. "If you're still concerned about anything, feel free to give me a call at anytime. I still suggest sending the young man you're seeing over for peace of mind."

"I'll take that into consideration. Thank you." I folded the piece of paper in half and stuck it into my purse with a sigh.

"Just check out at the front desk before you leave."

"Thank you again," I said before hurrying out of the office.

As soon as I exited the office, I pulled my phone back out. My finger hovered over the spot to give Grant a call back. I should have told him about coming here, but I hadn't wanted to freak him out over nothing. I still didn't want to freak him out.

"Ugh!" I exited out of the screen and dialed my brother's number instead.

"Aribel?" he answered.

"Hey, Aaron."

"What's up?"

"Just having a slight mental breakdown, and I needed to talk to my big brother."

"*You're* having a mental breakdown?" he asked in disbelief. "What? Is O-chem causing you problems?"

I laughed hollowly. "No. School is fine. It's more…guy-related."

"I see. Well, this is a first. My little sister is all grown-up." He chuckled softly.

"This isn't a joke, Aaron! I just left the doctor!"

"What? What happened? Are you pregnant?" He sounded pissed.

"No! Christ, Aaron, no," I said, flustered. I hadn't meant for this conversation to happen this way. I opened the door to my BMW and sank into the driver's side. "I don't know how to be this girl."

"What kind of girl?"

"Look…I don't even know what I'm saying. I really like this guy." No way was I about to directly tell him about Grant. He wouldn't understand why I was dating someone like Grant. "But being with him terrifies me. Have you ever been in that kind of situation?"

"Sure. I know what you mean. You're in love, kiddo."

I threw my head back onto the headrest and closed my eyes. Maybe that was all it was. Maybe I was just in love and scared. "We had an argument a couple of weeks ago, and now, I feel as if we're trying to pretend nothing happened."

"Aribel, calm down. It'll be fine. You don't have to tiptoe around me. I know what happened with Henry over break. I'm sure it will be fine."

"With Henry?" I asked, sitting up straight.

"Yeah, when you left Le Petit Parlor," he said, referencing the bar we had gone to after the New Year. "He's a good guy for you. Don't let one argument get in the way."

"I…"

"I've got to get back to work, Aribel. If it's about Henry, then don't worry. You guys were meant to be together. I wouldn't be surprised if Mom is already planning your wedding." He laughed again. "See you, sis."

The line went dead in my hand, and I stared down at it in shock. *Aaron thought that I had slept with Henry? And that we were now dating?*

Ugh! Not good.

This afternoon had gone from bad to worse in the span of one conversation.

"She sent me to fucking voice mail!" I threw the phone onto the couch and stormed over to my guitar.

"Maybe she's busy," Miller suggested.

"She's been acting fucked up all day—no, all week. Let's just play." I threw my guitar over my head and mechanically tuned her.

"That's what you get when you deal with uptight pussy," Vin said.

I didn't even have the energy to fight him on that. I couldn't figure out what Ari's fucking deal was. She had never struck me as the kind of girl who would sneak around and avoid me. My favorite thing about her was her fucking mouth. She wasn't afraid to say the shit that everyone else held back. She couldn't start acting like every other chick, or I was going to lose it.

"This might not be the best time, but—" Miller started.

"Then, save it," I growled. "We've already lost most of rehearsal."

Miller glanced between McAvoy and Vin. McAvoy shrugged, and Vin just looked irritated. Vin needed to keep his stupid mouth shut. Nothing good ever came from a conversation with him.

"Bro, we need to talk about meeting up with Hollis," Miller continued.

"I don't want to talk about Hollis right now."

"We need to get serious about what is going to happen. If you don't have your head on straight about this, then we need to know now." Miller crossed his arms over his chest.

As a united front, he stood with McAvoy and Vin.

"Chill, Miller. Grant's in. He's always been in," McAvoy said. "Look what he did with the EP."

"Are you fuckers forgetting the time he said that he didn't even want to get signed?" Vin asked. "I didn't fucking forget."

I slid my hand back through my hair and cursed under my breath. "I explained that shit, and I'm in. Just don't say anything to Ari about it yet."

"How can we? She's not fucking here," Vin said.

My eyes traveled around the garage, and I gritted my teeth. No, she wasn't. "Thanks for reminding me, asshole. Now, can we play?"

The guys didn't argue with me as they picked up their instruments and began playing our regular set. Breathing heavily, I opened a bottle of water and guzzled it before we got to work on the new song I'd given to Miller last week. "Life Raft" was the first song I'd ever written for the band, but with the way things had been going with Ari, I'd been incredibly inspired to put pen to paper. Now hearing the words I'd written about us made my anger simmer until it was boiling over. The fifth time through "White Hot" did me in.

"Fuck this. I can't play this shit anymore." I removed my guitar strap and thrust my cherry red Gibson back onto her rack.

I didn't miss the glance that Miller and McAvoy shared before agreeing we should take a break.

"If you have something to say, why don't you just say it?"

McAvoy shrugged. "You're acting like an asshole."

"What else is new?"

"Normally, I'd say let's go get fucked up and find you some ass to make it all better, but…" Miller said.

"But what? Let's go." I grabbed my jacket and headed to the door. "I'll drive."

The guys followed me out without complaint. Even if they had one, I didn't want to hear it. I didn't care that I was acting like an asshole. I'd been in a shitty mood all day. I'd thought that the EP and rehearsal would have helped things, but it hadn't. So, now, I was going to go back to things I knew worked for numbing the pain and dousing the anger.

We walked into The Ivy League and grabbed a table in front of the empty stage. A hot waitress sauntered over to our table with a round of beers. Her tits bounced in her tight white tank top.

"Hey, guys. My name is Kat, and I'm new here."

Vin chuckled behind me. "Pussy."

I cracked a smile, and she blushed deep red.

"I, uh…brought you these from Hurst." She leaned over and placed beers in front of us.

"Thanks, Kat," I said, reaching for my beer.

She pushed her dark brown bangs out of her eyes. "You're Grant McDermott, right?"

"The one and only."

"I *love* your music," she crooned.

"Well, why don't you pull up a chair and tell us all about it, pussycat?" Vin said. He raised both his eyebrows at her.

"Pussycat," she mumbled. "I've never heard that one before."

"Ignore Vin. He's a five-year-old stuck in a 'roided-out body," Miller said.

Kat giggled and leaned her hip into my chair. She had on this skimpy little skirt, and all I could think about was how a couple of months ago, I would have grabbed her by her waist, tugged her onto my lap, and found my way up that skirt.

But somehow, I couldn't harness that feeling. All I could see was that her hair was the wrong shade, her lips were too full, her eyes were too brown. She just wasn't Ari.

I stood abruptly, forcing Kat to take a step away from me. "I've got to take a piss. Here, Miller will take care of you." I pushed the girl onto Miller's lap and then left the table.

I skipped the public restrooms and walked backstage. Hurst, the owner, was lounging in the back room. I nodded at him.

"Grant, my man!" he called, jumping up. "When am I going to get you guys back in here? Are you too big to play my venue?"

We slapped hands together, leaned in, and clapped each other on the back.

"I'm never too big for The League, Hurst. I'd play tonight if I had my guitar."

"You don't bring it with you everywhere?"

"Not tonight."

"Where's your girl anyway? Isn't she the other thing you bring with you everywhere?" Hurst asked.

I shrugged noncommittally. I didn't want to talk about Ari. "No idea. I'm here for the booze."

Hurst nodded his head. "Trouble in paradise. I've got just the thing."

I followed Hurst out of the back room and to the bar where he fixed us a couple of shots. After three or four, I felt a thousand times better than I had earlier. *Why had I decided to let up on the drinking anyway?* I could drink and have a girlfriend. It wasn't like Ari didn't drink, and I could control myself.

It was just that when I was drinking…I didn't want control.

I wanted another drink.

A smile split my face as I poured alcohol down my throat. It was a welcome reprieve from thinking. I'd given up that shit when my dad went to jail. And just because he was coming back and Ari was acting like someone else didn't mean that had to change. I could fucking forget everything all over again.

I stumbled back over to the guys as a band took to the stage. It was some chick singer with four guys playing instruments. Normally, I didn't dig chick bands, but then she picked up a fucking badass seafoam-green Fender guitar. Her fingers played across the strings like the guitar was an extension of her body. I understood that right there.

"Hey Kitty Kat," I called. "Get us another round, will ya?"

"You haven't even had your first one," McAvoy pointed out.

"I found Hurst."

"Ah," McAvoy said as if that explained everything.

"Um...beer?" Kat asked, skirting around the table toward me.

I slung an arm around her and pulled her closer. "How about something a little stronger?"

"Anything you want," she murmured, fluttering her eyelashes. She slid a piece of paper into the front pocket of my jeans. "I get off at two."

"Whiskey. Make mine a double." I released her and fell back into my abandoned seat.

"Bro, you think that's a good idea?" Miller asked, eyeing the piece of paper I pulled out of my pocket.

"I was fucking moving in on the little pussycat while you were gone," Vin sulked behind me.

I tossed him the paper. "Have at it."

Miller looked relieved and seemed to relax for the first time tonight.

"Hey, everyone! I'm Killian, and we're Bank Avenue. Thanks so much for having us out tonight."

The crowd at The Ivy League applauded softly, except for a group near the front. They went crazy. Likely, they were people the band had brought with them.

But once they started playing, I couldn't figure out why they didn't have a large entourage.

"Hey, McAvoy, send out a blast, saying we're at the League tonight."

"But we're not playing," he said. His eyebrows knit together.

"The drinks are flowing. The music is really fucking good. I want *our* crowd," I said, sinking back into my chair. "Make it happen."

6 — Aribel

"Grant, sorry I missed your calls earlier. I got stuck at school and just got home. Call me when you get this."

I ended the voice mail and frowned down at my iPhone. It was strange for Grant not to answer my calls. That was the third one in a row.

After I'd spoken to Aaron and calmed down, I'd realized that I was overreacting. And some of his advice sank in. Maybe I was just in love and scared about what that meant. I had never been in this position before.

I'd treated love like my chemistry homework. Every equation had an answer, and when combined properly created a fixed outcome. But there were no fixed outcomes with Grant. There wasn't even an equation. It was just a whole lot of insanity.

I didn't want to be afraid of it, but in my world, nothing changed, and Grant was an unbelievable amount of change. When I had lived at home in Boston, I'd thought that I was stifled in such a controlled environment, and maybe a part of me had been. However, living in a world without any control wasn't exactly me either.

The only thing I really knew was that I needed to talk to Grant and figure everything out. Grant got my blood boiling, raised my heart rate, and ignited passion within myself that I hadn't known existed under my cool exterior.

I didn't want to lose that. I didn't want to lose him. And I needed to lay it all out there like I always did. Either he accepted me, or he didn't. I lived life, freaking out over whether or not Grant would fit into my world and whether or not I'd fit into his. On so many levels, we already did.

Cheyenne appeared a couple of minutes later in a skintight black dress and stilettos with all her curly red hair piled on top of her head. "Hey, why aren't you dressed?" she asked.

"What do you mean?" I asked. "Why are you so dressed up?"

"Didn't you get the memo? The guys are at the League."

I scrunched my eyebrows together. "They don't have a show tonight."

"Well, they blasted all over social media that they're there and want all their fans to come down for the show for some Bank Avenue group."

"I've never heard of them." I entered the name into Google. There weren't many hits, but I found a small website that showed the band. "Oh Jesus."

"What?" Cheyenne came around and glanced over my shoulder. "Oh."

The lead singer was smoking hot. She had pixie-cut black hair and exotic almond-shaped eyes. In the picture, she had on black leather pants and a tiny lace bra with electric-blue high heels.

"Now, why would the guys want to go to see Bank Avenue and have all of their followers see them?" I asked.

"Someone wants to fuck that girl."

We glanced at each other, and Cheyenne sighed. "Come on. I'll do your makeup."

Ten minutes later, I was in a blue strapless dress that Cheyenne had insisted on. She was coating my face in products. I'd drawn the line at her messing with my hair. I wasn't going to the League to party. I was going to find out what the fuck was going on with my boyfriend. I knew that I'd been off, but that didn't mean he had a free pass. We'd been there before. He should know better.

"Are you sure I can't do something to your hair?" Cheyenne asked.

She brushed her fingers through it, and I swatted her hand away.

"Let's just go. Who knows what kind of debauchery they've gotten into already?"

"All right, Aribel." Cheyenne stepped back and knocked into my purse.

It fell over onto the floor and spilled the contents, including the prescription birth control I had picked up earlier from the pharmacy.

Cheyenne's eyebrows rose as she picked up the packet of pills. "Whoa. Things are serious, aren't they?"

I snatched the prescription out of her hand and stuffed it into a drawer, out of sight. "Forget you saw that." I quickly scooped up everything else on the floor and threw it back in my bag.

"What? It's just the pill. I've been on it since I was sixteen."

"Well, I'm not you, and I haven't told Grant. So, forget about it."

Cheyenne laughed. "Whatever you want, but I think he'll be excited. Then, you won't have to use a condom."

I blanched.

Her laugh turned into a cackle. "Oh, my sweet, innocent Aribel."

"Leave me alone, Cheyenne." I stuck my finger in her face. "And don't say a word."

She mimed zipping her lips. Her eyes twinkled with delight. She loved taunting me about this shit. I grabbed my purse, and we left the apartment. We got into Cheyenne's car, and she zoomed toward the League.

"Where are Gabi and Shelby anyway?" I asked.

Cheyenne shrugged. "Studying, I think. If I know them though, they're probably ditching the library and on their way to see the guys. No one ignores an SOS."

I sulked further into the seat. It was no wonder Grant was ignoring my calls. *How many groupies was I about to walk through to get to him?*

Another thought nagged at me. *What would happen if they got signed and went on tour?* He'd have all his vices around him all the time. I wanted to trust Grant, but everyone had limits with the amount of temptation surrounding them.

"Girl, I can see the worry all over your face. Just relax. Grant's crazy about you. I'm sure it's fine."

"He hasn't returned my messages today," I whispered.

"Probably because he was out with the guys and didn't hear his phone. Don't think the worst until we find out what's going on."

I narrowed my eyes. "Since when did you become the sensible one?"

"As soon as you fell in love with Grant McDermott of all people."

"Yeah. What was I thinking?" I asked.

"Best sex you ever had?"

I glared at her. "Honestly?"

"Oh, right—the only sex you've ever had."

"Don't fault me because I'm not a whore like you, Cheyenne."

She shrugged her shoulders and smirked as she pulled into the League parking lot. "We can't all have such high aspirations as me."

"Oh, is that what you call it?"

"So, I like rock-star dick. I don't see *you* complaining."

"No complaints here," I grumbled. No complaints about the sex at least. Just all the complications that came with it.

The parking lot was packed full. Cheyenne finally found a spot on the street a couple of blocks down, and we walked the short trek back to the bar. I braced myself for pandemonium before following Cheyenne through the door.

The League looked like every other night when ContraBand was in the house. Female bodies filled more than three-quarters of the room, and there was a crowd of screaming people by the stage. Cheyenne grabbed my hand as she elbowed her way through the crowd. We stopped once we reached the table where Miller, McAvoy, and Vin sat, staring up at the stage with shit-eating grins on their faces.

Where the hell was Grant if all the guys were here? My eyes traveled away from the table and up to the stage. My heart sank.

The entire time I'd been getting through the crowd, I hadn't truly paid attention to what was going on. I knew Bank Avenue was playing. I knew the lead singer was gorgeous. But I hadn't anticipated *this*.

Grant was on the stage, holding a microphone in his hand, singing with the lead singer of Bank Avenue. No, he was singing *to* the lead singer.

And not just any song...*my* song.

My hand fell onto the back of Miller's chair as ice filled my veins. *What the fuck was happening?*

"Shit, Ari," Miller cried over the music. He stood abruptly. "This is *not* what it looks like."

I threw my hand up in the air. "Save it."

He opened his mouth as if he wanted to say something more, but it was good for him that he realized it was a lost cause.

All I could do was stare as my boyfriend serenaded another woman with the song he had written for me. Cold fury took over, and rational thought fled my mind. The only thing that was there was Grant standing on stage in my favorite pair of his jeans and a black button-up, the sleeves rolled up to his elbows. His hair was perfectly tousled. His expression had the serenity that always took over when he got lost in his music.

Then, his eyes flickered open at the end of the second verse, and he stared straight ahead at the skinny bitch in an outfit much the same as I had found on the band's website.

The chorus seemed to play over and over again. Their harmony blended together as if they had done this before.

Every time I see you. You make me feel better.

Every single day. You push away the pain.
You push away the memories.
You're my life raft. In an endless ocean.
You saved me from drowning.
You saved me from myself.
You're my life raft. In an endless ocean.

I waited there, paralyzed, until the end. The crowd erupted into cheers. Grant cracked a confident smile, looking out across the room at his many admirers. I knew the instant his eyes landed on me, and I could read his lips all the way across the bar.

Oh fuck.

"Oh fuck."

Ari's face in the crowd silenced the cheers. Even through my buzz, I wasn't stupid enough to have wanted her to see that.

Thanks, I mouthed to Killian.

She winked at me and said something else, but I shoved the microphone in her face and jumped off the stage. The crowd was unyielding as I attempted to reach Ari.

"Fucking fuck," I grumbled under my breath.

I nearly knocked someone down while trying to get to her.

Her icy glare should have stopped me in my tracks, but I barreled right through the protective wall she had put between us. I grabbed her around the middle and pulled her against my chest. She smelled fucking amazing.

Fuck. I just wanted to take her home and forget this day had ever happened.

"Let's go home," I said into her ear.

She yanked herself from my grasp and crossed her arms.

"Great show, man!" one person said, clapping me on the back as he walked by.

I nodded at him, but I kept my focus on Ari. She hadn't said shit yet.

A series of interruptions kept us from speaking.

"That was amazing," one groupie said.

"Oh my God, you guys should sing it like that all the time."

"That's the best I've ever heard it."

I ground my teeth and tried to block it out. "Come on. Let's get out of here."

She continued to glare at me as if I were the only fucking person in the room who had done something wrong. *Why was she up on her fucking high horse when she was the one who had pushed me away this morning?* She had things to account for, too.

I roughly grabbed her by the arm and hauled her toward the entrance. She gasped and tried to pull away, but I held on to her tight. If she wasn't going to speak up, then she'd have to deal with this.

As soon as we stepped out of The Ivy League, Ari wrenched her arm free from me and walked around to the side of the building. I pursued her.

"What the fuck is your problem?" I demanded.

She turned around, crossed her arms, and stared at me. She just fucking stared at me. I could see she was seething. It was all bubbling up under the surface.

"The cold shoulder? You're not going to fucking say anything?"

Ari turned her head to the side, looking out toward the parking lot.

"Okay, fine. You know what? Don't say anything. I have enough to say for the both of us," I spat at her. "I thought we were over all this shit. I've never been in a fucking relationship, but I can pretty much guarantee that it's not supposed to work this way. You're acting like a fucking crazy person, Princess. If I wanted to fuck around, I'd be banging every girl in the League tonight."

"That's good to know," she ground out.

"But I'm not. I was fucking pissed tonight. I came here to get wasted. I wanted a distraction after you didn't fucking pick up your goddamn phone."

She turned her head back toward me. "Will you always need a distraction when one day doesn't go as planned?"

"I'm not a fucking saint, Princess. You knew that when you signed up for this. I play in a fucking rock band. Girls throw themselves at me left and right, but not a single one of them compares to you." I ran my hand along her jawline and up into her messy blonde hair. "What's going on with us?"

She stepped away from my touch and closed her eyes. I wanted to lash out at her all over again, but the ice was cracking. Pain was written on her face. Her eyes were scrunched together. She swallowed a couple of times as if she was trying to keep from…crying.

No, she couldn't cry.

"Ari," I groaned.

I pulled her into my arms. She rested her head against my chest and gripped my shirt in her hands.

"That song, Grant? My song?"

"I know. It was impulsive."

She pushed away from me again. "You're always impulsive."

"Killian called out ContraBand, and she said her favorite song was 'Life Raft.' Everyone went crazy, Ari. You should have heard them."

Her lips pressed together in a thin line.

"Everyone pushed me toward the stage and chanted for us to sing. What the fuck was I supposed to do?"

"I don't know," she admitted.

When she didn't say anything else, I kept talking, "Are you going to tell me why you ran out on me this morning?"

She shook her head.

"Fuck, Ari. Just tell me."

"No. I'm not ready to talk about it," she said. Her voice wavered, but she stared me straight in the eyes.

"Fine. Fucking fine. Take your time." I was itching for a cigarette right now like nothing else. "Maybe you should go."

Her eyes hardened but not before I saw a spark of hurt in her eyes. "Maybe I should."

"Find me when you're ready to talk about it." I turned and walked back toward the entrance to the League.

"Grant, wait."

"What?" I snapped. "What do you want me to say? Something is bothering you, and the most straightforward, outspoken, and mouthy person I know in the entire world won't tell me what it is. So, it feels a bit more like my princess is walking out on me now."

"No. I'm not...I'm not walking out. I just...I'm scared."

"Of what?"

Scared? Aribel Graham was scared? Now, I'd heard everything.

She closed her mouth. Her hands were shaking at her sides. Tremors traveled up her arms and through her whole body.

"Jesus, Ari, what is it?"

"I kissed someone else," she blurted out.

"You did what?" In shock, I stumbled backward a step. "You fucking cheated on me? What the fuck? Of all the people I've ever known...I never."

"No. No, Grant. It was while we were broken up. It was an accident. A total mistake."

"You're goddamn right it was a mistake. Biggest mistake you've ever made in your life, Princess," I snapped. "This was someone other than Donovan? Or was Donovan actually a real thing, and you were covering it up when we got back together?"

Ari closed her eyes. "This is why I was scared. I *knew* you'd react this way."

"How else am I supposed to react?" I yelled at her.

"It meant *nothing*. My parents were trying to set me up with Henry after New Year's when I thought—"

"When you thought I'd done what you did."

"No! I thought you'd slept with a groupie. I would never have..." She ground her teeth and sagged. "I'm sorry. I went out with my brother, and the guy showed up. We shared a bottle of champagne, and he kissed me. He tried to convince me to go back to his place, but I told him no, and I left."

"I don't know what the fuck you expect me to do with this, Ari. Your parents were setting you up with other guys over break. Do they even know we're dating?"

She bit her lip and cast her eyes away from me.

"Fuck, they don't know," I said, momentarily stunned. "What? Are you fucking ashamed of me?"

"Grant, no. God, I'm not. I just…with my parents. It's hard."

"Are you fucking kidding me right now? It's hard with *your* parents?"

"I didn't mean that as it being more or less difficult than anyone else's parents," she said. Her hurricane-blue eyes pleaded with me to understand. "All I'm saying is that it's hard when they expect so much from me. You're amazing, Grant, but I know my parents won't appreciate that," she said, the last part so soft that I had to lean in to hear her.

"Why? Because I'm in a band? Because I'm not on track to be a CEO? Because I don't have a fucking trust fund?"

"Yes," she whispered. "All those things and more. I don't care about that though."

"Maybe you will one day."

"I care about you."

"Enough to fucking kiss someone else and not tell your parents that we're together."

Ari straightened and crossed her arms. "I apologized for what happened, okay? Neither of us is faultless in this situation."

"What do you want me to do, darlin'?"

She frowned. "Darlin'? Really? We're back there?"

I shrugged and leaned my back against the brick building. "Tell me what you would do if I'd kissed someone else and no one in my life knew who you were."

"We've been through that before, Grant. I screamed at you and told you to sober up. More or less what I want to do now."

33

"You left."

She sighed heavily. The weight of carrying around her secret must have been killing her. I could already see that she didn't look as stressed as she had before. She looked uncomfortable as hell, which was fine by me, but not upset like I'd thought she'd be since I was yelling at her.

"Apparently, everyone makes mistakes," she said.

"Even a princess."

A tentative smile crossed her face at the use of her nickname.

Fuck, that smile ruined me. I sighed and gave up the fight. I wanted to be angry, but I was fucking happy to know what was wrong with her. If I were honest with myself, I was glad it wasn't *me*.

"Come here," I said, pulling her toward me.

My hands slid through her loose hair, and my lips greedily landed on hers. Her kisses were hot and needy. She pressed her body against me, and my mind raced ahead of me. *How fast could I throw her back against the wall and get under that dress?*

I was going to find out.

Grant swung me around and slammed my back into the wall. All the breath whooshed out of my lungs with the force of it. His lips crashed back down onto mine, and all that existed was here and now with him.

My fingers gripped his button-up and drew him closer to me. Suddenly, his hands were everywhere—dropping onto my shoulders, sliding over my waist, lifting the hem of my dress. I groaned into his mouth, and his tongue slid over mine. All of that built-up anger and frustration cracked open between us.

I had been so worried about what he would think once I finally told him what had happened that I hadn't even been able to be myself. I'd started acting like the person I thought he wanted. We'd been having a lot of sex and doing very, *very* little talking. For me, it had almost been easier. Maybe it was because it was all so new, but I couldn't let that continue forever. We had real issues that weren't going to be worked out with one conversation. At least we'd initiated the conversation though.

"Grant," I moaned.

"Just kiss me."

He gripped my hips in his hands and gyrated his body against mine. I leaned my head back against the wall. My eyes fluttered closed. Heat traveled up my body, flushing my skin and making my heart race.

"I fucking want you, Ari."

"I'm yours," I breathed.

"Right here. Right now."

He hitched my leg up around his waist and pressed himself against me. *Shit.* I could feel him through his jeans. My body ached for his touch. *This* most certainly had never been our problem.

I heard his zipper, and my eyes shot open. *Wait. Did he actually mean right here? As in, against the brick wall outside of the League where anyone could walk by and see us having sex?*

His hand brushed against my panties, and I squirmed beneath him. Fuck, I was already wet. I saw the moment when he realized that. A smirk crossed his face, and all the cocky arrogance that was Grant McDermott flooded to the surface.

I pushed him back a step and straightened my dress. "I'm not going to have sex with you against a brick wall. Who do you think I am?"

"My girlfriend?" He shoved me backward against the wall and ran his hand down my dress. "Be a little adventurous, Princess."

"That's right. I'm your girlfriend. Not some groupie slut."

"Can I treat you like one for a minute and fuck you backstage?" he asked.

"You're a real charmer."

He grabbed my face between his hands and roughly kissed me. "I'll charm you right out of your pants."

"I'm not wearing pants."

"It's already worked," he said, grabbing my hand. "Come on."

"Grant…" I groaned.

He dragged me around the side of the building and to a blank back door.

"What are you doing?"

"Taking what's mine."

And really…I had no argument for that. He yanked open the door and led me down the backstage hallway. The door to the lounge was ajar, but no one was inside, and the lights were out. He ushered me inside, slamming and locking the door behind him.

I reached for the light, but Grant was there before me. He grabbed my hand, keeping the lights off, and drew me toward the couch. Luckily, I was familiar enough with the back of the League to know where I was going, but still, I bumped into the coffee table as we went.

"Ow!" I yelped.

Grant laughed seductively in the dark room. He brought his lips down on mine, soft and sensual. He was in his element here. My heart beat in time with his as he clutched the material of my dress at my lower back. He traveled up the seam and tugged the zipper down to the base of my spine so quickly that I couldn't even respond. He pushed the material over my hips and let the dress pool at my feet.

"That's better," he said.

"If you think about laying me down on that gross scratchy couch…"

"I like where your mind is at. You can be on top."

He moved my hand to the waistline of his jeans. I took his lead and unbuttoned his jeans. My hand slid under his boxers, and I grasped his dick. He was already so hard and ready for me. It only intensified my ache for him. *How did he make me so desperate for his touch?*

"Fuck, Ari," he groaned as I stroked him. "If you keep that up, I'm going to throw you down on that couch whether you like it or not."

"You can tease, but I can't?"

He tensely gripped my shoulders. "That's right. Tease me later. Fuck me now."

A second later, his jeans and boxers landed in the pile with my dress and panties. He sank back into the couch and pulled me on top of him. He buried his face into my neck, sending chill bumps down my arms.

"I fucking love your body next to mine," he murmured.

Grant lowered me onto his dick. I shivered at the intimacy and connection.

A couple of months ago, I would have balked at the thought of doing this with anyone, let alone someone like

Grant McDermott. Now, there was no one else but Grant McDermott.

As I wrapped my arms around his neck, he trailed kisses across my shoulder. Slowly, he lifted me off of him and then rocked me back down. He started up a steady rhythm, bouncing me up and down on top of him.

The darkness, Bank Avenue's seductive rock tunes drifting backstage, and the intensity of our fight a minute ago made us push a little harder and go a little faster. My breath was coming out in short bursts, and I thought I was going to combust. I raked my nails across the back of his shirt and arched my back.

"Fuck," he growled. "I'm never going to get enough of your tight pussy."

I colored at his language. At the same time, my entire body tightened around him. He had a filthy mouth, but I'd be lying if I said it didn't turn me on.

"And you just got tighter."

I clenched even harder. Christ, I was so close. I couldn't believe that I was doing this. Oh my God, it was amazing. My body tingled from my head to my toes, and I couldn't hold it back any longer. I dug my fingers into his shoulders and shuddered as my orgasm hit me.

"Oh God," I cried out, leaning over Grant.

He pumped twice more into me and then followed suit.

"That was…amazing," I murmured.

"Yes, you are."

Knock, knock, knock.

"Fuck," he spat. "Someone's in here," he called out toward the door.

We both hopped up in a hurry and threw our clothes back on. My zipper got stuck, and Grant had to try three times before he secured it back in place. My hair was a disaster. I tried to wrestle it into something other than freshly rumpled sex hair. I was probably doing more harm than good.

Grant flicked the lights on. I blinked several times and then narrowed my eyes against the harsh light.

"Hello?" the person called again from the other side of the door.

"Coming," he said, winking at me.

Dear Lord…

He cracked open the door and smiled. "Hey, Killian."

"Oh, Grant, I didn't realize it was you," she said.

The door opened wider, and I got a better look at who was standing in front of Grant. The smile dropped off my face. *Really? The lead singer of Bank Avenue?*

Killian glanced from Grant to me and then did a double take. "Did I interrupt?"

"No, we were just finishing," Grant said with a dirty smirk on his face.

I coughed at the implication in Grant's voice. "Um…hi. I'm Aribel," I said, stumbling forward and offering Killian my hand.

"Killian." She took my hand in hers and smiled brightly.

"I'm Grant's girlfriend," I said.

"Oh, yeah," he said. "I'm bad with intros."

Killian still hadn't let go of my hand, and it was starting to get awkward. She peered over at Grant. "You have a *really* hot girlfriend."

"Would you expect anything else?" he asked smugly.

I pulled my hand away from Killian and stepped closer to Grant. "Well, it was nice to meet you." *Not really.*

"You, too," she said. She eyed us up and down. "I was coming to get my purse, and then I'm going to go hang out with the band. You should come, too."

"I think we're going to cut out early," Grant said with a wink.

I was relieved that he'd said that, so I wouldn't have to. I couldn't go back out there and face everyone right now. I didn't know what I looked like at the moment. Plus, there were too many emotions swirling around between us to act like a happy couple around everyone we knew in Princeton.

"Suit yourselves," she said. She sauntered into the room, grabbed a studded black purse, and then turned to leave. "Bye, Grant,"

"See you around, Killian."

She stopped when she walked through the door and invitingly looked back at us. "You know…if you would ever be down for a threesome, I'd be interested."

My mouth dropped open. "What?"

"I love little blondes," she said. She bit her lip and stared back at me.

"Oh!" I gasped.

Grant laughed. "I love where this is going."

"Grant," I said, smacking him on the chest.

"Give me a call if you're up for it." She walked away.

Grant moved to run after her. "Wait!"

I grabbed his arm and yanked him back to me. "Grant…no. Just no."

He looked pained. "But she's *into* you. It would be so fucking hot."

I arched an eyebrow at him. "No."

He slumped back against the doorframe. "Damn, this girlfriend thing is hard."

"Hey!" I said. I walked over and stood before him. "Grant, are we going to be okay?"

"Did I fuck someone else?"

I shook my head at him and rolled my eyes. "Grant…"

He pulled me flush against him. "That guy meant nothing to you?"

"Absolutely nothing," I whispered.

"And you're going to tell your parents?"

I bit my lip and nodded. "Yeah. Eventually."

"Okay. Then, we're good."

"Just like that?" I asked, wondering where the catch was.

He nodded. "Just like that."

"You want me to go in there?" I pointed at the brick library building in front of us.

"Come on," Ari said. "I have my O-chem study session, and the girls are already inside. We can go get dinner afterward like a totally normal couple who do things other than live in your bedroom." She raised her eyebrows at me.

"I didn't realize other couples lived in my bedroom, but I'm liking the way this sounds."

She laughed and shook her head. "Please."

"The library really isn't my thing, Princess." I glanced away from her hurricane-blue eyes and shifted uncomfortably from one foot to the other.

The next morning after Ari and I had left the League, we'd agreed that we wanted things to go back to the way they'd been last semester—before the ski lodge when she had caught some groupie, Kristin, trying to seduce me in my room, before the band had started taking off, before she'd kissed someone else. I'd fucked Ari and then fucked it all up that weekend, and then she'd been too afraid to tell me about what had happened with her. Now, we were both trying to compensate for those problems.

To her, that meant we should tone down our time in the bedroom and put more effort into talking.

With disdain, I stared up at the imposing building. I hadn't realized that our conversation would lead to...the library.

"I know." Ari ran her hands down the front of my shirt. "But think of all those books...so many dark corners in the stacks..."

"Are you bribing me with sex?"

"Is it working?" she asked hopefully.

"Yes. Let's go." I grabbed her hand and dragged her toward the entrance.

"Oh my God. Why am I not surprised that worked so easily?"

"Because I'm a guy."

She laughed lightly, and it was all I could do not to throw her up against the wall right then and there. She'd said she didn't want to fuck against a wall outside of the League, but she hadn't said anything about outside the library.

I pressed her against the wall next to the sliding glass door and silenced whatever she was about to say with a kiss. I didn't need to hear her complaints. She wanted me, and I wanted her. If she was planning to be adventurous tonight, then I was only going to encourage her.

"Grant," she groaned between kisses.

I slipped my hands underneath her shirt and touched her warm soft skin. She shivered at my touch.

Fuck. I wanted her.

"Ahem." Someone coughed behind us.

Ari pushed me a step back and straightened out her top. "Sorry," she mumbled.

"Can we help you?" I asked, annoyed.

A blonde stared back at me. Her cheeks were bright red, and she couldn't meet my eyes. "Uh…hey, Grant. I just—"

"What are you doing here, Kristin?" I wouldn't forget that face soon. She had slipped through the cracks one too many times for me not to remember her now. Fucking whore had tried to ruin everything.

"She's in my study session," Ari spoke up. "We have a couple of classes together this semester."

"Right. You mentioned that," I grumbled.

Didn't seem like the best idea for me to stick around with Kristin here. Ari had said she was over it, but I didn't want to fuck things up right when everything was good again between us.

"I was seeing if you wanted to walk up to the session together," Kristin peeped.

"Maybe I should go," I said.

"No!" Ari and Kristin said at the same time.

I raised my eyebrows in question.

"I mean…not on my account," Kristin murmured.

"I'll meet you in there," Ari said.

Kristin nodded in understanding and fled into the building.

"I can't believe she's even fucking talking to you," I said.

"Don't remind me. I have to see her all the time, and I have to refrain from stabbing her eyes out."

"Now, *that* is something I'd like to see."

She quizzically looked at me. "You want to see me stab someone?"

"It'd be fucking hilarious. Completely out of character."

"Speaking of things out of character…"

She grabbed my arm and pulled me into the library. I groaned but kept walking. I clearly would do anything for her. I was proving that shit every time I put one foot in front of the other in this place.

We walked through the front room and into a long open corridor. My eyes widened as I took in the sheer number of books. Every shelf was filled several stories high. *Who had the time to read all of this shit?*

"Maybe you'll find something you like," she whispered into my ear.

"They have porn here?"

"Sometimes, I don't have words for you, Grant."

I smirked. "That's not how I remember it. You're actually pretty vocal."

She flushed. "Can we go five minutes without you talking about sex?"

"Why would we want to?"

"Upstairs," she said, pointing to the stairs. "If we keep talking about this, you're going to steal me away, and I'm going to miss my study session."

"You say that like it's a bad thing."

"I have a huge O-chem test tomorrow. It *is* a bad thing!"

I couldn't help but chuckle at that. "O-chem." I snickered.

"Ugh!" she groaned.

I was still laughing by the time we reached her study session. Her O-chem group was tucked away in a private study room while Cheyenne, Gabi, and Shelby were seated at a table nearby with their computers and papers strewn all over the place.

"I'll see you after," Ari said.

She gave me a peck on the mouth, but I didn't let her go. I deepened the kiss and sank into the desire that always flared up between us. When she finally pulled back, her pupils were dilated, and she was breathing heavily.

She swallowed and then glanced down at my lips once more. "You're dangerous."

I smiled as if that were the best fucking compliment she'd ever given me. "Don't I know it?"

"I'll see you after."

She sauntered over to the private study room and closed the door behind her.

With a sigh, I sank into the chair across from Cheyenne. She gave me a seductive smile and wink before returning to her homework.

I pulled out a notebook from my back pocket and fiddled with the lyrics I'd been working on this week. It was so new that I didn't even have a title for it yet. I was pretty sure that it fucking sucked and would never see the light of day, but writing lyrics had taken the place of most of my vices when Ari was away.

I scribbled through the last line and shook my head. "Fuck."

Cheyenne looked at me and raised her eyebrows. "You know this is a library, McDermott."

"Yeah." I shrugged and doodled in the margins.

"What is that?"

"What is what, Cheyenne? Don't you know this is a library?" I pressed my finger to my lips, and she glared at me.

"That, dipshit." She planted her finger on my notebook.

"That would be an *arrow*. Maybe Princeton is too hard for you, and you should return to kindergarten for shapes."

"Oh, ha-ha." Cheyenne rolled her eyes.

Gabi and Shelby leaned over to take a peek at what I was working on.

"What she meant is, it's good," Gabi whispered.

"I didn't know you could draw," Shelby said.

"I can't draw. I drew a fucking arrow in the margin of a notebook."

"Okay," Shelby said, putting her hands up in defense. "It was a compliment."

I went back to my notebook and tried to ignore them. The thought of Ari was making me draw things now. *God, I'm such a pussy.*

"So, what are you getting Ari for her birthday?" Cheyenne asked.

"What am I—what? When is her birthday? I was just getting caught up on fucking Valentine's Day."

"Aw," Shelby crooned. "You have Valentine's Day plans?"

I closed my eyes and breathed in heavily. *What the fuck had I gotten myself into?*

"Let's focus on one thing at a time. Birthday?"

"You have time, lover boy. It's March fourth," Cheyenne said. "We were thinking of throwing her a surprise party."

47

My phone buzzed in my pocket. I fished it out and saw that my cousin, Sydney, was calling. "I'm in, but I have to take this," I said. I walked away from the table. "Hey, Syd."

"Grant, I'm glad you answered."

"Of course I answered."

"I can barely hear you. Why are you whispering?"

"Sorry. I'm in the library."

There was a pause on the other line before she started laughing. "I'm sorry. I was trying to reach Grant McDermott with something important. Can you put him on the line?"

"You're fucking hilarious," I drawled. "You know, while we're talking, what are you doing on March fourth? I'm throwing Ari a surprise birthday party. You should fucking fly up for it."

"That sounds great. I'm sure I can make it."

"Good. I'm thinking the League."

"Grant," she muttered, "that's not why I called."

"What's up? You fucking too many dudes right now?"

"Grant!" she cried. Her voice wavered and then broke. "I-I'm sorry."

"What's going on?" It was as if she'd flipped a switch, and suddenly, I was in big-brother mode. No one fucked with Sydney on my watch.

"Have you…have you heard from my dad lately?"

"No. Should I have?"

She hesitated before responding, "I wasn't supposed to tell you, but I think this is too big to keep from you."

My heart sped up as I waited for whatever she was about to say. "Tell me what?"

"Your dad came by the restaurant tonight."

"Sorry," Grant said, peeking his head into the room. He looked right at me and tilted his head out into the hallway.

Everyone stared at me, and I sighed.

Jesus. I had too much work to do to deal with this right now. I wanted to flirt and have sex with him in the stacks, but couldn't he wait until after my study session? I knew I'd led him on to believe it would happen soon...but not right now.

"Give me a minute," I said. I put one finger up and finished writing in my notes.

Grant stood by and waited for me.

How embarrassing.

"I'll be right back." I hurried out of the room and after Grant. Closing the door quietly behind me, I groaned in frustration. "What? I'm in the middle of this session, and things aren't going that great."

"Ari," he said softly. His arms were crossed over his chest, and he wasn't meeting my eyes. He had this hollow look on his face as if he'd seen a ghost.

"What's wrong?"

"Sydney called. My dad showed up at Duffie's."

My hand flew to my mouth. "What did he want? Why didn't anyone tell you that he was out already? Last we heard, he was going to get out on parole, but—"

"Well, it looks like he's out. Sydney said that my uncle called her to see if she had spoken to me. She thought that was weird, and he ended up telling her that my dad had called a couple of times. Today, he showed up at the restaurant."

"What does he want?"

Grant sighed and then finally looked at me. His eyes were hard when he answered, "Me."

I blew out the breath I'd been holding. *Great.* Just when things were finally going right, his dad had to force himself into the picture. *Why would he even think that Grant would want to see him? After killing Grant's mother and attempting to blame the whole thing on Grant, didn't his dad realize he'd done enough damage?*

"So, what does this mean?" I asked.

"I…I don't know." He walked down an empty row of books empty of people.

It killed me that he was going through this. All I wanted was to be there for him, but I didn't know where to start. It wasn't as if I could call his dad up and tell him to leave Grant alone.

"Grant," I said, following after him. I latched on to his shirt and stopped him in place. "Talk to me. Tell me everything that Sydney said."

"That's it. She didn't really know anything."

"Are you going to call your uncle?"

He shrugged. "Maybe."

"I know this is hard," I said, rubbing my hand up his arm, "but you can't ignore it."

"I'm not ignoring it. I'm trying to fucking deal with it. The thought of him being out of prison, stalking me…" He breathed in heavily and ground his teeth together. "You don't know what it's been like the last thirteen years he's been locked up. I carry this guilt with me that I'm somehow responsible for my mother's death."

"You're right," I said softly. "I'll never know what that's like." I looked down at the ground and then back up at Grant. I needed to be strong for him right now. "But I'm here for you…for everything you're going through."

I slid my hand into my shirt and pulled out the dog tags that Grant had given me when we decided to become exclusive. They'd belonged to his dad, and Grant had worn them daily until we started going out.

"I keep you close to my heart. Keep me close to yours," I whispered.

Grant pulled me into a hug, sinking into me. I wrapped my arms around his waist and held him as tightly as I could. I knew that I couldn't keep him together like this, but I would damn well try.

"Ugh," he groaned, tearing away from me. "I can't do this right now."

"Do what?"

"This." He gestured between us. "I need to get out of here."

"And do *what?*"

"Who cares?"

I reached for him, and he pulled away.

"No. Don't do this. Don't shut me out. I'm here for you."

"I can't talk about this right now, Ari. Go back to your little study session."

He waved his hands to shoo me away and then took off toward the stairs. I raced after him. I was not going to let him walk out on me in the state he was in. His dad made him insane. He had been all right on the beach when he first found out his dad was getting out of jail because it was some far-off reality. Now that it was here, I didn't know what he would do.

I jogged to keep up with him through the entranceway and out of the library.

"Would you stop?" I yelled as soon as we were out of the building. "You can't run away from your problems!"

"I'm not running from my problems. I'm running from you." He continued walking to the parking lot.

"I must be the only person here who sees that as a problem."

"Must be."

He reached for the handle to his blue pickup truck, and I threw myself in front of him.

"I know you're being an asshole because you're pissed off. If you missed the old Aribel, well, then she's back. Don't act like I mean nothing to you because you got

51

some upsetting news. You can't run from me. I *tried* to get away from you, Grant, and I couldn't. You fought for me tooth and nail. There is no way I'm letting you storm off, get plastered at the League, and do something you'll regret."

Grant stared back at me, expressionless, but I could see the dark brooding thoughts underneath the exterior.

"What do you want from me?"

I sighed and took a step toward him. "I want you to be rational about this. Sydney doesn't know all the facts. You should call your uncle and find out what happened."

"Next thing I know, you're going to be pushing me to see my dad."

"No. I'm not trying to push you into anything! I'm trying to get you to think about this for a second."

I leaned into my hip and looked up at him. My body was shaking, and I wasn't sure if it was from the arctic temperatures tonight or the conversation I was having. We'd gotten over a fight this weekend, only to stumble into one that I didn't even want to happen.

"I thought about it. You want me to talk to my uncle. I want to forget that conversation with Sydney ever happened." He brushed me over to the side and popped open the door.

"So, what? You're going to run away like always? Get drunk with Vin the Enabler?" I croaked.

My face was hot, and I could feel the tears springing to my eyes. I was so not this girl. I didn't get upset about guys. I didn't continually confront them in parking lots. Grant McDermott was turning me into such a typical girl, and I *hated* it. I could really use some of that indifference right about now.

Grant laughed hollowly. "Vin the Enabler. He'd probably like that nickname."

"I don't give a shit what he likes. He's a prick who tried to drug me at the beginning of the year!" I ran my hands back through my hair and then brushed the tears from my cheeks. "I'm sorry. This isn't about Vin. I want what's best for you."

"The best thing for me right now is to go blow off some steam."

I opened my mouth to tell him that I'd go with him, but he held up his hand.

"Alone, Princess. I have to deal with this my own way."

"Fine. If you want to be alone, we can be alone together."

I pushed past him and climbed inside the cab of his truck. He wasn't thinking straight tonight, and there was no way I'd let him drive off without me.

"Ari, all your stuff is still inside."

"I'll text the girls, and they'll bring it home later."

"What about your test tomorrow?" he asked.

I swallowed. I hadn't really thought about that. The test tomorrow would be a huge part of my grade, and I couldn't afford to do poorly. My stomach crawled as I thought about abandoning my studies for the night, but Grant was of more immediate importance. He couldn't do this by himself. I'd still do well without a few extra hours in the library.

"You're going to abandon your study session for me?" He looked utterly mystified.

I reached my hand out to him through the open door. "I *love* you. Not just when it's easy."

He sighed heavily. "It's not going to be easy tonight. Scoot over."

As soon as I got out of my truck and inside my house, I stormed into the kitchen and grabbed a bottle of Jack Daniel's. I didn't bother with a glass before tipping it up and drinking it straight.

"So, it's one of those nights?" Miller asked from his position in the living room.

"Yes, it is," Ari said. She crossed the threshold into my house and slammed the door behind her.

"Fuck yeah!" Vin cheered. "Let's get fucked up!"

"I'm so thrilled this is happening," Ari said sarcastically.

Vin hopped up from his seat and made his way to the kitchen. "And we're fucking thrilled you brought your buzzkill with you, bro."

I lifted the bottle to my lips again. No way was I in the mindset to get between Ari and Vin. They could get their hatred out of the way while I downed this bottle, and then maybe Ari would be down for some angry fucking. That sounded like a perfect fucking night.

"I don't want to deal with you tonight, Vin," Ari said. She slumped onto the couch next to Miller. "Can you text Shelby and tell her to take my stuff home?"

"Weren't you guys at the library or something?" Miller asked. He had the video game controller in his hand and was staring at the TV.

Vin laughed. "The library? You must be talking about someone else. My bro would never do any of that stupid shit."

"Why is going to the library stupid shit?" Ari asked. Her voice was on edge. "Cheyenne was at the library with me. Last I heard, you two were still sleeping together."

"Chey's hot, but I wouldn't fucking follow her to the library like my pussy-whipped friend."

"Pussy-whipped," Ari said softly. "You make a relationship sound like a tragedy."

"Now, you're fucking getting me. Relationships are a disease."

"And you'd know because you've *been* in so many relationships?" she asked pointedly.

The guys all cracked up in the living room at Ari's comment. I attempted to tune them out.

I was already halfway through the bottle, and everything was getting really warm. The liquor loosened my muscles and clouded my mind. This was fucking perfection. Soon, I wouldn't be able to think about my shit dad or my uncle who hid things from me. Hopefully, I wouldn't have to hear anyone arguing either. I wanted to get lit up and black out.

"McAvoy, you got a joint on you?" I asked, interrupting Vin and Ari's argument.

"What do you need a joint for?" Ari asked.

"Uh…nah, man. My stash is running low," McAvoy said.

"Since when? You always have the good shit."

"Grant, seriously?" Ari demanded.

"You decided to come along, darlin'," I slurred. "McAvoy, will you get me something?"

"I'll see what I can do, bro." He apologetically glanced over at Ari before handing over his controller to Vin. He left the house through the garage to where he lived next door.

"Fine. Whatever," Ari grumbled.

Miller leaned into her, and they whispered to each other, but I didn't give a shit what they were talking about at this point.

My phone vibrated in my pocket. I pulled it out and tossed it onto the counter. Now was not a good time.

"You going to answer that, bro?" Miller asked.

I glanced down at the screen.

Uncle Randy.

Fuck no.

"No chance in hell."

Ari hopped up off the couch and walked into the kitchen. The phone went to voice mail. She frowned when she saw my uncle's name on the screen.

"You should call him back."

"Fucking hell, Princess. No! I'm not fucking doing this tonight."

"Just talk to him," she said quietly. "What if he wants to tell you about it? What if there's news?"

The phone buzzed again on the counter, and I shook my head. She snatched the phone up and answered the call.

"Hello, Mr. Duffie. This is Aribel."

"Aribel," I growled.

"Let me see if I can find him for you, Mr. Duffie." Ari laughed lightly. "Yes, Randy. Of course. I'll remember that for next time."

She put the phone on mute and then pushed it toward me. "Talk to him."

"What the fuck do you think you're doing?"

"Grant, please. See what he wants, and then decide if you want to hear it or not." She ran her hand up my sleeve and smiled sadly. "I'm here if you need me."

"You're killing me, woman." I grabbed the phone out of her hand and stalked up the stairs and into my bedroom. I brought the bottle of Jack with me because I had a feeling I'd need to finish it by the end of this conversation.

I took a deep breath and unmuted the phone. "Hey, what's up?"

"Grant, hey! How are you doing?"

Why was he so fucking peppy? Shouldn't he sound as fucking scared and confused as Sydney had?

"I'm all right."

Remain calm. Try to get through this one conversation without blowing up on him.

He was as close as I had to a real parent, and he wasn't the person I was actually pissed at. I kept trying to remind myself of these things, but it wasn't working.

There was a long pause before my uncle responded, "That's good, real good."

"Yep."

"So…I was calling to make sure we're all set for this weekend."

"This weekend? What are you talking about?"

"Valentine's Day. The big dinner you have planned for your girlfriend. I think I was on the phone with her." He chuckled softly, but all I felt was panic.

Fuck! I'd completely forgotten about Valentine's Day. I'd been planning to take Ari to Duffie's and to our beach. There was no fucking way I could do that now. *What if my dad was fucking waiting for me to show up? Was he in the area? I couldn't chance it.*

The whole thing pushed me over the edge—not only was my uncle refusing to tell me about my father, but I also had to cancel my fucking plans because of this shit.

"Do you really think I want to come to your restaurant right now?" I asked.

"I don't understand. Why wouldn't you?"

I blew out my breath heavily, plunked the whiskey bottle down on my nightstand, and threw my fist into the closet door. "Why do you think?" I shouted.

"Grant—"

"No. I'm not a little kid anymore!" I shook my hand out in frustration. "You're supposed to fucking trust me and come to me like you did when you found out about my dad getting out of prison. You can't fucking choose when to tell me important things."

"Sydney called you," he said softly. "Grant, I'm sorry."

"No. Don't fucking say that!"

"I know you're upset, but I wanted to try to make this easy for you."

"By lying?" I shouted.

"No. I was going to tell you in person on Saturday. I thought it would be better to hear about it face-to-face rather than over the phone. I only checked with Sydney to make sure that your father hadn't already reached out to you."

"And you thought it was a good idea for me to come see you when you know my father has been in the area?" I asked.

"When I asked him to leave, he told me he was going to head out of town for a little bit, but he'd check back in."

I shook my head. *Was my uncle that idiotic?* Even if what he was saying was true, I was halfway into a bottle of whiskey, and I still fucking knew it was a setup.

"Yeah, he's going to check back in when I'm there."

"And would that be so bad?" he asked.

I cursed under my breath. "What the fuck do you think is going to happen? We're going to sit around and sing 'Kumbaya'? He killed my mom! This conversation is over. I don't want to have any contact with my dad. Maybe you'll get that one day."

I hung up before he could say anything else, and I hurled the phone. It smashed against the wall and then fell to the floor. At this point, I didn't give a shit if it completely stopped working. Every phone call was getting worse and worse.

The bottle of Jack temptingly smiled back at me. I grabbed it and tipped it back.

Disappear.

Foggy.

Numb.

The pain ate away at me, and I was so fucking tired of feeling. One day…one day, I wouldn't feel it. But if all I had now was this bottle, then I'd let it do its fucking job.

59

"Shit."

I peeled my eyes open, my vision bleary. *What the fuck happened? And where the fuck was I?*

I propped myself up on my elbow. A wave of nausea hit me, and I collapsed back down. *Holy shit. I might still be fucking drunk.*

After a few minutes, I forced myself to sit up again. I leaned over the couch and rested my head in my hands. *Why was I on the couch? Fuck, I didn't remember shit.*

"You awake, bro?"

I looked up and saw Vin crashed on the opposite couch in the garage. *Why the fuck was I in the garage? Jesus!*

"No. Stop talking."

"That was some fucking party."

"Party?" I groaned.

"Yeah. Half the city was here last night."

"What? No. We were just supposed to drink and smoke and get fucked."

Vin laughed roughly. "Sure, man."

I held my head as I stood and left the destroyed garage to head back into my house. It was a mission, getting up the stairs to my room, but it was all worth it to see Ari passed out in my bed. I fell into the bed next to her and pulled her body against mine.

"Princess," I murmured.

Ari rolled over and groaned. "Hey."

"What happened last night?"

She popped up. "Oh my God, what time is it?"

"I don't know. Maybe slow down a bit. I'm still messed up."

"Shit, shit, shit. I have to go, Grant. I have my O-chem test today, and I didn't study last night."

She bolted out of my bed. I'd forgotten about her test. I shouldn't have taken her away from her study session yesterday. *Shit!*

"Hey, take my truck. Keys are…downstairs. I think," I offered.

"Okay," she said, rushing toward the door.

"Ari," I called before she could leave. "Thanks for being here for me."

"You know I love you, Grant. I realize you're going through some awful shit. I'm here for you. But I can't sacrifice my career like this again."

She left my room in a hurry, and I sighed.

Yeah, I'd royally fucked that one up.

B.

I'd been staring at the letter long enough that most of the rest of the class had emptied out of the room. My professor still stood behind the lectern, but I was too embarrassed and horrified to speak to him. I wasn't certain that I wouldn't break down into tears if I opened my mouth right now.

"Miss Graham, it's time for you to leave," Professor Williamson said.

I hadn't even noticed that he had snuck up on me. "My paper has a B on it," I told him.

"Yes. I was surprised by that as well."

"I can't get a B." My voice didn't even sound like me. It was high-pitched and squeaky as if I might combust at any moment.

"You've done exemplary the rest of the semester, Miss Graham. I'm sure if you study harder for the next one, then you'll keep that A you've earned thus far."

Study harder. Ha! Maybe I would have if my boyfriend hadn't gone off the deep end.

I realized I was sneering at my professor in my attempt at a smile, and I stopped. *How the hell was I going to get out of this?* I'd never gotten a B before in my life.

"But you do have to leave," he insisted.

"Right. Of course." I robotically packed up my stuff and then slung my bag over my shoulder. "Just have to study harder. Do better. All that."

"Feel free to stop by during my office hours, and I'd be happy to discuss the problems that you missed."

I laughed maniacally and then swallowed down the crazy. I needed to get a grip.

"Thank you, sir. I'll take you up on that next week." I rushed out of the room before I could freak out anymore in front of Professor Williamson.

I fumbled around for my phone as I walked out of the building.

Grant picked up almost immediately. "Hey, Princess, are you all ready? I had to do some rearranging, but I think I have everything perfect."

"I got a B on my test," I croaked.

"Congrats! That's awesome."

"Are you kidding?" I nearly screeched. "I've never gotten less than an A-minus. Not even a B-plus. Definitely not a plain old B. Do you know what this could do to my GPA?"

"Oh…well, it's not like this is the final grade. You probably still have an A in the class or something, right?"

Just the thought of not keeping straight As was making me hysterical. "I have to cancel tonight," I hollowly told him.

"What? You want to skip our date? It's Valentine's Day."

"Tomorrow is Valentine's Day. It's Friday the thirteenth, and I received my first B. Yes, I want to skip. This night is only going to get worse."

"Aribel, come on. Don't do this," he pleaded. His Southern accent was more pronounced than ever.

Dirty tricks. It was a good thing I couldn't see his smile.

"I need to stay in to study and figure out how not to ruin my life."

"It's one bad grade. Let me take you out to make you feel better. That's what's supposed to happen in these situations, right?"

I shook my head and plopped down onto a bench. "I'm not up for it. I'm emotionally devastated."

"I didn't know you had a flare for the melodramatic."

"Grant McDermott! Do not make fun of me in my time of need!"

"Princess, I'm not making fun of you," he said earnestly. "I'm the reason you didn't study as much as you normally do. I've spent a lot of time getting everything ready for the ride into the city. We can't cancel now. I will resort to kidnapping your ass."

"Just try it, *darling*," I spat back.

"If you're not ready by the time I get there, you might get your wish."

"Grant—"

"See you soon."

The line went dead, and I glowered at the phone. I didn't even know what to wear to this Valentine's Day date. *Since when were we going into the city anyway? Ugh!* I had a horrible feeling about this.

I spent my afternoon trying to figure out where Grant was taking me. It was better than obsessing over the B staring back at me from my desk. There had to be a way for me to make that grade up. I couldn't get halfway into the semester with a B average.

Oh my God! Here I was obsessing all over again. I glared at my test and then flipped the paper upside down, so it couldn't continue to mock me.

Back to Grant.

What kind of Valentine's Day would Grant McDermott plan?

I Googled *Valentine's Day dates in New York City*, and an insane list populated, including everything from ice-skating and a horse-drawn carriage around Central Park to hot chocolate and Netflix. There was no way he was going to do any of these cheesy romantic things. That was so not Grant.

After late-night swimming at a hotel, horseback riding, and watching a sunset on the beach last year…maybe I was wrong?

Nah, he'd be more likely to take me to some concert in the city. I wondered who was playing. As I was investigating all the possible concerts we could attend, my phone buzzed with a message.

> *Be there in twenty. I brought handcuffs. I hope I need them.*

My cheeks heated. That damn man could make me blush over a freaking text message.

I exited out of the phone and went to get ready. I only had twenty minutes, and I spent most of the time straightening out my hair in the bathroom and the other time debating between my pink cardigan and my cream sweater. I decided on the sweater as I heard a knock on the door.

"I got it!" I called out.

Gabi had already left for her plans with McAvoy. In a few hours, Cheyenne and Shelby were going to some anti-Valentine's Day party off-campus that would basically result in everyone coupling up with strangers.

I opened the door, and my jaw dropped.

Grant was in a tuxedo.

I blinked.

He was still in a tuxedo.

I blinked again. It wasn't going away.

"Hey, Princess," he said with that signature smug smile.

"*What* are you wearing?"

"You've never seen one before? I find that surprising."

"I've seen a tux but…not on you."

He leaned down and planted a firm kiss on my lips. "I wanted tonight to be special."

I glanced down at my cream sweater and cringed. I hadn't thought he would want to do something…fancy. It was completely uncharacteristic.

"Just…give me a minute."

I ducked back into my bedroom, undressed, and tossed my sweater and jeans onto my bed. *Ugh!* I had not been prepared for this. After rummaging through my closet, I located a short black dress my mother had bought me the last time she and my father had been in Paris. She had insisted I bring it with me to college. It was coming in handy now.

There was no time to change my hair or makeup. I slid on a pair of high heels, grabbed my peacoat and black clutch, and then hurried out of my room.

"Wow," Grant murmured when I walked into the room.

"Good wow or bad wow?"

"You look amazing."

"Thanks. I did what I could on short notice."

"Sorry. I should have forewarned you, but I wanted it to be a surprise."

He gestured for the door, and he followed me out into the brisk evening air.

"Where exactly are you taking me?"

"You'll see."

I shrugged. It was much colder out without my sweater and jeans, but I guessed if he wanted to do this, then I'd play along. He really didn't have to though.

A black town car was parked on the street, and I glanced around. "Where's the truck?"

"No truck tonight."

The driver hopped out of the front seat and opened the back door.

Oh.

Oh!

My brain wasn't catching up quickly enough with what I was seeing. "You got a car? To drive us into the city?"

"Don't act so shocked," he said. "I can afford to do nice things for you."

"Of course you can. I didn't think you would want to."

67

"That I wouldn't want to do nice things for you?"

"No," I said plainly. *God.* I needed to get myself together. I wasn't trying to insult him. I was trying to understand. "That you'd want to get all dressed up. Ignore me. I'll get in the car now."

Grant climbed in after me, and then we were off.

I couldn't believe the things I'd said and the way I had acted. Yes, it was surprising he had shown up in a tuxedo and was driving me to New York City in a town car. *Wouldn't most girls be jumping up and down for this?*

I couldn't place where my unease originated. It was probably a result of the bad grade I'd gotten today, and I was simply being dramatic. That was what I was going with.

The traffic into the city was horrendous, thanks to the holiday weekend, and it took us forever to make it to our destination. I was jittery by the time we pulled up, and I was anxious to find out where we were.

When the car door opened and I stepped out onto the noisy city street, I teetered on my heels in anticipation. Grant slid his hands over my eyes. His breath was hot against my ear, and it sent a shiver up my spine. *Where had this all come from? What had happened to my manwhore rock-star boyfriend?*

"Ready?" he breathed.

I nodded.

He walked me inside a building, into an elevator, pressed me back against the wall, and then dropped his mouth down onto mine. I returned his kiss that was layered with a hint of desperation and desire with my own need for him.

We broke apart as the elevator dinged before opening to our destination.

My face fell. *Oh.*

"Surprise!"

Orchids filled the room of the restaurant with the same name, and they assaulted my senses. I'd been to

Orchids more times than I could count. When my dad did business in the city, we always ended up at Orchids. It was one of the nicest places in the city, and they catered to a certain clientele that made me wonder what kind of backroom deals Grant must have done to get us seated on such a prominent holiday.

I immediately felt bad for thinking it. He was trying to do right by me. It was sweet, charming. He was treating me like the princess he always called me.

"Reservations for two. McDermott," Grant said to the host.

"Ah, yes, Mr. McDermott," the man said, looking him up and down. "Right this way."

We were seated at a little candlelit table by a window with a bottle of champagne waiting.

"Okay, seriously. How did you get us into Orchids on Valentine's Day?" I asked.

Grant shrugged and gave me his most devious look. "Connections."

"But this place is next to impossible to get into on a regular day."

"You said you wanted to come here, so I brought you."

I narrowed my eyes. "What? I never said I wanted to come to Orchids."

"Well, I heard you mention it to your friends. Same thing."

"Oh. No, it's where my dad always comes for business."

His face fell as the news hit him.

"Not that it isn't nice. It's a great restaurant."

"Did you want to go somewhere else?" he asked.

I caught his eye and shook my head. "No. This is perfect. Really."

Perfect. Really.

I'd never heard so much bullshit come out of her mouth in one night.

I'd put in all of this work to get her the kind of Valentine's Day I thought she would want. Fancy dinner, town car, tuxedo—I thought these things were a fucking prerequisite. But she had been more uncomfortable since I picked her up than I'd seen her since I pursued her like a fucking maniac last semester.

She sweetly smiled back at me and then opened her menu.

Man, I'd better be getting laid after this.

"So, you like French food?" she asked.

French food? I opened the menu. Half of it was in French. *Well, fuck me.*

"Sure." I shrugged as I tried to understand what the fuck was in front of me.

The waiter came by and introduced himself. Ari asked for a bottle of some French wine I couldn't come close to pronouncing, and she did it all in flawless French. The waiter was enamored with her. He left with a skip in his step.

"You speak French," I said tightly.

"Not fluently."

"Uh-huh."

I peered over my menu at the people surrounding us. It was a myriad of older couples who were barely looking at each other and flighty gold-digger types with sugar daddies. We were the youngest people in the room by a long shot, and the longer I sat in here, the more uncomfortable I felt. I had been a fool to think that by putting on a tuxedo, I'd suddenly belong here. *You can take the boy out of the trailer, but you can't take the trailer out of the boy.*

When the waiter returned, he uncorked the bottle, poured a small amount into my glass, and then handed it to me. *Really? That was all I was going to get?* I could down that bottle myself in a couple of minutes.

"Is this not the bottle you requested?" the waiter asked carefully.

"You're supposed to taste it," Ari whispered across the table.

"Right." I sipped from the glass. "Uh…yeah, that's great."

The waiter arched an eyebrow and then poured the wine for both of us. "Are you ready to order?"

I'd stared at the menu for ten minutes, and the only thing that sounded appetizing was the steak, but it was a hundred fucking dollars. *Who paid that much for a steak?* I could buy one and grill it at home for ten bucks.

"You go first," I offered.

She swiftly spoke in French to the man. *Who knew what she was getting?*

When their eyes turned to me, I took that as the cue to order. "I'll have the steak. Medium rare."

Ari blanched as I handed him the menus, and then he left the table.

"That steak is really expensive," she murmured.

"It'd better be fucking good then."

She giggled. It was the most amazing sound I'd heard all night. She slapped her hand over her mouth and shook her head. She couldn't stop laughing. Her shoulders were shaking, and soon, tears formed in her eyes.

"What is so damn funny, Princess?"

"Honestly? This whole night. No! This whole damn day."

A few people were peering over at us because she was still laughing uncontrollably.

I couldn't help it. A smile appeared on my face, and then I was laughing, too.

"People are looking at us," I told her.

"Since when have you ever cared?"

That was a good point.

"I've got an idea," she said. She took a deep breath to try to control her laughter and pressed a hand to her side. She must have had a stitch from laughing so hard. "Oh my God, my cheeks hurt."

"You're fucking insane."

"To be dating you? Obviously." She winked at me.

Who was this chick in front of me? This gorgeous, confident girl. When we had first met, I would never have thought she would be like this.

"Are you ready for my idea?"

"This'd better be good."

She leaned forward and whispered, "Let's ditch this place."

"And go where?" I threw my hands out.

Her eyes twinkled. "I have an idea."

"All right." *Who was I to stop her from being spontaneous?*

Aribel promptly stood, grabbed my hand, and walked out of the restaurant with her head held high. I'd dined and ditched before but never at a place like this. Definitely never at a place where I'd ordered a hundred-dollar steak. Then again, I'd never fucking been at a restaurant like this before either.

Before I knew what was happening, Ari threw her arm out, and a yellow cab zoomed up in front of us.

"But what about the town car?"

"We don't need it," she said. She reached forward, undid my bowtie, and pulled it off. "Or that."

I grabbed her by the arm. "Are you sure about this? I thought this was what you'd want."

"I know," she said with a smile. "If I wanted all of this, I could have it. But I just want you."

That was all I needed to hear before I claimed her. Her lips felt so fucking good, and if she kept clutching at me so desperately, I was going to skip whatever her idea was and find the nearest hotel. She groaned into my mouth, and I nearly lost it.

But the cab honked at us and ruined the moment. Ari laughed and then darted inside, apologizing along the way. She gave the driver our destination.

"So, where are we going?" I asked.

"To do what I thought you might have planned all along. I have to admit though," she said, looking me up and down, "you might be overdressed for the occasion."

"Now, *that* would be a first."

She giggled again and snuggled up next to me. It was a short drive to our destination. Ari threw the guy some cash and then hopped out of the cab.

I did a double take when I realized where we were. "The Zell?" I asked in disbelief.

Ari had taken me from a fancy-ass restaurant to a mosh-pit music venue.

Forget everything I ever said about missing how easy it was to get ass. Who needed that when Aribel Graham shocked the shit out of me at every turn?

Okay…I still wanted pussy. But I fucking loved this girl.

"Who's playing?"

"Edge of Reason," she answered immediately. She purchased two tickets for us at the door. "Let's hope they don't suck."

I laughed. *At this point, who cared if they sucked?*

Better yet, it turned out that they didn't. The band was already playing the opening to their set for a medium-sized crowd. The bar was a dive. ContraBand had played here once when we first got started but never since. It had a good atmosphere but terrible acoustics. But I was so high on my night with Ari that nothing else even mattered.

A couple of songs in, Aribel left to take a phone call. I stayed to bask in the energy and adrenaline of the performance. At the end of that song, it was pretty fucking clear I needed a beer. I grabbed two from the bartender, so Ari could have one when she got back.

I meandered back toward the stage when two chicks in way too much fucking heavy black makeup stopped me. Their tits were out on display in their too tight shirts, and I made the mistake of glancing down. *Well, they were fucking out there, right?*

A smile crept up on one, and the other looked as if she was ready to pounce. "Hey," one of them crooned.

"What's up?" I grunted.

The girl on the right nudged her friend and giggled. "Uh…you're Grant McDermott, right?"

Whoa. I wasn't fucking used to getting recognized at gigs that weren't my own.

"Yeah, we saw you at The Drift show on New Year's. You were brilliant. That 'Life Raft' song. Oh my God."

"She listens to it on repeat," the other girl cut in.

"Well, thanks."

The first one was kind of hot in a trashy sort of way. Her friend looked a little more put together, but it was probably because she didn't have as big of a rack as the first girl.

I bet they'd be down for a threesome. Nah, maybe I'd just go with the first chick. She had some serious dick-sucking lips. Chick could probably suck a fucking golf ball through a garden hose.

"So…are you guys here for the band?" I'd never made small talk to groupies before. It usually consisted of smile, smile, grope, fuck.

"Yeah, we are," she said, leaning into me and running her hand down my arm, "but if you want to get out of here—"

"Sorry. I'm here with my girlfriend," I tested the words out. They might have been the first time I'd ever officially said no or told a groupie I had a girlfriend.

"She won't mind," the other girl said with a giggle.

"You clearly don't know my girlfriend."

Ari would murder them before being okay with me leaving with them.

I scooted around them as Ari reappeared before me. She looked flustered.

Her eyes landed on the two girls standing nearby, and she glared disapprovingly. They frowned and then scurried away.

"That was my parents. My dad is coming into town this weekend for my birthday."

"And you're upset about that?"

"What? No. I miss my dad. It'll be nice to see him." She fidgeted and then cocked her head back toward the show. "Is that for me?" She grabbed a beer out of my hand and took a swig. "You want to get back to the band?"

"Yeah, but are you going to tell me what the fuck has you upset?"

She sighed and glanced down. "My parents got a letter in the mail from the health insurance company about my test work."

"Test work? Are you okay?"

"Grant, I got a pregnancy test."

My body stopped functioning, and the music seemed to disappear. *A pregnancy test? What the fuck! She couldn't be pregnant.*

"No, no, no!" she said quickly. "I'm not pregnant. It was a routine exam. I, uh…got birth control," she said.

Her voice was so quiet during the last bit that I almost didn't hear her.

But when I puzzled it out, my face lit up. "That's fucking great! Princess, that's great news."

"Yeah, and well, Plan B after we had sex at the League."

"That's good, too. I know I'm not fucking ready to have a kid. But why didn't you tell me before?"

"I don't know," she said. "I was worried you'd be angry that I wanted to get, um…STD tests."

"Are you fucking kidding? Do you know who I am? Do you know how many times I've been tested? And birth control! Fuck condoms."

"Grant," she groaned, "we're in public."

I picked her up around the middle and crushed her to me. "I don't care where we are. This all sounds like great news to me."

She teetered when I set her back on her feet. "Yeah. I mean, not being pregnant is good, but uh…my parents got the insurance letter. Now, they're asking questions. I didn't want to have the I-lost-my-virginity talk over the phone on Valentine's Day just because they read the medical insurance paperwork."

"How exactly *did* you want to have that talk?" I asked, amused.

"Preferably, I never wanted to have that talk."

"Well, did you tell them about us then?"

She cringed as if she had been waiting for this. With that reaction, she didn't even have to answer. It was clear she still hadn't told her parents we were dating or that she was even seeing anyone. *Did they think she had fucked a stranger?*

"I know. I know. I should have said something, but it wasn't the right time."

"Is there going to be a right time?"

"Yes. Yes," she said. She pulled me closer and stared me in the eyes. "I'll tell my father next weekend when I see him. It'll be better in person. I promise."

I would have laughed when I'd gotten the message from my father to meet him at Orchids in the city only two weeks after Grant and I had dined and ditched at the same restaurant, but I was too nervous.

My father loved me fiercely. He'd always had high expectations for Aaron and me, but since I was three years younger, I felt the weight of his disapproval so much stronger. The thought of disappointing my father was debilitating. He never explicitly came out and said he wanted me to graduate with a practical degree and marry someone successful, like him, but he didn't have to.

And it wasn't as if I hadn't tried.

I'd dated loser after loser, trying to force the feelings for the *right guy*. I hadn't even known how sad that was until Grant.

A smile touched my lips. I was going to tell my father about Grant tonight. Maybe it wouldn't be so bad. *What could he really do about it anyway?*

He'd probably call it a phase or something equally hurtful, but I had been dealing with that my whole life. This wasn't a phase—for me or Grant. I didn't need to prove anything to my father. I just needed to tell him, so I wouldn't feel so guilty that my family didn't know about Grant.

After valeting my car at The Kimberly Hotel where my father had made a reservation for me, I took a cab over to Orchids. A weight sat in the pit of my stomach as the elevator carried me up to the restaurant.

When the doors dinged open, the scent of orchids assaulted my senses. I sneezed twice as I walked over to the host. By chance, it happened to be the same one from the night I had been here with Grant. He looked at me as if he were trying to place how he knew me.

Before he could figure it out, I spoke up, "Reservation for Graham."

He slightly shook his head to clear his thoughts and then plastered a smile on his face. "Right this way."

He directed me to a perfect booth in the corner. I saw my father's smiling face as I approached. He was always so stern, but he looked so happy to see me. Then, everything seemed to slow down as I captured this one moment.

My feet kept moving even though I realized someone else was in the booth with my father. He swiveled around in the booth. His blue eyes caught mine with that same predatory gaze I had come to associate with him.

Henry.

I stumbled a step in disbelief before righting myself. *What the hell was he doing here?*

Henry stood from the table like a gentleman. He touched the small of my back as he gestured for me to take the seat next to him. "Aribel, it is so good to see you again."

I opened my mouth to speak, but anything polite would be a lie. He looked handsome in a very expensive suit, but he also was only interested in me because my parents had arranged this entire thing.

"Henry," I sputtered, "what are you doing here?"

"I'm here for your birthday, of course." His smile widened. "Happy birthday."

"Thank you," I said automatically.

My eyes slid over to my father. He looked amused by the exchange.

"Hello, Aribel. I knew you wouldn't mind that I invited Henry to your birthday celebration."

End of discussion.

I closed off the retort I had in mind. My father wouldn't care to hear what I had to say. He would have invited Henry against my protest. If he wanted Henry to be here, then he would get his way.

The only problem I foresaw was that I hadn't intended on telling my father about Grant in front of anyone else. I was already nervous enough. Having another witness wasn't making that any better. Of course, I'd told Henry I had a boyfriend when he kissed me earlier this year, so he already knew, but it was still awkward, considering my family was trying to set me up with him.

"I didn't realize Henry would be in the city with you," I said as I slid into the booth.

Henry sat next to me.

"Well, we're celebrating more than your birthday tonight, Aribel. Henry received a promotion," my father said.

"Congratulations," I muttered.

"He's a very promising employee, doing really well for himself."

"Thank you, Jim," Henry replied. "I'm happy to be a part of the company."

"We should have a toast." My father gestured for the waiter to come over, and he ordered champagne for the table.

Once the waiter delivered the champagne and it was in hand, he raised his glass. "To my Aribel's birthday and Henry's promotion!"

"Cheers," I whispered, lifting my glass and clinking it against my dad's and Henry's before taking a sip.

After we ordered our dinner, I plucked up the courage to interrupt their conversation about banking. I couldn't believe I was doing this, but I had *promised* Grant.

"Um…Dad?"

My father tore his attention from whatever Henry was saying to look at me. "Yes, Aribel?"

"I wanted to tell you I'm sort of seeing someone," I said in a rush.

He looked between Henry and me, and then he let loose a short boisterous laugh. "You don't have to be afraid to tell me. Aaron let it slip a couple of weeks ago. Your mother and I are thrilled by the idea."

"You are?" I asked dumbly. Then, my mind caught up with me. *Aaron.*

Aaron thought I was seeing Henry…that I had slept with Henry.

"Of course. Henry is a great match. Just the kind of person I would entrust with my only daughter."

"Right." The words caught in my throat. The *kind of person*, as in successful, wealthy, highly educated—not someone in a rock band, who had slept with half the state of New Jersey, who had a father who had been in jail for thirteen years.

Anger flared inside of me. *How fucking elitist to say something like that!*

Grant was a good person who loved and cared about me. Just because he wasn't like Henry, who had honestly been more willing to sleep with me and then forget about me, didn't mean he wasn't the right guy for me—or even that we couldn't date and find out.

"Actually, it's not Henry," I said boldly. "I didn't mean to give Aaron the wrong impression, but Henry and I aren't together." I gestured between us.

Henry kept an amused look on his face as if he liked watching me squirm.

A storm cloud rolled in over my father's face. "I thought, with the insurance paperwork your mother received—"

"Dad, please," I groaned. *How could he bring that up in front of Henry?*

"Is he a Princeton student? Did you meet him in class? What is his major?"

"God, the third degree," I muttered. "No, he's not a student. He, uh…works in a recording studio."

Henry scoffed next to me and then tried to hide it by taking another drink from the champagne. My father just looked increasingly more frustrated with the conversation.

"Is this some kind of phase? You know your brother went through something similar before he met Sarah."

I distinctly remembered Aaron with his arm around some random girl when we had gone out over Christmas break. If he'd had a phase, it didn't seem to be over.

"It's not a phase!"

"Aribel," my father said sharply, "we're in a public place. Why don't we discuss this at another time?"

"Fine."

All I'd wanted to do was be honest with my family about my relationship with Grant. I'd known it was going to go down like this. I'd told Grant it wasn't going to be easy. But then again, I hadn't promised him that my parents would accept him. I'd just said that they would know he existed. Now, they knew.

With the conclusion of our meal, I stood and followed my father and Henry out of the room. I'd secretly hoped my father would want to stick around and do something together, like maybe go ice-skating in Central Park, but I could already tell he was all business.

"It was good to spend some quality time with my baby girl," my father said. He kissed the top of my forehead and then handed me a box. "Happy birthday."

My eyes lit up with surprise. I tipped open the box, and my mouth dropped open. Inside was a small platinum ring with a string of diamonds around the band that decreased in size from the center. "Oh my God! Is this mom's ring?"

He smiled, but there was something under the surface. "Our original engagement ring. Yes."

My father had replaced my mother's ring many times over the years. They had gotten more and more extravagant as the years went by, but I always coveted the very first ring.

"Your mother and I thought it was appropriate for you to have something befitting the woman you are turning into."

I slipped it out of the box and onto my right hand. It shined brilliantly, and it made my heart ache. Staring at the ring made me miss them.

Then, unexpectedly, the sight of it on my finger made my stomach flip. *Would I one day wear a ring like this from Grant?* I was way too young to think about marriage. I needed to finish school and probably get a good job before I ever saw wedding bells in my future, but still, the glittering ring did make me wonder, if even for a moment.

"Thank you," I murmured, giving my dad a hug.

"You're welcome. Now, I have to meet one more colleague tonight before I can get back to the hotel."

"I'll get her home, sir," Henry said.

"Good man," my father said, clapping him on the back. "Take care of my baby girl."

There was no way I wanted Henry to take me home. I was turning twenty this week. I could get myself around New York City. It wasn't as if I was staying in a sketchy part of town. My father had gotten me a suite at The Kimberly after all.

My father lightly squeezed my shoulder. "Let's have brunch at Norma's tomorrow, sweetheart. We can talk more before I leave the city."

I sagged and nodded. "Okay, Dad."

With that, he turned and left the restaurant, no good-bye necessary. I swallowed back my rising anger. This was not the night I had bargained for.

"Come on. I'll hail a cab." Henry pressed his hand against my lower back and guided me outside.

"Really, I'm fine. I can get there by myself." I pulled away from his hand and walked to the elevator.

Henry followed me with a smirk. "So, this guy you're seeing, is it the same one you forgot to mention on New Year's?"

"I don't really want to talk about this with you," I said.

"All right."

They got into the elevator, and it let us out on the bottom floor. Despite my annoyance, Henry hailed a cab.

"I can do that."

"I'm sure you're capable, but I wanted to do it for you." He opened the door for me.

I turned to look at him before I got inside. "You can catch the next one."

He smiled smugly and leaned forward into me. "Then, how am I going to give you your birthday present?"

I leaned away from him to deter him from doing anything drastic, like kissing me. "You didn't have to get me anything."

"Trust me. You'll like it."

"Are we moving or what?" the taxi driver yelled at us.

"You heard the man," Henry said, helping me into the cab.

"Where to?" the cabbie asked.

"The Kimberly Hotel, please."

"Beacon Theatre," Henry corrected.

"What? Why are we going to Beacon?"

From his jacket pocket, Henry produced a pair of concert tickets and passed them over to me.

I looked down at the tickets, and my stomach turned. "You got us tickets to see The Drift?"

The flashy bright sign outside of Beacon Theatre on Broadway glared down at me. I glared back.

This was the last fucking place I wanted to be tonight. But I'd agreed. I'd made a deal with the devil, only for it to be thrown back in my face. Hollis had been the connection I used to get Ari and me into that snooty restaurant on Valentine's Day. All the good that had done me. Even though it hadn't worked out how I had intended, I still had to keep up my end of the bargain.

That meant I had to walk backstage with the rest of the guys and hear Hollis out.

"Come on, bro," Miller said, clapping me on the back. "Showtime."

I wished we were playing this fucking venue tonight. The Drift had sold out the theatre for the evening on the kickoff of their new tour for their album that had dropped last week. It had soared into the Top Ten on the *Billboard* charts. As much as I wanted to hate them for it, the music was good, and Donovan's lyrics were better than ever.

I followed the rest of the band backstage and navigated through the controlled chaos. They had a crew that clearly knew how to run this place like a well-oiled machine.

A pretty brunette in a short skirt gave me a once-over as we passed by. Her friend nudged her forward, and they both broke down into giggles.

Fans, not groupies. It was strange to notice a difference. Before Ari, I'd have probably lured her in. It would have been so fucking simple, too. Now, I just turned my back on the girl I would have had on her back in about ten seconds.

Hollis stood at the end of a hall, talking to some Asian chick in a pantsuit. She looked pissed and not caught up in his charm like every other fucking person around him. His eyes lifted from the woman as we walked down the hallway and landed on me. I couldn't tell if his smile was relief or smugness that I'd shown up. I clenched my fists at my sides and resisted the urge to knock the smile off his overconfident fucking face.

"ContraBand!" Hollis called. He shook Miller's hand, fist-bumped McAvoy and Vin, and then clapped me on the back. "Glad you showed."

"Bet you are," I muttered under my breath.

"Guys, this is Mia Lu. She's a face I hope you're going to get to know around here. She's our PR rep from Pacific. She keeps your ass in line."

Mia gave him a thin-lipped smile of disapproval. She didn't exactly look like the kind of chick I'd expect to work PR for a record company. She clearly had a fucking stick up her ass. I wondered if she liked it up the ass. In my experience, the girls who pretended to be prudes were usually total fucking freaks.

"So nice to meet you boys. I truly hope once you're a part of the Pacific team, you won't need my assistance as much as Hollis insinuates." Her forced smile turned into a flat-out glare before she disappeared.

What the fuck was that about?

And they were awfully fucking sure that we were going to sign with them. By looking at my bros' eager faces, maybe they had a reason to be. I wasn't even sure I could convince my bandmates to give this up.

But if I needed to, I'd make a fucking effort.

Hollis gestured for us to follow him, and then we entered The Drift's room backstage. As the door opened, a cloud of smoke billowed out.

The first thought I had when I entered the room was, *Ari was going to fucking kill me.*

If she had been pissed about what the backstage looked like at the Poconos music festival with The Drift, she'd fucking blow a gasket here.

Half-naked groupies littered the room. If I squinted through the smoke-filled room, I even recognized some of them. Jaci and someone…Jennifer maybe, were two of the girls who had been at Donovan's penthouse party where I'd decked him.

I picked out the other guys in the band in different stages of inebriation. Ridley had his head in his hands, looking as if he might puke. Nic and Joey were cutting cocaine into a straight line in front of a blonde who had her tits out. Trevor was making out with some chick against the back wall. The only person I didn't see was Donovan.

Then, he walked in from a door across the room— shirtless and zipping his fucking jeans.

In that moment, all I could picture was Donovan getting anywhere near my girl. Anger boiled through me, and McAvoy and Miller grabbed me before I'd even realized I started storming across the room.

Hollis laughed like an idiot next to me. He'd known this was going to happen. I could see it on his face. I was really fucking glad I hadn't told Ari that I was coming up here with the guys tonight. She would never have been okay with me walking into this kind of shitstorm. I couldn't tell her until I had everything figured out.

"Why don't you guys grab a beer and relax? The set starts soon for the opener, and Drift will have a short meet-and-greet. No rush," Hollis said.

"Actually," I snapped, taking point and ignoring Miller's exasperation, "I'd like to get this shit over with, Hollis. You dragged us out here. Let's fucking talk."

Hollis had a moment of anger blaze in his eyes before attempting to smother the initial reaction. It worked about as well as cheap cologne covering the smell of a men's locker room.

"We can stay and have a beer first," Miller said. "Right, guys?"

"You know I'm fucking down!" Vin said.

"No. McDermott is right," Donovan chimed from across the room. He still hadn't bothered with a shirt. "You should finish your business here and then get the fuck out."

A chorus of laughter followed his outburst, and Miller tightened his grip on my arm. It was a silent plea to not fuck this up.

"With pleasure," I growled.

"Now, now," Hollis said. "We're all adults here." He sounded like a condescending parent. "If this all works out, then you guys will be working together."

Donovan let out a short laugh that sounded more like a bark. "You're going to need to fucking pay me more for that, Hollis."

"You'll get every penny you earned and not one more than that. Now, go put on a fucking shirt and meet your fans who paid to see you."

As Donovan turned around, grumbling about not being able to find his shirt, Hollis directed us out of the room.

He led the guys into another room down the hallway, but then he pulled me aside. He spoke low so only I could hear, "Look, whatever went down between you and Donovan is in the past. This animosity needs to end. I believe in ContraBand, Grant. I want you in the studio. I want to release an album. I want you on the road with them. I want you headlining in the future. Work with him, and make everyone's lives easier."

I was momentarily shocked by his candid behavior, but then reality crept back in. Hollis would use anything and everything he could to get what he wanted. The truth was, he didn't know what the fuck had gone down between Donovan and me. He was trying to get me to spill by offering me everything he thought I fucking wanted.

I shrugged away from him. He would have to try better than that. I gave him credit for realizing I was going to be the hardest sell but not that much credit.

"Let's get this over with," I grumbled.

Hollis grabbed my leather jacket and pulled me in close again. "I don't fucking get you. When we first met, I thought I'd found exactly what I was looking for—the right band, the right sound, the right vibe. I'd thought Frank Boseley had been an idiot for passing on the whole group and just going for you because I saw it from the beginning. You only shine amid your guys. I get it. I know someone just fucking like that. His name is Donovan Jenkins, and he's about to play for a sold-out show in New York City. His album debuted in the Top Ten of the *Billboard* charts. So, what the fuck is your problem? Don't you fucking want that?"

"Yeah, man, I want that," I told him without hesitation.

I fucking hated the dude, but maybe Hollis actually did understand. The only problem was, he didn't get what Ari meant to me one bit.

"But if you ever interfere with my girl again, I'll fucking end you," I growled.

Hollis stuck his hand out. "Deal."

"I appreciate the sentiment, but I don't want to see The Drift."

Translation: I don't want to get anywhere near Donovan Jenkins or that fucking creep Hollis Tift.

"You don't like them? I thought every girl liked them with that one song playing on repeat on the radio," Henry said.

"'Tell It Like It Is,'" I filled in for him.

"So, you do know it."

"I think everyone knows that song."

"Well, good. It's not Paris, but it'll have to do…for now," he said like that closed the discussion.

I just rolled my eyes. Henry might have met me when I was depressed about Grant, so I had been slightly malleable, but under no circumstances would I consider myself that otherwise. And he was about to see it firsthand.

"I'm not going to The Drift concert. I don't like them or their music. In fact, I despise their lead singer. He's an asshole."

"You speak as if you know him personally." Henry looked over at me with interest.

"Whatever. Just tell me why you're doing all of this."

"It's your birthday weekend. I like Jim, and I want to take care of his daughter tonight."

The way he said that made me question exactly *how* he wanted to take care of me. I knew what Grant would be thinking in this moment even though I wasn't sure if he was exactly an accurate representation of the male population. But the way Henry's eyes seemed to be laughing at his own implications, I was sure he was talking about having sex with me.

"Do I need to reiterate that I have a boyfriend?"

"Of course not," he said mockingly. "He comes up every time we're alone."

"I'm glad you got the memo then. So, let's turn this cab around. I want to sleep."

"I didn't realize you were in such a hurry." He arched an eyebrow in question and leaned toward me. He was visibly holding himself back from touching me.

"I'm in a hurry to get some sleep. Just sleep. Plus, I have homework to do." I would have all day tomorrow to do it, but that didn't matter. I'd been working my ass off to make up for that bad grade in O-chem, and I needed to keep it up. I wanted any excuse to get away from Henry.

"Well, we're celebrating my promotion, too, and I want to take you to this concert, so we're going. I can be as stubborn as you are."

Apparently, that really was the end of the conversation because he didn't take to any of the other attempts I'd made at trying to change his mind. He just sent me a devilish smile and cast his deep blue eyes over my face. I gave up, crossing my arms over my chest and sinking back into the deflated cushion.

Soon enough, the cab pulled up in front of Beacon Theatre. Henry handed over a few bills before helping me out of the vehicle. I reluctantly walked into the building. Our tickets were scanned, and the attendant let us know the opening band had already started playing—as if it wasn't obvious by the noise coming from the theater.

And it really was noise. The Drift needed a better opener than this. *What were they thinking?*

I was so lost in my thoughts about the opening band that I didn't realize Henry wasn't walking us into the auditorium seating, but toward a roped-off door.

"Box seats?" I asked, confused. I wasn't familiar with Beacon Theatre, and I didn't know the layout.

"Better."

It wasn't until I was already backstage, staring at the dwindling line of squealing teen girls, that I fully comprehended what Henry had meant by *better*.

I stopped dead in my tracks. "No."

Henry gave me a perplexed look. "Come on. Backstage passes," he said, flashing the shiny passes he'd held back from view until that moment.

"Don't care."

I turned to go, but Henry latched on to my arm. "What's with you?"

"I said no," I spat at him. "Are you fucking deaf? I don't want to be here. I don't want to see the band. I don't want to meet them. Now, let me go and stop this ridiculous charade. We both know why you're doing all of this, and it's not going to work."

Then, I heard *his* laugh from over my shoulder. I could practically feel his green eyes boring into my back. When I turned around, Donovan was smiling as if he'd just won the lottery, and I was the cash prize.

I groaned as Donovan abandoned the group of girls vying for his attention and strolled over to me. "Now, that is a face I've missed seeing." His eyes flickered to Henry and then back to me. He arched an eyebrow. I knew he was enjoying this. "New beau, beautiful?"

Henry looked stunned, which was the only good part about this entire ordeal.

"Hello, Donovan."

"Did you miss me?"

"Hardly. We were just leaving, weren't we?"

"You know the lead singer personally?" Henry asked.

"Astute deductive reasoning skills. I'm going to give you an award for your brilliance," I said dryly.

"How do you know him?" Henry asked.

"Well, there was this time over New Year's—" Donovan began.

I slapped him on the chest. "Do *not* finish that sentence." I glowered at him.

Henry stared between Donovan and me as realization seemed to cross his face. "So, when you said he was an asshole, you meant because you guys were together," he guessed.

I closed my eyes and pinched the bridge of my nose. "Yes, I'm a total groupie slut. Obviously. That's how I know everyone. Let me call up Adam Levine and John Mayer. We're like besties." The sarcasm dripped off of every single word. I couldn't hold back my disdain and disbelief that this was happening.

"Oh, come on," Donovan said, laughter in his eyes. "An asshole is all you've got? I distinctly remember you comparing me to the wolf in 'Little Red Riding Hood' and something about acting as if I were from the sixteenth century or something. I know you have better comebacks."

"Seventeenth century. And you *are* an asshole, Donovan. I'm glad Grant got in a good hit. You deserved it."

"Who is Grant?" Henry asked.

Donovan stuck a thumb out at Henry. "He doesn't know about your boyfriend?"

"Stop! Both of you. This is enough. I'm leaving." I spun on my heel and started for the door.

"Huh. Interesting," Donovan mused.

I was not going to give in to him.

"I thought you were here to see him, and I just got to you first."

My stomach twisted, and my heart thumped wildly in my chest. *What was he talking about? No, he was baiting me. I wouldn't ask.* Regardless, my steps slowed.

"Now, I'm starting to wonder if you even know he's signing."

That stopped me short.

"Signing?" I asked. My voice came out breathy.

"He's in there with Hollis right now."

My mouth dropped open. Donovan was a liar. This couldn't be true. Grant would never sign with Pacific without at least talking to me about it. I didn't have any delusions that I would change his mind. This was everything the band wanted, but I wanted to be a part of the process. It was a life-altering decision after all.

An Asian woman came over and tapped Donovan's shoulder before speaking softly in his ear.

"Well, I have a show to play right now. If it doesn't work out, stick around. I'd be happy for a revenge fuck or, you know, whatever you're into." He threw out the suggestion so casually that I couldn't even respond before he walked away.

"So, your boyfriend is in a band?" Henry asked with barely concealed humor. "No wonder you didn't say anything else to your father."

"I can't talk about this right now."

"Do you want to go?"

Yes, I really did. I didn't want to stand here and wonder if Grant was backstage, talking to Hollis and signing a recording contract. I didn't want to wonder why he had lied to me and held back information after our big blowup about communicating. He'd known I was coming into the city to meet my father for dinner. *Had he used that as his excuse to get out of telling me about it?*

This wasn't exactly something he could hide. I'd find out what was going on one way or another. Eventually, ContraBand would record an album and go on tour. *Why hide it?*

My overactive brain raced through possibilities that I wanted nothing more than to ignore. I wouldn't jump to conclusions. Maybe he was just here to talk to Hollis and find out what the fuck he wanted. Maybe it wasn't a recording contract. Maybe Grant hadn't come to a decision. Maybe…

Maybe I should leave.

But I couldn't.

"No, I should stay. You should go."

"I'm not leaving you here alone."

"What part of *go* don't you understand? I'm not a child. I can take care of myself."

"You're the boss's daughter. I'm not abandoning you in New York City while backstage at a rock concert with some asshole lead singer and your supposed boyfriend. I'll take my chances with those odds," Henry said. Crossing his arms, he gave me a look that said arguing with him would be like trying to take down a brick wall with my bare hands.

I threw up my hands in defeat and wandered further backstage. I was stopped almost immediately by a staff member.

"I'm just looking for ContraBand."

"Sorry. No ContraBand here," he said. "This is The Drift show."

"Yeah, I realize." I tried to contain my sarcasm while I talked to this idiot. It was difficult with the mood I was in. "But another band came in here to talk to the manager for Pacific Entertainment. I'm looking for them."

"Haven't seen another band, and the meet-and-greet is over. So, you should probably get to your seats. The Drift will be playing shortly."

I cursed under my breath and then walked back to Henry.

"No luck?" He gave me this sly smile that said everything I needed to know.

"I'm just going to wait here."

"Suit yourself."

Goddamn smug smile.

"Good doing business with you boys," Hollis said, shaking our hands.

I couldn't believe this was happening. After all this time, we were going to get signed. Our dreams were becoming a reality. Everything was fucking falling into place. It felt too good to be true. Victory showed on everyone's faces.

Miller wanted to have a lawyer present before we signed, or we probably would have gone through with the whole thing tonight. The terms Hollis had suggested sounded fucking awesome. I didn't know how it had happened, but in the space of a conversation, I was sold.

"I'll be in contact when we have the contract in place."

Vin was the first out the door, barreling through it like a bulldozer leveling a building. "Fuck yeah. We're going to be on a fucking world tour soon. I'm going to get all sorts of foreign pussy."

McAvoy laughed. "More likely, foreign dick."

Vin punched him, but it was halfhearted. Even Vin couldn't get upset right now, which was saying something.

I was on cloud nine. "Thanks for dragging me out here tonight," I told Miller.

"Someone has to be the sane and rational one in the group."

"Well, it's not Vin."

We both looked up at our friend and shook our heads.

"Definitely not." Miller scratched the back of his head. "I hate to bring this up because I don't want to burst your bubble. But...Ari?"

My steps slowed. "What about her?"

"You going to talk to her about this? I know it's none of my fucking business, but I do like the sanity-inducing effect she has on your idiotic self. I don't want this to come out of left field."

"Let's get a fucking drink!" Vin called as we exited the hallway.

"It won't come out of left field. Ari gets it," I confidently told him. "It'll be fine."

Miller tightly grabbed my shoulder in his hand. "Bro, you sure?"

He nodded his head to the left, and I followed his gaze. I gaped in shock at seeing Ari standing backstage at The Drift show.

What the fuck was she doing here? Did she know the band had driven up here? Had she followed me under the pretenses of seeing her father?

No, I knew she had this dinner with her dad. She couldn't have known about this show.

Maybe she wasn't here to see me. Maybe she didn't even know I was here. Maybe she was here for Donovan.

The rational side of my brain fled the building. *If Ari wasn't here for me, then what the fuck was she doing here?*

All I knew was I was going to find out.

I stalked across the room. Ari shifted as if already sensing my eyes on her. Her mouth dropped open in shock, only confirming my belief that she hadn't even fucking known I was going to be here. My hackles rose, and I couldn't shake the nagging feeling of betrayal. Ever since she had told me she'd kissed someone else while we were apart, I'd had a hard time disconnecting.

"What are you doing here?" I demanded without thinking.

Ari's defenses immediately went up. "What am *I* doing here? What are *you* doing here?"

"Don't make this about me. You didn't even know I was here. Were you here for someone else?"

Her mouth dropped open in shock, and then her hurricane-blue eyes stormed over. "How dare you! You're the one hiding your location and the reason you're here, yet you're accusing me of coming here to see someone else. Have you lost your mind?"

"Technically, you are here with someone else," a guy said from behind her.

I hadn't even fucking noticed him. I definitely hadn't thought he was with Ari. He was in a suit and looked like a trussed-up preppy douche bag. Then again, Ari was in a pretty hot black dress. It made me want to simultaneously rip it off of her and demand to know why she would wear it for some other asshole.

"Stay out of this," Ari snapped at the guy.

"Who the hell is this guy?" I demanded.

She deflated under the question, which set my blood from simmer to high.

"This is Henry," she murmured softly and then kept speaking in a rush, "I had no idea he was going to be here tonight. My father invited him. I didn't even know he was in the city. This isn't what it looks like."

I saw red. "You're here with the douche you kissed when we were split up."

"You didn't say you were split up," Henry accused.

"Henry!" she snapped.

"And you never even told him?" I asked.

"Stop. Just stop!" She ran a shaky hand back through her hair, which was when I saw the glittering diamond on her finger.

"What the fuck is that?" I pointed at her hand in shock.

"What?" she cried, exasperated.

"Is that a fucking engagement ring?"

Ari looked down at the ring on her finger and then groaned. "No! Oh my God! I can't believe you would even think that."

"What am I supposed to think when you show up here with him and are now wearing a *diamond*?" I was about to combust.

"I *don't* know. Maybe trust me! This is from my father! It's a birthday present! It was my mother's original engagement ring. He wanted me to have it. Jesus!"

I shook my head. I was a little thrown off. Ari had fucking parents who gave her family heirlooms. Not to mention, it was a bigger rock than anything I'd *ever* be able to afford for her. *How was I supposed to compete with that shit?*

"And you don't find it suspicious that your dad would give you something like this around the fucking dude he's weirdly trying to hook you up with?"

"It was a birthday present! This is *not* about Henry. This is about you being here. Why didn't you tell me you were coming to the concert? Did you sign? Is that what this is about?"

"I didn't tell you because I knew you'd freak. I had to figure out what we're doing, what's right for the band. I can't do that with you in my goddamn head."

"I don't even know what that means!"

"It means, if I want to sign, I don't want to deal with your judgment."

Her mouth dropped open. "I don't judge your music! I've been completely encouraging."

"Keep telling yourself that, Princess."

Her lips drew into a thin line, and she looked as if she might rear back and punch me. Maybe I deserved it, but if she thought she wasn't judgmental, then she was delusional. She hated the lifestyle—the groupies, drugs, booze, sex. She hated the other bands. She hated the thought that we would be on tour with our vices. She hated it all.

Until that moment, I didn't realize how true that really was…and how much it pissed me the fuck off.

"Fine. Fine!" she spat. "I'm not going to stand around and argue with you. If you want to believe the worst about me, then *fine*, Grant. It's much easier to assume I wouldn't want you to be here, signing, then to simply ask me."

"I don't have to ask you. I see it on your face."

"I thought we already talked about all of this! You know what? Forget it. You've made it clear the business side of the music industry isn't something you want to talk to me about. Obviously, you'll be the only one affected by the changes, so it's not important to discuss them with me." She held up her hand. "I'm going to go. When you figure it out, come talk to me."

She turned on her heel and walked toward the door. I stared after her retreating back with a mixed bag of emotions eating away at me. On one hand, I wanted to rush after her and tell her she wasn't allowed to fucking walk away from me. On the other hand, I just wanted her to be gone. As she walked away from me, her judgment weighed heavily in the air.

"Thanks, man," Henry said with a nod of his head in my direction.

"What?"

"I couldn't have asked for a better performance."

I glared at him. "Get the fuck out of here."

Henry laughed at me before following Ari out the stage door.

My stomach sank as soon as they were gone. I'd let her walk out. He'd gone with her. It was as if I'd been pitched headfirst into an ice bath. I'd pushed her away...right into the arms of someone else. *What the fuck was wrong with me? Why did she drive me up the wall?*

Everything was either fiery passion or icy-cold arguments. Either way, I couldn't get my head on straight around her.

"Bro, what just happened?" Miller asked, appearing at my side.

"Honestly, I've no fucking clue."

"Why did she leave? You fuck up?"

I nodded. "I..."

I tried to process.

"She was here with the guy who she kissed over break, and I fucking lost it. It's as if she's got this goddamn vise grip on my brain, so it stops functioning when she's around."

"Because you love her, dipshit," Miller said as if it were the most obvious answer in the world.

"Fuck. Fuck!" I cried. "She can't be with him."

"Then, what are you still doing here?" Miller shoved me forward. "Go after her."

I was running through the backstage area as soon as Miller finished his sentence. My feet pounded on the carpeted floor, out the lobby, and onto the sidewalk. I thrust my hand out into traffic to catch a passing cab with only one thought on my mind.

I have to fix this.
I have to fix this.
I have to fix this.

18 · Aribel

That motherfucker.

I couldn't believe he had come all the way out here without saying one word to me beforehand. I couldn't believe he had hidden the fact that Pacific was trying to sign them. I couldn't believe he had called me judgmental. He hadn't even *asked* my opinion on it. He was too chickenshit to even find out.

I had finally confessed about kissing Henry. I'd thought everything was out in the open, but he'd been holding back.

What did all of this say about us? Were we too fucked up to have a realistic relationship? Was I blinded by the fact that I loved him?

I felt deluded by how desperately I wanted to be with him. It shouldn't be this hard. It shouldn't hurt this bad. It shouldn't feel as if he had just punched me in the gut when I could see in his face that all he'd wanted to do was hold me close.

My world had always been ruled by logic, but Grant had pushed all logic aside. In its place had grown this inexplicable fear.

Fear of losing him.

Fear of losing myself.

Fear of it all crashing down.

Fear of it not being worth it.

I was so *mad* at him—for everything. But I was equally mad at myself.

I slammed my finger on the elevator button and ignored the hulking presence behind me. I hadn't even fought Henry about the cab on the way back to the hotel. Grant hadn't tried to stop me or come after me, so what would it matter if someone else got me back to my hotel?

We stepped into the elevator, and I pressed the button for the top floor. My father had gotten me a suite, and all I could think about was tumbling headfirst into the king-sized bed and burying my heartache under a mound of pillows.

The elevator opened up onto my floor, and I found my suite number. Sliding the key card into the door, I turned the handle, flipped on the lights, and walked into the room. Henry followed right behind me inside my suite.

"What are you doing?" I demanded.

He gave me this little smile, and I had no idea what it meant, but I was sure I wasn't going to like it. Then, he pushed past me, heading further into the hotel room and going straight toward the phone.

"Henry?"

He held the phone to his ear. "Calling for a bottle of champagne—unless you'd like something stronger?"

My mouth dropped open. "No. I don't want anything. I want you to leave, so I can go to sleep."

"You can't sleep in your condition," he said matter-of-factly, entirely ignoring the rest of my statement. "You need to wind down and relax." He dialed the number for room service. "Yes, would you send up your best bottle of champagne and a glass of Johnnie Walker Blue?"

"Scotch and champagne?" I asked indignantly. This was not what I needed when I was pissed about Grant.

"We are celebrating, aren't we?"

As if that was the reason he wanted me to drink.

"No. I don't feel like celebrating."

He sat down on the plush black leather couch in the living room and crossed his leg at the ankle. He ran one hand back through his messy dark blond hair before responding, "Then, we'll just drink. You can close the door. Room service will knock."

I turned away from him as I wavered with indecision. I was mad and frustrated, but my anger wasn't directed at Henry.

I was mad at Grant. Henry was collateral damage in all of this. He was a reminder of the lengths my family would go to keep me on the straight and narrow. Even though Grant and I were…complicated, I still had no intention of making things worse by hooking up with Henry. The thought alone made my stomach turn.

With Grant…I always knew that, one day, he would get signed. ContraBand was on the rise. It made sense to me that they would try to secure a recording contract. None of this had come out of left field for me. I just hadn't anticipated that he would sneak around behind my back about an offer.

My eyes found Henry's blue ones once more.

Oh, right.

Henry had been my secret, one that completely fit into my perfect life where I never had to keep secrets.

While Grant was very talented and was going to be very successful, it would be doing something my parents would never approve of.

The whole thing gave me a headache. Sleep was sounding more and more inviting.

"Aribel," Henry said softly, "it's just a drink."

I sighed. "Fine. One drink."

I shrugged out of my coat and threw it on the back of the couch.

A couple of minutes later, room service arrived with the drinks. The guy popped the top off the bottle for us, poured two glasses, and then left after Henry handed him a crisp twenty-dollar bill. I took a sip of my drink and tried to let the bubbles soothe my temper, but it really wasn't doing that great of a job. Anyway, I didn't even want to be drinking. I wanted to be sleeping away the anger, so in the morning, I could think clearly about what to do.

Henry downed his glass of scotch before I'd even gotten through half of my first glass of champagne. He reached for his champagne and finished that, too.

Classical music came through the surround-sound system, and my head popped up in surprise.

Henry smiled down at me and held his hand out. "Dance?" he offered.

"No, thank you."

"Oh, come on," he said, taking my hand that I hadn't offered and pulling me off the sofa.

He twirled me in place as if he'd had years of formal ballroom training, which I supposed he probably had. Then, he tugged me against him, all to the time of the music.

I squirmed and tried to pull away. "Really, I don't feel like dancing. Just stop."

"But you're so good at it." His head dipped down into the crook of my neck and nuzzled the soft skin.

"Henry!" I cried. "Stop it."

I tried to get away from him, but he had me locked in a tight embrace. His right arm wrapped around my back, and his left hand clasped mine in a death grip. His right hand traveled to my ass, and he pulled back to look at me with a dirty gleam in his eye.

"Come on, Princess."

"Get away from me." I wrenched out of his embrace. I couldn't believe he had used Grant's nickname. "What the fuck do you think you're doing?"

"I was just helping you relax." He gave me the sweetest smile he could muster up, and still, it didn't hide the snake.

"I think our definitions of relaxing are different."

"You're in a bad place right now. You need someone to be here for you. I want to be that person, Aribel. That idiot can't take care of you. He can't even seem to appreciate what's right in front of his face. Just let me stay the night."

I rolled my eyes. *What a crock of shit.*

"I don't need *anyone* to take care of me—least of all you. So, you can turn around right now and get out of my hotel room. I might be angry, but I'm not an idiot."

"You'd have to be an idiot to want to be with me?"

"Yes! You just tried to sexually assault me! Now, get out!" I stormed across the room and jerked open the hotel door. "You've overstayed your welcome. In fact, you were never really welcome. And if you don't leave, I'll have security escort you out!"

19 GRANT

By the time I pulled up the GPS on my phone to find out where the fuck Ari's hotel was, the cab had already driven me five blocks in the opposite direction. He had claimed to know where we were going. It had taken everything in me not to punch him in the back of the head for his stupidity and get in another cab. All I wanted to do was get to Ari and talk to her like a civil human being. I couldn't ever manage that shit when it mattered.

I couldn't stop running through what I was going to do once I got there. *Find her, apologize, fuck her.* Things would get better.

She needed to know I trusted her, that I wanted to tell her about these things. I'd just freaked the fuck out at the thought of leaving her. If I signed, then we'd be on tour, no doubt about it. Hollis would ship us out with some shithole band, and then who knew when I'd see her next? I didn't want to have to face that before I was ready. I didn't want Ari to have to face it at all. She deserved better.

But that didn't mean that douche bag Henry could have her.

I hadn't understood what he was saying when he thanked me. I'd been so pissed off at everything that was going on that I hadn't realized he was thanking me for sending Ari straight into his arms. I'd never let that happen, not if I could help it.

I jotted out a text to Ari, letting her know I was on the way.

> *Coming to The Kimberly. Please meet me downstairs. We need to talk.*

The cab stopped outside of The Kimberly. As soon as I paid the fare, I jumped out of the car and into the drizzle that had started on my way over here. I ducked under the overhang, and the doorman pulled the door open for me.

"Hey, man. Did you see a girl walk in here? Blonde about yea-tall," I said, holding my hand up to my shoulder, "in a nice black dress and jacket. I don't know. Maybe ten minutes ago?"

"Sure, I saw her. She was here with a man in a suit," the doorman offered.

He was warily eyeing me, and I realized I probably looked like shit compared to the normal clientele at this place.

"Yes. Most likely. Did you see where she went?"

"Last I saw, she went up in the elevator with the gentleman she was with."

Fuck.

Fuck, fuck, fuck.

Fucking fuck.

My first instinct was to ram my hand into the side of the brick building. Pain exploded through my arm, and I cursed loudly.

"Sir, are you all right?" the doorman asked. He looked as if he wanted to find out what the hell my problem was and force me to leave, but instead, he stared at me as if I were some strange specimen.

My knuckles were throbbing, and it looked as if I'd broken the skin. I shook out my hand, trying to ignore the pain. The real issue here was that Ari had gone upstairs with Henry.

Upstairs to her hotel room.

With Henry.

My brain wasn't wrapping itself around the concept. *What the fuck?* She had said they had kissed over break, but that he meant nothing to her. Now, he was here in New York. It all seemed so...coincidental. *Too coincidental.*

She wouldn't cheat on me. She wouldn't fucking do that to me. I needed to talk to her. I needed to hear it out of her mouth that she wasn't fucking some dude in an expensive-ass hotel room to forget about me.

I fumbled with my phone and went back out under the awning. She hadn't responded to the text message I sent earlier. I clicked her number and hugged the phone to my ear. It rang three times before going to voice mail.

"Hey, this is Aribel. Leave a message after the tone."

"Ari, answer your phone. We need to talk. Call me back."

I hung up, feeling like a complete fucking idiot. *Who was I to chase after a girl like this?* My whole fucking life, chicks had pursued me. Now, I was turning into a goddamn lunatic at the thought of Ari being with someone else. I'd do anything to make this right.

Maybe she was already in the lobby. Maybe she'd gotten my message, and she was coming down to see me. I pushed past the doorman in a hurry.

My eyes scanned the small lobby in earnest. An older couple was sitting on a sofa. Otherwise, the place was empty.

No Ari.

No Henry.

Nothing.

I stormed over to the front desk and tried to put a smile on for the female desk clerk. I could be charming even with this fucking thundercloud over my head. I could get what I wanted. She would tell me how to find my fucking girlfriend.

"Hey," I said.

The woman glanced up at me and then back down at her computer screen, unimpressed.

Right. Classy-ass joint. I'd need a bit more of my usual swagger than what I was mustering up at the moment.

"Hello, sir. How can I help you?"

"Hi, Rachel," I said, reading the gold name tag on her chest. I ignored the small amount of cleavage peeking out of her top and directed my gaze into her almost black eyes. "I'm trying to locate someone who is staying here."

She gave me a look that told me to explain, so I jumped right in.

"I'm trying to find Aribel Graham's room. She told me she was staying here, and I'm supposed to meet her, but she didn't tell me what number she was in."

Rachel's eyes narrowed slightly. "I'm sorry. I can't help you with that. We keep all our customers' information private."

I laughed confidently and leaned against the desk. "I get it. I totally hate asking, but I think her phone is dead. I just got into the city. See, I'm on tour with The Drift and wanted to see my girl when I was finished."

"The band, The Drift?"

"That's the one," I lied.

She seemed to look at me a tad more appreciatively, but I still hadn't moved her. "I really wish I could help, but if she didn't give you that information, I absolutely cannot provide it."

"All right. I don't want you breaking any rules." I shot a smile that said I'd love for her to do nothing more. "But can you call up to her room and let her know I'm down here?"

"I would if I could, but I can't," she said diplomatically. "No outside contact with customers. You have to understand."

She cast her eyes back to the computer monitor. It was a dismissal. I couldn't fucking be dismissed.

"Please," I begged.

I was fucking begging. *Shoot me now.*

"Please, I need to see her."

Her eyes softened for a second, and then she shook her head. "Don't ask again. It's against company policy. I'd lose my job."

I nodded numbly. I understood. I didn't want to get the poor girl fired. I just wanted to see my girlfriend. I wanted to make her understand.

Why was that so difficult? She could walk down from her room, and we'd talk like normal people instead of the insane people who took up residence inside of our heads when we argued.

I loved Ari. That was really fucking obvious. But I couldn't keep letting our alter egos take over during our conversations. I needed to remain calm.

I needed a fucking joint, but I wouldn't go get one.

No, I'd sit right here on the fucking couch near the old couple and watch the elevator doors. Even if Ari never came down, Henry would have to at some point. I just had to keep fucking telling myself that.

She'd never do anything with that motherfucker. She would never let him stay. She was smarter than that.

I sat down and stared. Every time the elevator doors dinged open, I'd jump up from my spot and wait for him to exit. Anticipation settled in my stomach as I imagined all the horrible things I'd do to him when I saw him, and then I'd make him tell me which room Ari was in. Intermittently, I'd call her cell phone, but after the third time of no answer, I stopped trying.

My best bet was to wait. I ignored Miller's curious and worried text messages asking me where I was and wondering if I was going to go back to Princeton tonight.

I told myself Henry would come downstairs. I told myself that same fucking phrase so often that I almost believed it.

But after four solid hours of nothing, I realized the truth. Henry wasn't leaving. Ari wasn't coming downstairs.

And I was a motherfucking idiot for hoping...for trying.

Rachel gave me a sad look and a farewell wave as I stood, but she had never changed her stance. I left The Kimberly Hotel, feeling like a steamroller had flattened me.

The doorman was still there. He asked me how my hand was, but I waved him off with it. *Who cared how my hand was when the rest of me had been blown to smithereens?*

When I never returned to Beacon Theatre, Miller had texted me the address to the hotel the band had gotten for the night. It was surprisingly easy to get to, and since Miller had left my name at the front, it was even easier to get a key from the woman at the desk. As I plucked the card out of her hand, I felt utter disdain for the bitch who had refused to let me up to see Ari.

Sliding the card into the slot, I pushed open the door and found Vin and McAvoy passed out and snoring. Miller looked exhausted, but it was clear that he had been waiting for me.

"What happened, bro? You look like shit," Miller said.

"I feel like shit."

I ran a shaky hand back through my hair. Maybe I was in fucking shock.

"You and Ari okay?"

"I never fucking saw her."

Miller's eyebrows shot up. "You've been there the whole time and didn't even talk to her? I thought you guys were arguing or some shit."

"No. I couldn't get up to her, and she didn't answer her phone. She left with Henry, he went up with her, and he never left. In four hours, he never left. So, the fucker is staying the night…with my girl."

"Nothing happened."

"How the fuck do you know?" I asked, kicking off my shoes and wishing for something to take the edge off.

"Because she loves you."

"Yeah. You feel that way about Sydney, and you're fucking around on her."

Miller glared at me. "Don't fucking bring Sydney into this situation. You know she doesn't want anything serious, and Ari does. Completely different people."

TAKE ME WITH *you*

"Fine," I grumbled. I was too mentally and emotionally exhausted to argue. My heart was shredded. I just wanted everything to go back to the way it was before.

"Talk to her when you get home. Things will be fine."

"She's not going to be able to handle the road, bro. She doesn't even like the League, and you and I both know the scene on the road is going to be so much fucking worse than that."

"You don't know what she can and can't handle. Maybe she can't," he said quickly when I glared at him. "But...maybe she can. Give her a fucking chance. She won't need to worry about life on tour if you can show her there's no reason to worry."

"Yeah, man, and how the fuck do I do that?"

He shrugged. "You'll figure it out."

I clenched my fists, and pain rushed through me again. "If she fucked that other dude, I'll fucking murder him."

"Ari isn't fucking anyone but you. As soon as you realize that, you'll be fucking solid, man."

Miller turned over and closed his eyes. He was out like a light, leaving me all alone to think about what he had said.

I just needed to trust Ari, yet all I could see was the anger in her eyes and the blinding madness she drove me to. *How could we make something like that work?*

How had everything spiraled so far out of control?

One minute, Grant and I would be happy. The next, we would be arguing. We'd talk and figure things out, and it'd seem that everything was all right again between us. Then, everything would fall apart.

How could loving someone hurt this bad?

All I wanted to do was make things right, but I wouldn't make the first move. I couldn't swallow my pride and go to him. He was the one who was in the wrong. Nothing was happening between Henry and me, and I certainly wasn't *stalking* Grant to find out about what had happened with Pacific.

He didn't trust me. He didn't trust that we could get through this together. It was a blow, and I'd be lying if I said it didn't hurt.

It hurt like a bitch.

The next morning, while I was on my way to have breakfast with my father, I saw the missed calls from Grant, but I couldn't bring myself to return the messages. I had told him to come talk to me when he figured out his problem, but *I* wasn't ready to talk to him. I was still mad. I needed more time to cool off, or we would keep repeating the same disastrous mistakes over and over again.

I knew he would call me again when he was ready.

Except he didn't.

Not that day or the next or the next.

I hadn't heard one word from Grant in three whole days.

When I woke up the next morning, the day of my birthday, I was struck with all this hope that things would be different today. Grant would show up at my apartment and wish me a happy birthday. We'd fall into bed together, the memories of our argument drifting from our minds with the feel of our bodies pressed together. I'd cry out his name, feel release wash over me, and know I hadn't made a horrible mistake in walking out of the theater and refusing to return his calls the next day.

But there was no Grant waiting for me when I woke up, not even a call. There was just my unfinished O-chem assignment on the kitchen table and a package from the girls, wrapped in little kids birthday paper.

My hope winked out like a flame deprived of oxygen.

"Happy birthday!" Cheyenne cried.

She walked into the dining room carrying a stack of pancakes with a candle lit in the middle. Shelby and Gabi followed behind her. They all started up with a chorus of, "Happy Birthday," and I just stoically stared at them. I wasn't really in the mood to celebrate.

Cheyenne unceremoniously plopped the plate down in front of me.

"I know it's not a cake, but we know you love blueberry pancakes!" Gabi said.

"It's great. Thanks, guys," I responded automatically.

"Make a wish!" Shelby crooned.

I wasn't much in a wishing mood. The other wishes I had made weren't coming true, but I couldn't deny my friends this after they had gone through all the trouble.

I leaned forward and closed my eyes. *I wish for everything with Grant to be all right.*

It felt dumb wishing for something I could fix by picking up the phone and giving into my stubbornness. But I didn't feel in the wrong here. So, I blew out the candle and hoped wishes came true.

The girls had splurged on a new outfit for me. It was nothing like anything I owned, and I assumed it was Cheyenne's influence, but they all looked so happy I couldn't even muster up the sarcasm to ask.

"Where am I going to wear this?" I asked, holding up the sparkly sequined backless dress that secured around my neck. They'd paired it with shiny gold hoop earrings, heeled booties, and a matching hair clip.

"Tonight of course!" Cheyenne said. "We're taking you out for a drink!"

"Oh no," I said. I pushed the dress back into the box and then held my hands up. "I don't want my birthday to be a big deal. I have to finish my homework and go to class, and then I'd rather stay in, eat ice cream, and watch Netflix."

"No way!" Shelby cried.

"Not in the plan," Gabi agreed.

"Please, please, please, guys! I don't want to do this. Maybe this weekend?"

"Don't think for a second we believe you when you say this weekend. We've lived with you for over a year," Cheyenne said, sinking into her hip and giving me a dirty look. "If we don't get you out tonight, you'll never go out with us."

I groaned. *Why did my birthday have to fall on this week?* All I wanted to do was crawl into bed and forget about what had happened with Grant.

"You better be ready to go by seven tonight, or I'm going to get a free-for-all with your hair and makeup."

Cheyenne was teasing, but I wouldn't put it past her to doll me up to an unrecognizable state. The girl could work makeup like no one else I'd ever known. I knew enough to brush a mascara wand over my lashes, dab some blush on my cheeks, and apply a coat of lip gloss. The rest I tended to ignore.

"Fine," I muttered. "Besides, I could probably use a drink."

Somehow, Cheyenne got her claws into me anyway. She added curls into my typically stick straight hair and made my dark blue eyes smoky. I suddenly had high cheekbones and rosy cheeks. My lips were full and red. I hardly recognized myself.

I slipped into the black sequined dress and booties, slid the hoop earrings into my ears, and adjusted the diamond ring on my right hand that my father had given me this weekend. Seeing my reflection in the mirror made me anxious.

This was not the Aribel Graham who had dated Benjamin Curtis and cared more about her calculus homework than the breakup.

I almost felt…powerful.

It was a feeling I'd never associated with getting dressed up like this. I knew I was powerful because I was smart and determined to succeed. I knew I was powerful because I wouldn't let other people stand in my way or make me feel like less for knowing who I am. Now, for the first time, I felt powerful as a woman.

If only Grant could see me like this…

My heart sank.

No Grant tonight though.

I rolled my shoulders back and stood up straight. If he didn't call me before midnight, then I'd have to take this into my own hands. I would not be the girl who sulked over a boy on her birthday.

Determined and with a plan of action, I left the house with my girlfriends.

Cheyenne pulled up to the League, and I nearly groaned.

"Isn't there anywhere else in town we can go to get a drink?"

"Yes. But why would we want to?" she asked.

"Oh, I don't know. Maybe because I haven't heard from Grant in four days, and I don't want to be reminded of him."

The silence constricted the air in the car. Cheyenne exchanged a look with the girls in the backseat.

Shelby finally responded, "It's going to be okay. Try not to think about Grant tonight."

"Do I have any choice in the matter?"

"Nope," Cheyenne said, popping the door to her car.

I counted to five before following her out of the car. I walked precariously on my high heels toward the club. A sense of foreboding washed over me. I didn't want to be here. Tension pricked at my skin, and the hairs on the back of my neck stood on end.

"Maybe we shouldn't go in," I said, stopping before the entrance. "I don't feel good. I want to go home."

Cheyenne gave me an exasperated look. "You cannot go home, looking like that."

"I can do whatever I want."

"What she means"—Shelby wrapped her arm around mine—"is that you cannot get down on yourself so hard, all because of one boy."

"Guys are all idiots," Gabi agreed. "Grant is super hot, but he's still just a boy."

"Going home now would be giving in," Shelby said.

"Yeah. You're better than this," Cheyenne said.

I closed my eyes in frustration. They were right. I was better than this. I didn't need a guy to make it okay for me to go out like this.

I just wished he were here to see it. I wished he were here constantly, even when we were arguing. I missed him. The thought struck me harder than the rest of it. I needed to call him, and he needed to come see me.

"I'm going to make a phone call, and then I'll meet you inside."

"We'll wait for you," Gabi said quickly.

"Seriously, it'll only be a minute."

Cheyenne grabbed Gabi's and Shelby's arms. "Come on, girls. Let's go inside. We'll see you in a minute, but if we wait longer than five, we're sending out a rescue squad."

"Fine," I said, fluttering my fingers at them.

As soon as they were gone, I dialed Grant's number. It rang forever before clicking over to voice mail. I sighed with regret.

Guess he doesn't want to talk to me after all.

I'd made the effort. I'd felt so guilty for holding back from calling, but now that I had, he hadn't answered.

Wishes really didn't come true. It had been silly to hope that we could fix everything that had gone wrong.

One drink. I'll stay for one drink, I told myself as I walked into the League.

The room was dark, pitch-black, and I couldn't see a thing.

What the hell? What was going on? Where were my friends and all the other bar patrons? Had the lights gone out? There wasn't a storm or anything.

Then, all of a sudden, light flooded the room, and people burst from their hiding spots as they yelled, "Happy birthday!"

Icy wind whipped at my leather jacket as my motorcycle zipped down the narrow side street. My fingers were numb inside the thick gloves gripping the bike. My lips were chapped and raw behind my helmet, and my lungs ached from breathing in the wintry air.

Yet I throttled the accelerator, leaned into the bike, and pushed it to the max. The hum of the bike and the winds high-pitched whistling were my only companions. I was outrunning my problems as usual. I kicked the bike into overdrive and hit the ground, going over a hundred miles an hour. Maybe I could outpace my demons, outpace the fact that my world was crumbling about as fast as a demolition team could take down a building.

My father was out of jail.

My band was picking up steam at the exact wrong time.

My girl wouldn't even speak to me.

Why had I thought all of this would fucking work out? It made no fucking sense. *I'd let Ari in and for what? So she could get pissed at me, fuck some other dude, and then ignore me?*

The logical side of my brain, otherwise known as Miller yammering in my ear, had told me I was being stupid. Ari would never go off with another guy. She had picked me. I had taken her virginity. I was the *only* one for her. She wasn't a groupie. She wasn't some slut who would throw herself at the first guy she saw when we were in an argument.

But the other side of my brain, my devil on my shoulder, had told me I was a chump for believing, for even wanting to believe that was true.

The doorman had told me she had gone up to her room with Henry. She had ignored my phone calls. I'd stayed there for over four hours, and he had never come downstairs. He had never left. *If they weren't upstairs fucking, then what the fuck were they doing in her hotel room all night?*

I slowed as I came upon the next turn. The roads were shit this time of year. I couldn't get the same traction I liked during the summer. I wanted to push faster, but it was starting to get dark, and my vision was blurring with the decreasing speeds.

I basically had no fucking clue where I was at this point. I'd turned off the interstate fifteen minutes ago, and these back roads were looking less and less familiar. I wasn't sure I'd ever gone this way.

But it didn't fucking matter. I wanted to keep speeding away, to stop thinking about Ari. Even out here in the middle of fucking nowhere, I couldn't escape her. She clouded my thoughts worse than anything else ever had.

I'd wanted to call her and rush over to her apartment to make things right. I'd wanted to wish her a happy birthday and fuck her until the fighting stopped.

But when I'd hopped on my bike, I'd driven in the opposite direction and kept driving until I was fucking freezing cold and hungry as a dog. I'd driven away from the surprise birthday party I'd planned and her happy smiling face when she realized why everyone was there, and I'd kept driving even though I knew she'd be there, looking for me.

But I couldn't go to a party I'd planned while wondering about our relationship. I couldn't fake being okay with her…even on her birthday. And I couldn't show up and ruin the whole thing either. She'd be better off without me tonight. I'd just end up doing what I do best— make her miserable.

With Ari on my mind, I rounded a sharp blind turn, and I realized my mistake a minute too late. I slammed on my brakes to try to stay upright. The tires squealed against the black pavement. They found little purchase against the slick roads. I tried to bend my body against the oncoming crash, but I only managed to slow my descent marginally.

It made little difference.

My body collided with the ground so hard that my head whipped back at a painful angle. The snow-scattered earth soaked through my clothes as I skidded across the ground, mercifully away from my motorcycle. I bounced once more, hard, and a guttural cry escaped my mouth before I slipped over the edge of the road and down an embankment.

I rolled down the hill at lightning speed, hitting rocks, twigs, and branches. Mud coated my visor, and the world went dark. After what felt like forever, I landed with a dull thud at the bottom of the drop-off. I lay face-first in a pile of snow that had collected from the last storm.

I gasped out for breath as my brain attempted to process what had just happened. Sticky fingers removed the helmet that had saved my life, and I laid my head back in the cold. My heart was thrashing around in my chest. I could feel the blood rushing to my ears.

Shock.

I was in shock.

Oh fuck.

Breathe.

Ari.

Breathe. I saw stars in my vision.

Ari, I love you.

It was the last thing I thought before I blacked out.

"Surprise!" Cheyenne cried, pushing her way through the crowd and to my side.

"Uh...what is all of this?" I asked, dumbfounded.

"A birthday party, of course!"

I stared around at the crowd of faces—all of my friends, the band, a large portion of the groupies that I had started to recognize, even Sydney. I hadn't seen her since the ski lodge. My eyes searched through the crowd for the face I was sure to find among them.

But no.

No Grant.

For a moment, I'd been sure that Grant hadn't answered my call because he was here for the celebration. But I didn't see him.

"Oh. You put this all together?"

"Well, no," Cheyenne admitted.

Gabi came up next to her. "Grant planned it all. Got everyone to keep it quiet and come tonight. He's been planning it since that night he came to the library."

"Oh," I muttered again lamely. "Well, uh...where is he?"

"We don't know," Gabi admitted finally. "We got here with you. We could go ask the guys."

"No," I said quickly.

The last thing I wanted was to be the desperate girl asking about her boyfriend. I couldn't believe he had put this whole thing together for me. It was unbelievably sweet. I didn't know if he had been planning it this whole time, and that was why he had avoided me this week. Maybe the reason I hadn't seen him had nothing to do with our argument.

But if that were the truth, then where was he?

Nowhere.

No, one decent action by Grant McDermott didn't make up for last weekend and his silence the past couple of days. When I saw him again, I was seriously considering wringing his neck.

Asshole.

"It's fine. Let's get a drink," I said.

The last thing I wanted to do was bring attention to myself about the situation. The girls knew things were weird with Grant right now, but that didn't mean I needed to alert anyone else. There were too many vultures at the party. Groupies were here because Grant had invited them, and they would quickly rush to his side if they knew we were in trouble.

Ugh!

Trouble. I couldn't even think about that word.

I realized how irrational that sounded even in my head. I was mad at Grant, mad at myself, but I didn't want anyone to know. I didn't want anyone else to get close to him. It was all so confusing.

We walked over to the bar, and I was handed a beer.

"Birthday shots!" Shelby cried.

"Later. I want to let this settle first," I told them.

"Oh, come on," Shelby pleaded. "I need to get fucked up."

"Well, get one now, and I'll get the next round."

"Shelby, you do not need to get fucked up," Cheyenne snapped.

"Yeah, you shouldn't have to compete with that," Gabi whispered, leaning over forward.

"What am I missing?"

Cheyenne rolled her eyes. "Seriously, Aribel, do you not pay attention to anything?"

I glanced between them. "Not really."

Gabi cracked a smile and then smothered it under Cheyenne's glare. "Sydney is here."

"I know. I saw her."

"And hello? Shelby has been dating Miller since Sydney left." Cheyenne gave me an exasperated look.

"I didn't know it was serious," I mumbled.

Actually, I'd spent more time around the guys in the last two months, and I knew firsthand that Miller did *not* think they were serious. He thought she was fun to hang out with and fuck. He liked that she was here in Princeton and with his friends' girls.

But he still had a thing for Sydney.

As did Vin.

That was the last topic to bring up around Cheyenne even though none of us had any fucking clue why she liked the meathead douche bag.

"Well, it's not been *defined*," Shelby muttered.

"Because you won't ask him to define it," Cheyenne said.

"Have you asked Vin?" Shelby snapped.

"No, but I don't want a relationship. I'm cool with this limbo we're in. I get to fuck him when I want, but I don't always have to listen to the stupid things that come out of his mouth."

"At least you're talking some sense now," I said. "Sometimes, I wonder if you even remember he tried to drug me."

"I don't think he intended anything *bad* to happen."

It was my turn to roll my eyes. "Please. He wanted to sleep with me."

"Well, nothing bad did happen, and he doesn't do that shit anymore." Cheyenne leaned forward and sighed. "He'd kill me if I ever mentioned this, but he told me once he felt really bad about what happened that night."

"Vin has feelings?" I asked in disbelief.

"All I'm saying is, I think a little bit more is up there than he lets on." Cheyenne held her hands up. "Don't let him know I said that."

I shrugged. I couldn't change what had happened or that Vin was a fact of life around Grant. My eyes left the girls as they chatted more about what Shelby should do.

Seriously, Grant…where are you?

"I am *not* going to go hang on him like some desperate tramp!" Shelby cried.

"Oh my God. Miller probably didn't even invite Sydney. Grant probably did. Just act normal and things will be fine. There are more important things to worry about," I said before tipping back my bottle.

All three girls looked at me, surprised.

"Look, Aribel is giving good relationship advice," Cheyenne said. "You should take it. It's probably the first and last time."

"Ha-ha. You're hilarious." I grabbed Shelby's arm. "Come on. Let's go say hi. It'll be fine."

"What? Now?" Shelby asked frantically.

"No time like the present."

Really, I wanted any excuse not to think about or talk about Grant.

"Sydney!" I called, walking over to Grant's cousin.

She was a vivacious brunette, wearing one of her tamer outfits—a studded white sleeveless crop top and skintight leather leggings with a sheer stripe down the sides, starting at her hips and disappearing at the knees where they met her heeled black leather boots. The last time I had seen her she was in a miniskirt and cowboy boots at a ski lodge.

"Ari, hey! Happy birthday." Sydney rushed forward and threw her arms around me. "It's good to see you."

"Thanks. You, too."

Sydney and I hadn't necessarily bonded the last time we were together, but despite all the craziness she brought, I found I did like her.

"How is Tennessee?" I asked.

She currently went to the University of Tennessee in Knoxville. I couldn't believe she had driven up during the middle of the week for my birthday while she had school. I never would have done that.

"Fine. Still plenty of Southern cock to keep me occupied," she said rather loudly in Miller's direction.

My eyes bugged, and I looked away. "Well, that's…great."

"Did you say cock?" Vin asked. He grabbed his junk in his right hand and adjusted himself through his pants. "I've got some for you right here, baby."

Sydney smiled sweetly. "Let me think about it." She tapped her lips twice and then dropped her smile. "Thought about it. No, thanks."

I shifted, so I couldn't see the glares passing between Vin and Miller. Having Sydney here was dangerous for everyone involved.

"So, what crazy plan does Grant have cooked up?" Sydney asked. "I'm sure you've heard rumors or some shit, right? Is he going to fucking jump out of a cake? Is he bringing strippers? He's not answering his damn phone, and I want the juice."

"You're asking me? I'm the birthday girl. I didn't even know he was throwing this party."

"How could you not know? He's been planning it for a month!"

"Well, we've been kind of…" I didn't know what to say or why I was even considering confiding in Sydney. "We got into an argument about the band."

"What about the band?"

I sighed. I didn't really want to talk about this right now. "Nothing has happened yet, but they're still being scouted pretty hard by Pacific."

"What? That's amazing! I can't believe Miller hasn't said anything!" she cried. "I mean…not that we're talking."

She tried to play it off so cool that I instantly knew that Sydney wasn't just fucking around with Miller. She liked him as much as he liked her.

Oh, boy.

"God, you two shouldn't be fighting over that. You should be fucking celebrating! Where is Grant fucking McDermott? We need to drink!" She dug around in the bag hanging at her hip. "I'm going to give him another call. He should be here by now."

Yeah...

My eyes searched the crowd again as if I could make him appear out of thin air.

Why wasn't he here?

I couldn't move.

What the fuck? What the fuck? What the fuck?

My eyes slid open, and I stared up into the night sky. My brain had turned to mush. I could barely think. *How long had I been out?* It was hard to tell since it was so dark outside.

I scrambled to come back to my body, but it was as if I was treading through water. I blinked rapidly and then tried to make sure nothing was broken. I twisted around in the snow, and while everything hurt like a bitch, I didn't feel like something had snapped. I could still be in shock though.

With a deep breath that seared my chest, I tried to push myself into a sitting position, and I cried out in pain when my hands touched the freezing ground. The gloves I'd been wearing were destroyed on the palms and fingertips, which had been scraped up when I tried to stop myself. I forced myself up anyway, ignoring the lingering aches and pains on my body.

My leather jacket was torn, and I had a visible gash along my left arm where the material had been shredded. My neck hurt like hell. I could barely turn it from side to side without wincing. My breathing remained labored, but at least it didn't seem like I'd punctured a lung or anything.

I was lucky that when the motorcycle had fallen, I'd been thrown from the seat, so the weight of the bike hadn't crushed my legs. My legs seemed to be the most functional part of my body, especially compared to my upper half.

Against my better judgment, I attempted to stand, but I fell forward onto my knees at the effort. My legs were jelly.

My whole body was trembling. I'd never felt so shaken and helpless. I couldn't even stand. I could hardly breathe. I couldn't see. I had no idea where my motorcycle was.

My breathing came out in short gasps as panic set in with the shock.

Oh my God, I was going to die out here, all alone. I'd never make it out of this embankment, and even if I could, I had no idea of the condition of my motorcycle. If it were half as bad as me, I wouldn't be able to drive the thing home.

I'd never get to talk to Ari. I wouldn't get to tell her that I was sorry and that I loved her. I wouldn't get to see her smiling face.

My stomach twisted at the thought.

How could I have been so stupid?

God, I was a fucking idiot. I should never have driven out on these roads. I should never have taken the chance.

All I knew was, I needed to get back to her.

Please just let me get back to her.

A bright light fell down onto me, and I squinted up at it.

"Are you okay down there?" a woman called.

My eyes lifted to the road where an older woman stood, holding a flashlight. I raised my hand and then dropped it back down.

Shit! I hurt everywhere.

But at least someone was here. I wasn't going to die—not yet.

"Down here," I groaned. "I'm fine. Just a little banged up."

"Stay put. Don't try to move! I'm going to call an ambulance!" she yelled.

"No," I croaked. I didn't do hospitals. "No, hospitals, please. Please don't call for an ambulance."

She wavered with indecision before calling back down to me. "Let me send my husband down there to help you up. Don't try to move."

A few minutes later, the woman's husband was hauling me up the drop-off. I hated to admit how much I was leaning on him. I was too shaken up to assess my injuries, but it could have been so much worse. Aside from my wounded pride, I suspected my arm and neck were the worst of it.

"Oh dear," she cried when she saw me. "We should take you to a hospital right away. Look at you."

I took a deep breath and then stood on my own two feet. I rocked back and forth before regaining my balance. "I'm really…I'm okay."

"You most certainly are not!"

"Please, I don't want to make this a big deal."

"You just fell off a motorcycle and down a hill!" the woman cried. "It *is* a big deal."

"I'm sorry. I appreciate you helping me, but I avoid the doctor's office at all costs."

"Joe, tell him!" she sternly said to her husband.

"Sherry, we can't force him to go to the doctor."

"Yes, we can!"

"Thank you for your help. Honestly, I don't know what I would have done without you, but I feel fine," I lied. "How is my bike?"

The couple both frowned at that question.

Fuck.

When I found it, I realized I was in *much* better shape than my motorcycle. I was lucky that I'd been thrown off the bike before falling down the hill onto a pile of built-up snow from the last snowfall. My bike was not as lucky. It had skidded twenty feet past me, crashed into the guardrail, rolled down the hill, and wrapped itself around a tree.

She was completely totaled.

Undrivable.

Potentially not even salvageable.

As sad as I was, I was equally thankful that nothing that bad had happened to me, that I wasn't as mangled as the bike, that I wasn't *dead*.

The thought shook me to my core. I could have died tonight.

Sherry patted my shoulder. "I think it's best to leave it here. You can come back for it in the morning. No one else is going to take it in that condition."

I blinked. *What the fuck was I going to do? Where the fuck was I supposed to go?*

"We can take you home if you'd like," Joe offered. "Where do you live?"

I looked between them. My mouth had fallen open, and I quickly recovered. "Thank you. That's…I appreciate it. I live in Princeton. Downtown."

"It's about an hour drive, but we can get you home safe. Get into the truck, and tell us what you were doing out here, driving around on a motorcycle in this weather."

I didn't know what to say.

Because I was an idiot?

Because I'd thought a spark of adrenaline and a dose of danger would cure the real heartache?

Because I'd never realized I wasn't invincible until that moment my bike tilted and I slid off the road?

So, I shrugged and climbed inside before giving them the address to my place.

"Thank you again," I repeated. "I don't know how I can ever repay you."

Sherry turned around in her seat and smiled at me. "No need to repay us. We were happy to find you alive."

"Me, too."

As they turned the truck around and drove back toward Princeton, I peeled my ruined jacket off my body. I hissed at the pain that shot up my left arm. There was a gash about four inches long. The skin had been scraped back, bleeding a thin trickle of red down my arm, and dirt and debris had collected in the wound. I used my jacket to stanch the bleeding, and I tried to ignore the pain as I pressed down on the injury.

Everything else hurt, and I was faint and dizzy. *When had I last eaten anything?* I couldn't remember. I closed my eyes to try to fight back the pain, but my body slid toward slumber.

I woke up to the feel of someone lightly shaking me. I must have passed out in the back of the truck.

"I'm awake," I grumbled.

"Maybe we should take him to the hospital," the woman said. "He's so banged up. What if there's internal bleeding?"

"I'm not forcing him to go, Sherry. Let's get him inside and make sure he's all right. If he's too banged up once you can look at him, then we'll take him."

"I don't like it."

Somehow, I made it out of the truck and inside my house. After Sherry checked me out, she conceded. I needed a shower, some Tylenol—which she located in the cabinet—and a lot of rest. We exchanged numbers, and she promised to call to check on me, and I promised to go to the hospital if anything got worse.

When they left, I peeled my shirt over my head and stared in horror at myself in the mirror. It wasn't just my arm. The skin was broken all the way down my chest, ribs, and hip. My ribs were already turning a wonderful shade of purple, and I wondered if I had fractured something. It hurt to breathe, but I didn't know if it was because it was tender or from something worse.

After I showered and wrapped up my arm, I came to an abrupt stop in the doorway to the bathroom. My phone. *Where the fuck was my phone?*

I patted down the jeans and jacket I had worn, but I found nothing. *Shit.* I must have lost it on the road.

I needed to call Ari. I needed to tell her what had happened. I should have asked for Sherry's phone, but I'd been so out of it up until I took that shower that I couldn't think in coherent sentences. With the shower and pain medicine working its magic, my thoughts came through with sharp clarity.

Ari.

She was what mattered.

She was all that mattered.

I threw on another pair of jeans and a T-shirt, and I grabbed a black jacket from the hook. At the last second, I remembered I had bought her a birthday present. I seized that, too, and then darted for my truck.

This probably wasn't the smartest thing I'd ever done, but neither was taking a joyride in shitty conditions and crashing my motorcycle. If I had survived that, I could survive driving to the League...but I couldn't survive without Ari.

A cheer went up from the front of the League and gradually grew. I turned around to figure out what was going on, and then I saw him.

Grant.

He was here.

Our eyes locked across the room, and I wasn't sure what I saw reflected back in his eyes. Desperation, fear, hope—it was a strange combination, one I certainly hadn't expected after the last time we had parted.

Ignoring all the people around him, Grant practically bounded across the room until he was directly in front of me. The room fell silent at his approach. My pulse thrummed in my throat, and I swallowed hard. I tilted my chin up to meet him with determination in my face. I was not going to break down. I had no clue what he was going to do, but I could handle it.

Then, his hands were cupping my cheeks so tenderly that it was as if he thought I might break in half. Without a word, his mouth dropped down on mine, and the kiss was as light as a feather. It was a question, a soft and delicate question, one he had never asked before—permission.

When I didn't pull away from him, he received his answer. The kiss deepened, and he coaxed all the anger out of me. He drew it out as if sucking venom from an open wound. He kissed me so heatedly and lovingly that not even a drop remained. All that was left was a bottomless well of emotions of how much I loved and missed him.

When I came back into the moment, I heard the catcalls and yells from the people around us. It was then I remembered that we were in a crowded room, surrounded by people for my birthday, and Grant had kissed the breath out of me. I flushed from head to toe at the attention, but he wouldn't let me pull away.

"I'm sorry," he whispered. "I shouldn't have blown up on you. I shouldn't have done anything. You're all that matters."

I stared up at him in confusion. "Who are you, and what have you done with Grant McDermott?"

He laughed that beautiful glorious laugh, and a smile lit up his whole face. It was that damn smile that had won me over in the first place.

"Run away with me," he murmured.

"What?"

"Run away with me. Let's get out of here."

"Where are we going?"

"Anywhere. Everywhere."

"You're not making any sense," I said.

But his determination was contagious. I didn't even know what he was talking about or what had made him act like this, but I suddenly knew I'd go to the ends of the earth for him.

"Isn't that the beauty of it?"

I shook my head in confusion, but I couldn't keep a hint of a smile off my face. "I guess. But you set this all up."

"And now, I'm stealing you away."

He grabbed my hand and pulled me back through the crowd before I could offer an argument. *Really, what argument could I have?* He had done everything I had hoped for in the span of two minutes, and I had no idea why.

But I was carried away with being with him. Exhilaration and excitement flared up every time I was around him. It was like the first time all over again—when I had tried so hard to resist him and it was all for naught. Because Grant wasn't anything like I'd thought he'd be. He loved me, and tonight, it was written all over his face.

How had I let that slip my mind when we were angry at each other?

Suddenly we were outside in the bitter cold and I was following him to his blue truck that was illegally parked in front of the building.

"You weren't planning on staying long, huh?"

"Hurst wouldn't have towed it, but no, I wasn't."

He opened the passenger door for me, and I stared at him.

"Why are you in such a hurry?"

"Because I need you, Ari. I need you now. I didn't see that before." He ran a hand back through his hair.

I noticed his knuckles were scraped up, and I wondered if he had been fighting or something. He grabbed my hand and pulled me in closer.

His gaze was electric. "I was an idiot. We should never have argued like we did. I love you—plain and fucking simple. Everything else, we'll figure out."

"Okay," I said hesitantly.

I wasn't sure what had caused this complete one-hundred-and-eighty-degree turn in him. It was as if the last couple of weeks had never happened, and our relationship was starting over with a clean slate. I appreciated it, but I was also wary of it backfiring in my face.

"But we're going to talk more later about what happened, right?"

He reached out and stroked my hair. "Whatever you want."

Then, he was kissing me again. Fire burned through my skin, and I reached out for him. I grasped on to his sides, and a guttural cry broke free from his mouth.

I stepped back in shock. "Wha-what's wrong?"

He held his side. His eyes were closed, and he ground his teeth together.

"Did something happen?"

"I'm fine," he said slowly after a labored minute.

"You are absolutely not fine. Were you fighting? Did someone hurt you?" I asked. Terror washed over my features.

"No, no fighting. This is all my doing. Let's talk about it when we get back to my place."

"Are you okay to drive?"

"Ari," he said softly. The pain was gone from his face, but I didn't know if he was hiding it or if it was gone from his body, too. "We'll talk once we get there."

"All right." I hopped into the car without complaint only because I didn't think he would give up information otherwise. I didn't want him to be hurt. That cry had been inhuman.

When Grant sat down in the driver's seat, he handed me a large plain brown box. "Here, I, uh…got this for you."

I took the box from him as he drove down the street. After everything that had happened between us, I was still a bit in shock over the lengths he had gone to for my birthday. First, the surprise party—which we hadn't even stayed at—and now, a gift, a pretty big one by the size of the box.

"Thank you." I found the lip of the box and tugged it up. Inside, the present was wrapped in dark blue tissue paper. I was surprised he had splurged on tissue paper. It seemed to contradict the plain box, but it made me smile nonetheless.

I carefully tore the paper aside and pulled the contents out of the box. Unrolling the hastily put together package, my mouth dropped open when I realized what I was holding in my hand—a black leather jacket. The sleeves were quilted. There were double buckles at the wrists and one across the back. The jacket was a moto design that crossed the body and zipped up the left side with a wide open collar. I brought it to my nose and inhaled. The smell of new leather was unbelievable, and the whole thing was so amazingly soft.

"Wow."

He glanced over at me. Concern creased his features. "Wow, good? Or wow, this sucks? Why would you ever get this for me? It's so dumb."

It wasn't me at all. I would never have bought myself something like this. It had grunge and rocker written all over it. I also tended to prefer faux leather—not that I was an animal rights activist by any means, but it was how I'd been raised.

But it was from Grant.

"It's...beautiful."

"Are you just saying that?"

"Would I do that?"

He shrugged. "Maybe."

"No, I wouldn't."

"I love your cardigans, Princess, but I think you'd look fucking hot in leather."

I laughed. "When you say that, I imagine you're not thinking about a leather jacket."

He smirked. "I'm imagining you naked."

Of course he was.

My cheeks heated as I slung the jacket on. It fit perfectly. It was warm and molded to my body. Considering I hadn't even asked for a present, this was pretty amazing. Grant couldn't have done better.

I reached out for his hand and linked out fingers. I knew I needed to talk about our argument even if Grant didn't want to discuss it. "Grant, I'm sorry about this weekend."

"It's okay," he said dismissively. "We just got into an argument."

"I know. I...feel like we should have talked about it afterward."

"Well, I went to your hotel, and no one would let me contact you. Plus, you never answered your phone."

"It was stupid. I just wanted to sleep."

"Sleep." Despite how loving he'd sounded just a minute before, his face looked tense and tight.

"What?"

"I waited for you almost all night. The doorman said Henry went upstairs with you, and he never came back downstairs."

"You waited all night?" I asked, my heart contracting.

"Yeah, more or less. Uh…were you with Henry?" he asked.

I could tell he wasn't trying to accuse me, and I felt so terribly bad for not calling him.

"No. He tried to kiss me, and he tried to force me to let him stay." I shuddered at the memory. "But he had a room in the same hotel. That's why he never left."

It was like a weight he had been carrying around all week had suddenly been lifted. I brought his hand to my lips and softly kissed it.

"I love you, Grant. We might have been in an argument, but I would never do that to you."

"I know," he said at last. "I know. I love you, too."

And the sigh out of his mouth showed how utterly relieved he was.

When Grant finally pulled up in front of his place, he eagerly escorted me out of the car, inside, and up to his bedroom. He kicked the door closed behind me and removed the jacket he had given to me. My fingers worked just as quickly, stripping him out of his own jacket and reaching for the button on his jeans.

His lips found mine again, and all the gentleness from earlier was gone. He kissed me with primal desire. He wanted me, and nothing would stand in the way. His hands tugged on the new dress the girls had gotten me to wear tonight. I found the zipper and tugged it down to the base of my spine where Grant then dropped the material to my feet.

His hands grasped my breasts, and he massaged them. He rolled the nipples around between his fingers, causing me to squirm, but he kept kissing me. He dragged my bottom lip between his teeth. My eyes fluttered closed at the practiced ease with which he ignited my body.

Soon, he released my lip and dropped his mouth to the hollow of my throat. Then, he replaced his hand with his tongue. He circled my nipple and then lightly tugged on it. I shook with desire.

God, how did he do that so well?

My mind was having a hard time coming up with any logical thoughts, except that Grant was pretty amazing at this and my body had missed him.

Grant pushed me backward, so I was lying on my back on his bed. He grasped my panties and tugged them to the ground, and then he hitched my legs up onto his shoulders. There was only a second before his tongue touched my clit, and I was arching off the bed. His fingers probed inside me, and then I felt the world spinning.

"Oh my God," I breathed.

With Grant, I had learned to just let him have his way with me. He liked to get me so worked up that I thought the world was going to shatter all around me. I already felt as if I was reaching that point.

"Are you going to come for me, Princess?" he murmured between my legs.

"Come with me," I pleaded.

I dug my fingers into his hair, hoping to coax him upward, but he just flicked his tongue across my clit again and again.

"Please…"

But he didn't listen to my begging. He worked on my body until I was soaking wet, soaring through my climax, and panting on the covers.

Grant dropped his pants and then crawled onto the bed, lying down flat. His dick was hard and throbbing, and I got to my knees, reaching out and grasping him in my hand. He groaned and grabbed me by the hips, positioning me on top of him. I slipped against him, coating him with the wetness he had created between my thighs, before slowly dropping down on top of him.

"Fuck, Princess."

I lay there for a minute without moving, feeling how deep he was inside of me. A few months ago, I hadn't felt this comfortable in my own skin. *But how could I not be when Grant was staring up at me as if I were a real-life princess?* I was one who he had properly deflowered, and he was ready to make me into his own sex goddess. It was enough of a boost of confidence to make me forget about clinging to my apprehensions.

Grant's hands slid up my bare back, and he drew me down to rest lightly on his chest. I ran my fingers up into his hair. He cast soft butterfly-light kisses all over my face, and his right hand brushed the hair out of my eyes.

"I love you," he murmured in a sexy dazed voice.

"I love you, too."

Then, he started moving. Slow, languid movements were in direct contrast with the way he normally took me. He wanted to take his time. He wanted to feel us skin-to-skin—my breasts against his chest, my fingers in his hair, his dick slipping in and out of my body. Our eyes locked, and I knew then that Grant wasn't fucking me. Our bodies might be meeting in time, but this wasn't just sex for him—or for me.

We were making love. Our hearts were connecting. And if the world ended in that moment, we would be at peace.

The orgasm that rocked through my body made me cry out and clutch on to Grant for support. He came with me, burying his head in my neck. I rocked back onto him one last time and then collapsed as if I'd just run a marathon.

He groaned in pain. "Ari, can't...I can't breathe."

I sat up immediately. "Are you okay?"

In the midst of our sexual encounter, I'd forgotten that Grant was in pain. *Oh God, had everything we done made it worse?*

"I'm fine, Princess. Go clean up, and we'll talk."

I stared down at him, concerned, but he nudged me off of him.

"Go on."

I dutifully cleaned up in his bathroom. When I returned, Grant had a soft light on in the room, and it was the first time I got a glimpse of his body.

I gasped in horror, and my hand went to my mouth. "Oh my God! What happened?"

He looked bruised from head to toe. His arm was bandaged. *How had I not noticed his arm was wrapped up? Jesus, I must have been so desperate that I had let this go on while he was injured.*

A phone rang loudly from under the bed. Grant scrunched up his features. "You have got to be fucking kidding me."

"What?"

"I thought I'd lost it on the embankment."

My eyes widened. "What embankment?"

"Can you reach down and get it for me?"

I glared at him. I was so pissed that he wasn't giving me a straight answer on anything. If he was this injured, then we should never have had sex. He looked like he needed medical attention.

But I dropped to the ground, grasped the phone, and held it out to him.

He stared at it. "Another unknown number."

It stopped ringing, and then immediately, it started up again from the same number.

"Just answer it, or turn the damn thing off, and tell me what happened!"

"Fine," he grumbled, choosing to answer the phone rather than address what had happened. "Hello?"

With my arms crossed, I waited for him to get off the line. *How could Grant have sustained that kind of damage? How had he had sex with that kind of bruising?* I was gradually falling from anger into panic. *Was he okay? Did he have internal bleeding? Did he need to go to a doctor? Oh God, how had I let him drive?*

Then, the next thing Grant said pulled me out of my troubled thoughts, "Dad?"

"Hey, son."

The world stood still. I forgot about the motorcycle accident, the feel of making love to Ari, the desire to avoid the conversation about what had happened. I forgot everything. The only thing in that moment was the sound of my old man's voice on the phone.

"How the fuck did you get this number?" I demanded.

"Grant, I've been trying to reach you."

I lost it. "Don't fucking say my name!"

I stood up off the bed and paced my room. All I wanted to do was slam my fist into the wall, but I was already too banged up as it was. Plus, I didn't want to scare Ari.

"Grant," she whispered, fearfully looking at me.

I held up my hand and shook my head. This could not be happening right now.

"Just give me a minute to explain," my dad said. "I've been trying to reach out to you since I…since I got out of prison. Randy told you I got out, right?"

"I don't need or want any of your explanations. I know bullshit when I hear it. So, let me fill you in. I don't want you to contact me. I don't want to see you. I don't want you talking to Uncle Randy or bringing *anyone* else into this."

"I'm not dragging anyone into this. Stop, and listen for a second," he snapped, dropping immediately back into his military tone of voice.

It was like a light switch when he talked to me. Suddenly, I was ten years old again.

He was standing over me, demanding obedience, always pulling the authority figure over my head. I saw him holding the gun out in front of him. I ran to my mother, but it was too late, and he pulled the trigger. I felt her blood on my hands.

I wiped my hands on my bare legs after reliving it. I'd relived it a thousand times in my nightmares. And here was my nightmare, coming to haunt me once more.

"You don't deserve a chance for me to listen to you. Did you give her a chance?" I growled.

"Don't bring her into this."

That was it. That was the end. As it was, I couldn't believe I had been on the phone this long with a raving lunatic.

"I can do whatever the fuck I want! I'm not a kid anymore. I'm not a ten-year-old you can blame for murdering your wife!"

"Is that how you feel?" he asked. His voice was deadly cold and devoid of emotion, showing me truly how much of a complete and total psychopath he was.

"You don't care about how I feel. I was there. I saw you holding the gun and pointing it at my mother before you killed her. So, whatever the fuck you have planned in that fucked-up head of yours, stop now. I want no part of it. I want you to leave me and everyone else I care about alone. If you get anywhere near them, I will not hesitate to kill you."

I hung up the phone and threw it on the bed. I wish I had lost the damn thing off the embankment. At least then, it would have saved me from that phone call.

My breathing was labored, and suddenly, all the events of the day came crashing back over me. I collapsed onto the ground.

Ari screamed and lunged for me. She placed my head in her lap and brushed my hair back. "Grant, oh my God," she murmured before kissing my forehead. "Everything will be okay. Tell me what happened."

I struggled to sit up, but she gently tugged me back down. I relented only because I had no energy left in my body. Her fingers trailed down my arm, over my bruised side, and to my hip. She brought my hand up to her face and kissed each and every inch of damaged skin. I lay there, mentally and physically immobilized.

"Grant, I love you. How can I help if you don't tell me what's wrong?"

She sounded near to tears, and I felt like a douche for pushing her to that.

I finally sighed and prepared myself for her anger. "That was my dad on the phone. He wants me to listen to him or some shit. Also, I got in a motorcycle accident."

"You did what?" she shrieked.

Then, she covered her mouth and shook her head. I could tell she was warring with herself on her reaction.

"Did you go to the hospital?"

"No, I was driven home by a couple who had found me."

"Found you?" she whispered.

"Yeah. I was thrown off the bike and fell down an embankment. The bike didn't fare as well."

"Oh, Grant, why didn't you call me? Why didn't you go to the doctor?"

"I'm fine," I repeated mechanically.

"If you weren't already bruised beyond belief, I would beat the shit out of you right now. Come on. I'm taking your truck, and we're going to the emergency room."

"Ari, no. I don't like doctors. I hate the ER. So much blood, and…" My skin felt clammy, and I thought I might throw up or black out.

Blood reminded me of holding my mother as she died. Blood ran thick and heavy between my fingers as I tried to save her. Doctors rushing around, trying to save a dead woman. Nothing could be done. The sound of the flat line. The questions. The nightmares.

"Grant," Ari breathed again, "I'm going to be there. If you die from internal bleeding, I'll never forgive you. So, we're going to the doctor. Now, get up. I'm driving."

"Princess—"

"I'm not taking no for an answer. You got into a serious car accident and *need* to get medical help—now."

There was no arguing with her. Everything I wanted to say about the accident, about my mother, about my dad…she'd sidestepped like a fucking pro. We were going to the hospital if she had to drag me every goddamn step of the way.

And I loved her even more for it.

Two broken ribs, eight stitches, and a concussion.

The doctor didn't look half as exasperated at me as Ari was. When she'd heard the news about the accident, I'd thought she might actually give me another concussion.

"How could you be so stupid?" she groaned. "You know how I feel about motorcycles!"

"You're more comfortable shooting a gun than being on the back of my bike."

"With good reason." She indicated my beat-up body.

"Don't have good experience with guns either, darlin'."

Her whole face softened with pity. I hated that look from her. No one needed to pity me. This was why I'd never told anyone about my past, not even Miller knew the sordid details.

I looked away from her. "Let's just get out of here."

"Grant," she murmured, reaching for me.

I stood and brushed past her. She grabbed my hand anyway. The pity was gone when I next looked into her eyes. It was replaced with determination.

"Whatever you're thinking right now, just stop. All we've been doing the past couple of months is fighting and running away from each other. I'm over it. I'm just over it." She balled her hands into fists at her sides. Her eyes were fierce. "We can't push each other away anymore. You trusted me with the information about your parents. I gave you…" She blushed furiously. "Well, me. Whatever. You know what I mean. And I can't keep up this cat-and-mouse game. Either, we're okay, or we're not—"

I wrapped my arm around her waist and silenced the rest of her speech with a kiss. She growled low in her throat and tried to fight me off. When I winced at her outburst and only deepened the kiss, she gave in. Her body went slack, and she leaned into me.

"Okay," I whispered against her lips. Then, I kissed her one more time.

She nodded. Her eyes were still closed as she stole another kiss from me. "Don't do that."

"Do what?"

"Make me forget what I was saying."

"I plan to do more than that."

She softly poked me in the stomach, and I groaned.

"You can barely stand up. We shouldn't have even done anything earlier."

I smirked down at her. "And here I thought you liked it."

She rolled her eyes and prodded me toward the door. "How about we get you home?"

I laughed but relented. I actually felt a lot shittier than I was letting on. After all the adrenaline had worn off, I completely crashed. As much as I'd claimed to want to take Ari home and fuck her all over again, I wasn't sure if I would be able to more than crawl into bed and pass out— if I could even make it to the bed.

Spending my birthday night in the ER hadn't exactly been what I had in mind. But I wouldn't have traded it for the world.

It felt ridiculous to me to be so happy in a stale sterile environment full of sick people, but it was the first time in a long time that things were right with Grant. Sure, we had a lot to talk about, but at least it felt as if we were getting somewhere. The complications that had been brought up with the return of his dad and the motorcycle accident seemed to have brought us closer. And I wasn't about to let that slip away.

I drove Grant home from the hospital, and despite his protests, he fell asleep as soon as he got into bed. I crawled in next to him, trailing my fingers over the mottled bruises on his bare skin. I fell asleep listening to his even breathing, thanks to the painkillers the doctor had given him for his ribs.

Sometime in the wee hours of the morning, Grant rolled over, wrapped an arm around my waist, and rested his chest flush against my back. My eyes slid open in surprise at the feel of his dick pressing through his thin cotton shorts and into the small amount of space between us.

"Ari," he groaned through his half-asleep daze.

His lips landed lightly on my collarbone. My body molded to his, and I felt the intensity in his desire. *How had I ever been too afraid to succumb to this? How had I ever thought that by saying no, when I'd really wanted to say yes, we'd somehow be able to talk more?* I didn't want to stop, not anymore.

Scrounging up some courage, I pressed my butt back against him and made teasing circular motions with my hips. He mumbled something incoherent in the crook of my neck and nipped at the sensitive skin. I arched back toward him, and then he grabbed my hip in his hand and pulled me back even harder against him.

I was fully awake at that point. Desperate to go further, our bodies rocked against each other, waking up the deep-seated desire coursing between us. Grant slipped his hand from my hip and moved it down between my legs. I was already hot and pulsing with anticipation. He squeezed his hand into the tight space and then massaged up and down, flicking his finger against my clit through the material, while I bucked against him.

A fiery inferno rose up all around us. We were barely doing anything, yet at any moment, I was going to combust. The room was so dark, and our bodies were so connected. The tension of the previous months stretched between us, snapping and pushing us over the edge.

I couldn't wait another minute. I rolled over onto my back and crushed my lips to his. "Fuck me," I breathed. I didn't even feel ridiculous requesting it of him. I'd come so far in such a short period of time.

Our clothes were quickly strewn across the bedroom floor. Grant eased himself over my body, pressing my legs open for him. My grinding against him had lengthened his dick, and I could tell he was already rock-hard as he slipped into my opening. My wetness coated the tip, drawing him deeper. I expanded and tightened all around him as he filled me.

Our breathing quickened in time with his measured thrusts. I buried my hands into his hair and tugged his lips back down to mine. I couldn't get enough of this moment. Grant made me feel alive as if I could conquer the world.

And I came apart while telling him how much I loved him.

I lay back, satiated and content. Grant fell back onto the bed and pulled me into him. He struggled to get his breathing back to normal.

I nuzzled closer to him. "Are you okay? Do you need medicine?" I whispered. I hadn't meant for things to get so out of hand, and I didn't want him to get worse because we couldn't keep our hands to ourselves.

He kissed the top of my head. "I'm okay, Princess. Just lie here with me."

I complied and closed my eyes. This was pure magic right here.

My nails scratched lightly down his chest. He sighed pleasurably, and goose bumps rose on his arms.

"That feels nice," he whispered into my hair.

"Good."

After ten minutes of silence, I thought Grant had finally fallen back asleep. I was about to hop out of bed and use the bathroom before trying to shut my brain down and getting some more sleep myself.

Then, Grant spoke again, "I still have nightmares."

I remained very still, unsure whether he was talking to me or to himself.

"After hearing his voice again, I don't want to go back to sleep."

His dad.

Grant was talking to me about his dad.

I didn't say anything. I just slowly reached out and twined our fingers together. If he wanted to talk about it, then I would be here. I would always be here for him.

"He wanted me to listen to what he was saying. But how could he fucking ask that of me? I don't want a relationship with him. I've spent my life escaping what he did, escaping him. I would be fine if it fucking stayed that way."

He sighed heavily and ran his thumb across my hand and then over my mother's engagement ring sitting on my right ring finger.

"What's it like to have a father who loves you, Ari?"

Unbidden tears sprang to my eyes. I tried to keep them back by blinking furiously. My throat closed up. I swallowed back the pain and anguish I'd heard in Grant's

159

voice. When I finally had my voice under control, I answered, "I'm sure your father loves you, Grant."

"No, I can't be sure of that. Your father wants what is best for you. He raised you right, sent you to get an Ivy League education, bought you a BMW, met you in the city to get dinner, gave you your mother's engagement ring as a birthday present. He even stupidly, if I do say so, tried to get you to date someone he approved of. That is a father who loves his daughter. My father only ever brought death, depression, and destruction on my family."

"People show their love in different ways," I whispered. "My father is a hard man. He works constantly. I hardly saw him while I was growing up. I can't compare it to what you went through, but I would never describe my upbringing as warm and loving."

"You'll never realize how good you have it," he muttered.

"I'm not denying I had a privileged childhood. But you have people who love you, Grant, people who took care of you afterwards. Your father did not make you the man you are today." I sat up on my elbow and looked down at him. "You're not half as bad as you think you are. Your aunt and uncle raised you right. Sydney loves you so much. The guys are your family. You didn't let your circumstances dictate your devotion to the people who matter to you."

Grant ran his fingers back through my hair and looked up at me as if I were a shining angel. "You matter to me, Princess."

"You matter to me, too." I bent down and softly kissed him on the lips. "Did your dad say what he wanted to talk about?"

"No." Grant closed his eyes and heavily blew out. "I didn't exactly wait for him to tell me."

"So, maybe he wants to get to know you?" I offered hopefully.

He fiercely shook his head. "No way. You don't know him. You didn't hear him. When I called him out on it, he immediately dropped into his military voice. I know that voice. He isn't a good person. He's a murderer, Ari. He doesn't deserve a chance to talk to me. And I'm sure he doesn't even want that."

"Okay," I said hesitantly.

"You don't get it. When he went to prison, the last thing he ever said to me was that I had killed my mother, and when he got out, he was going to make me pay for it," Grant said, a pained look on his face. "I don't doubt for a second he's waiting for the opportunity to kill me. You shouldn't either."

"I believe you."

I was chilled to the bone. *Who would tell a ten-year-old kid he was responsible for his mother's death? Better yet, who would tell a ten-year-old kid he was going to make the kid pay for what he had done?* Grant had had no part in what happened, and he had been torturing himself about it ever since. His dad's parting words hadn't helped anything mentally. The thought of having a psycho get out of prison to enact retribution was terrifying.

"Good. That's why I think you should leave with the girls for spring break."

"What?" I asked, confused by the subject change.

"I know your roommates are going to Florida for the break next week. You should go with them."

"Why? I was planning on staying around campus, so I can work on papers and get some extra lab time in."

He looked at me in disbelief. "Lab work over getting a tan?"

"I don't get tan. I go from pasty white to lobster red and back."

"Ari, I don't want you to be in town if he shows up," he earnestly told me.

I sat up straight. "Wait! You think he's going to show up here?"

Grant clutched his side as he struggled to right himself. "You're severely underestimating him if you think he won't." He reached forward and caressed my cheek. "I want you to be safe. I'd be worried about you if you were here. He tracked down my phone number. With his military background, I'm sure he could locate my address, or at the very least, get information on the band since it's readily available. Now that he's played his first hand, the second will follow."

"I'm not leaving you here if you're in danger!"

He leaned forward until our foreheads were resting against each other. "I know we've argued a lot, Ari, but you are *the* most important person in my life. And the bastard won't hesitate to use any advantage he has. You understand?"

"Grant…" I whimpered.

"Please—for me."

"Okay, Grant, I'll go," I consented with a sigh. "But you should go to the police if you think you're in danger."

He groaned and pulled away from me. "I'm not involving those idiots. They're not going to do anything unless he actually does something illegal. Trust me, they won't think a phone call constitutes that."

"It doesn't hurt to alert them—and me. You have to be sure to check in with me."

"If it looks like he's coming at me with a gun, I'll contact you and the police," he said in a sarcastic tone.

I playfully smacked him on his arm. "Don't joke about that."

After a pause, he sighed. "I wasn't."

"Let's get this shit out of the way," Hollis said, clapping his hands together. "Time is money!"

I glared at Hollis. I still couldn't fucking listen to the moronic things that came out of his mouth. And I couldn't believe that, after all this time, we were actually here in New York City about to sign with Pacific Entertainment. I wanted to be pissed about it all. Hollis gave me a bad feeling, but at this point, I also thought we had an understanding.

So, I couldn't stop my stomach from fucking flipping like an idiot at the thought. We were really going to be on a fucking record label!

It almost displaced the paranoia I had about my dad showing up in Princeton at any given moment and the constant pain from the motorcycle accident.

Almost.

At least I'd gotten Ari to go to Florida with her roommates. Peace of mind about that situation. She hadn't been happy to hear we were signing the week she was going to be gone, but at least she was excited for me, for all of us.

Neither of us knew what this meant going forward, but we'd fucking figure it out together. That was what we had decided before she left.

"I read over the contract you forwarded to me, Mr. Tift," the lawyer Miller had acquired for us said, "but I want to read the this document here before we hand my clients a pen."

"By all means," Hollis said. He waved his hand at the stack of papers on the table.

I walked a short distance away from Hollis with Miller. "This lawyer is legit, right? He's going to figure out if Hollis is fucking us over?"

"Best I could find on short notice, but I think we're covered," Miller told me. "Anyway, I don't see why it would be in Hollis's interest to fuck us over."

"Because he's a douche. It's in his job description."

Miller cracked up and shook his head. "Well, I think we're covered."

I punched Miller on the arm. "I can't believe I let my fucking cousin come up here with us today."

"Me either. How many dudes do you think she'll blow before the night is over?" he joked.

"I can't control her. I thought I knew someone who could help with that."

Miller raised his hands. "Don't look at me. No one can control that level of crazy."

"You seemed to handle her fucking fine at the ski lodge, if I remember correctly."

"Sometimes, I think she handled me."

I couldn't stop myself from laughing. "That sounds like Sydney. But, bro, she's still my little cousin. I don't give a shit what's going on with Shelby, but if you hurt Sydney…"

"No one can hurt Sydney," Miller said quickly. "No one and nothing. She does whatever the fucks she wants. We've all known her forever. We all know how she is. Just as much of a slut as you were."

"That's my cousin," I growled. There were few people I defended fiercely.

"Don't I fucking know it? I bet you'd love for her to find the equivalent of Ari."

"I think she likes dick too much," I regrettably told him.

"You know what I mean. Chick can't be tamed."

"My comment still holds. You're not a douche bag, Miller. Leave that to Vin."

I didn't clarify whether I meant to leave Sydney to Vin with all her crazy or for Miller to man up and claim his woman. In the long run, my two cents didn't fucking matter. I just hated that my boys were still arguing over my dumbass cousin.

"Everything seems to be in order," our lawyer finally said. "Same document I read earlier this week."

"Fucking great!" Vin cried. "Let's fucking do the damn thing!"

Miller and I moved toward the table where the other guys stood, and we all stared down at the contract that was about to change our lives. Hollis handed out pens, and then we signed page after page of a document that had so much fucking legalese that it read as if it were in another language. But we kept signing until every page was full.

I dropped the pen onto the table. All the fucking worries that had led up to this moment vanished. We were on a major record label. We were a part of Pacific Entertainment.

"Good to have you guys," Hollis said. He shook each of our hands and laughed at the shit-eating grins on our faces. "Time to celebrate. I wish I could stay and party with you, but I need to get back on the road and catch up with The Drift. I flew in from Dallas just for you guys!"

I didn't even care that he was feeding us his typical bullshit. I was high on life right now. It was unreal compared to all the other shit I'd had to deal with, but signing those papers would turn it all around. I wanted to fucking party. I wanted to get wasted and fucking go crazy tonight.

"McAvoy! Send out a blast, letting people know where we're headed. Let's make it a party!" I cried.

We all cheered, dancing around like fucking dopes and giving each other bro hugs. This was the motherfucking dream.

Hollis promised to be in touch about everything going forward. He kept using words like *tour* and *debut album* and *studio recording*—all these fucking things we'd never thought would fucking happen in a million years. Miller sending out those shit demos last year had seemed like such a joke at the time. Just last semester, I couldn't have foreseen any of this actually happening.

Once McAvoy had sent out the blast to our social media sites, we took a cab to a nearby bar. We'd played New York City enough that we had a few local groupies who came to all our shows. After the New Year's show in the city with The Drift, our fan base had grown. But I hadn't anticipated the number of people who would show up.

"Ugh! Look at all those sluts," Sydney said. She stood next to me in another tiny fucking skirt and shirt with cowboy boots.

Those goddamn cowboy boots.

"This coming from a girl who has fucked the entire Tennessee football team." I nudged her.

"Not the entire team."

"And half of my band."

"I can only fuck three-quarters of the band, cuz. Sounds like I'm missing out." She smirked defiantly.

"And how many dudes did you blow at the ski lodge?"

She shrugged. "How long were we there? I lost count."

"Long enough that you should remember. What's up with you and Miller?"

"Oh, stop, Grant. I don't want to talk about Miller. Just because you went and got your ass whipped doesn't mean I should suddenly change my ways. I like sex. I like lots of it. I'm not fucking waiting around for him or anyone else while I live three fucking states away."

"You know I don't give a fuck what you do, Syd. I'm far from a model fucking citizen. Just don't fuck with my boys."

"Whatever." She rolled her eyes. "Who else am I supposed to fuck?"

She gestured around the room, and she had a point. Practically everyone who had shown up was a chick. And at least half of them seemed to be trying to figure out who Sydney was, so they could make a move on me.

The chick in the front had on a skintight dress that showed off all her curves in all the right places. Two or three girls nearby were busting out of their tops. Christ, it was like someone had told them I fucking loved them busty. Another girl caught my eye who had a dark, mysterious vibe about her. I bet she could suck cock. Before Ari, I would have found out. Now, I made a mental checklist. I could appreciate a chick if she was hot and imagine what she would probably do to me without actually fucking wanting it to happen. At least I'd never go through with it.

"Your pick of the lot, and my pussy-ass cousin is waiting on his girl in Florida."

"Hey, watch your fucking mouth."

A smile crossed her face, and she playfully punched me on the shoulder. I winced, but I tried to cover it up. I hadn't told anyone else about the motorcycle accident because I felt like too much of an idiot to admit to it.

"Shots," I suggested. Alcohol could dull the pain of more than just the accident.

We rounded up the guys and toasted to our newfound success.

After a while, I remembered the number of shots I had taken about as well as Sydney remembered how many dudes she'd blown at the ski lodge. All I knew was, I felt wonderfully fucking numb everywhere and goddamn happy about the band.

I wandered away from the group and dug out my phone from my pocket.

Ari answered on the third ring. "Hello?"

"Hey!" I cried.

She laughed. "Are you drunk?"

"Barely had anything, anything at all."

"Right. That's why you're slurring your words."

"Okay, I might have had more than one." I crashed down onto a barstool and pressed the phone closer to my ear.

"I saw the status that was posted. Congratulations! How does it feel to be a signed band under a major record label?"

"Almost as good as your pussy."

I could practically see her blushing.

"Oh, Grant."

"Speaking of my favorite thing, can you bring her over tonight? We're fucking celebrating!"

"I wish I could, but it's kind of a long flight from Florida."

"Then, what am I supposed to fuck?" I asked.

There was a short pause before Ari answered, "Nothing. Absolutely nothing. You keep your dick in your pants, Grant McDermott."

"Oh, Princess, you know you're the only one for me."

"You're doing what?" I crossed my arms and stared at Grant in disbelief.

I'd been back from spring break for only a total of three hours. It had been a great vacation. I was glad I had let Grant convince me to go even though that had meant he had to deal with the band and his dad by himself. Luckily, there had been no sign of his father while I was gone, but there had been a *major* development with the band.

"Going on tour," Grant repeated.

"Already? I mean, doesn't that seem...I don't know...crazy?"

"Definitely crazy." He picked me up around the middle and swung me around in a circle. "Ari, ContraBand is going on a real tour. We're going to be playing multiple shows a week, making money off of our music, promoting 'Life Raft' and the upcoming album."

"The album you haven't even recorded yet," I reminded him.

"Yeah, well, we just signed. And we have so many songs that have never even seen a real album before."

"Besides the one from Corey."

"Forget about Corey," he said. "We're talking about a big studio album recorded in Los Angeles. We're talking about working with the best in the business."

As I recalled, Grant had been thoroughly impressed with Corey's work on their *Life Raft EP*, but I understood the enthusiasm. I wanted him to do well. I was being selfish. I didn't want him to go away. I especially didn't want him to go away when his crazy dad was on the loose and looking for him. Maybe it would be better for him. At least Grant would be gone. His dad couldn't get to him if he wasn't here.

"A tour and Los Angeles—big time."

"That's right, Princess." He drew me in close to him and dropped a soft kiss on my mouth. "You're dating a big-time rock star. How does it feel?"

"About the same as when you were a nobody rock star—totally and completely strange."

He laughed, wove his fingers through my hair, and kissed me again. "I like tilting your world off balance."

"You're rather successful at it."

"I'm going to keep it that way."

"Good," I murmured. "Now, tell me all the details about this tour."

The Drift concert I had stumbled into the weekend before my birthday was the beginning of a small nationwide tour. They were hitting medium-sized venues all around the country, trying to gauge interest in a blowout arena tour.

The opening band Hollis had scheduled would be pulled from the lineup halfway through the tour because of lack of audience interest. I wasn't surprised about that bit at all. The part I'd heard from them wasn't that great, not that it was exactly my kind of music. But I remembered thinking that The Drift needed a better opener. Well, it had turned out that they were getting one—ContraBand.

Hollis wanted to plug the guys in as The Drift traveled back up the East Coast for the second half of the tour. Grant claimed it would give ContraBand a huge boost building anticipation for their upcoming album. They'd gain a larger fan base that would be anxious for more of their music. "Life Raft" was already out there, and Hollis wanted to hammer it home to their audience. That way, when they were promoting, the song would already be a hot commodity.

It all made sense logically. I just found it surprising, not that I had any knowledge of how the music industry worked. Maybe this was more common than I thought.

Growing up, I'd rarely gone to concerts, and I had never been a teenybopper who religiously followed bands like some girls.

All I wanted was for Grant to be happy. If this record deal and the tour and the studio album made him happy, then I'd be there for the ride.

At the start of the next week, ContraBand was supposed to leave to pick up on The Drift's tour, which meant I only had one more week with Grant before he would be gone for two whole months. I knew we could make the distance work, and in the grand scheme of things, it wouldn't be *that* long, but I was going to miss him. I could already feel the ache of missing him settling into my chest. I'd finally found a boy who made my heart skip, and I didn't want him to go away.

I tried to smother those feelings when we were together. I needed to cherish the moments we had while we had them rather than obsess about the fact that he was going to be gone.

God! How had I become this girl? I'd spent my whole life trying not to be a lovesick sap. Somehow, Grant McDermott, of all people, had forced it out of me.

As much as I wanted to revel in every little moment, I still had classes, not to mention tests in my Molecular Biology and Calc IV courses. It hadn't been an easy semester, and it was even worse when I was trying to grab on to every minute with Grant.

But trying to hold onto time was like sand in a sieve, slipping away one grain at a time until there was nothing left.

Soon enough, it was the weekend, and after that, Grant would be long gone.

The guys decided to celebrate their upcoming tour with The Drift by playing at The Ivy League one last time for all their local fans. Hurst wasn't too thrilled about the fact that they were leaving since they brought in so much business, but I knew he was secretly pleased with their success. Everyone was happy for them. We were cheering on the hometown heroes.

When I arrived at the League with Cheyenne, Gabi, and Shelby, it was already at full capacity. The bouncer at the door was having trouble with people slipping inside on his watch. The packed building was a fire hazard, but no one seemed to care. They all wanted to be there, in that moment, to witness the beginning of the band's rise.

The crowd made me practically claustrophobic. Cheyenne needled people out of the way, but no one seemed to want to move. She was determined though. I almost told her that we should go through the backstage entrance and watch from there, but I liked the idea of being able to see the band front and center.

Eventually, we made our way through the crowd to a spot a short distance from the stage. Their instruments were already set up, even Grant's cherry red Gibson.

The crowd chanted, "ContraBand. ContraBand. ContraBand."

I held my breath and let the memories flood my mind. I'd first met Grant here. Listening to him sing and play guitar that first night, I'd actually seen *him*, and it had made me realize that he wasn't some idiot. He was pure passion and talent. On Halloween, he'd pulled me up onstage to kiss me. He'd written music for me and sang to me and loved *me*.

My throat tightened as Grant walked out. There he was, in all his glory, wearing jeans, a black T-shirt, and a new leather jacket. His dark hair was perfectly tousled. His eyes searched for me out in the massive crowd. The McDermott smirk made the girls all around me swoon.

My heart thudded in my chest in time with the beat McAvoy thumped against the drums.

Then, Grant found me.

His smile was one of pure devotion. It was *my* smile—the one that had won me over, the one I would never stop loving.

"Leaguers!" Grant cheered into the microphone.

The building shook with the enthusiasm of the crowd's screams, claps, and stomps.

"Thank you so fucking much for being here tonight. We're ContraBand! This is a special show for us. This kicks off our first ever tour with The Drift, who we'll be meeting in New Orleans on Monday!"

I smiled and shook my head, imagining how much trouble the band could get into on Bourbon Street.

"You'll always be our hometown, so we're going to start tonight off with a song we wrote about getting the fuck out of here!"

I laughed as the crowd went wild.

"This is 'Hemorrhage.'"

The girls were already dancing around like crazy to the music we'd listened to hundreds of times. I knew every word to every song, but nothing compared to when the guys performed live.

Grant took over, captivating the crowd and drawing them in with his sexy, seductive voice and flirtatious glances. I'd once said he owned the stage, and it had never been truer than tonight.

The other guys were drawing on his mood and the crowd's fervor. Vin rocked back and forth across the stage, raising his guitar high in the air. He jumped up onto one of the speakers and then crashed down onto his knees before sliding across the floor. The theatrics were ridiculous, but even I couldn't keep from smiling at how much fun he was having.

173

Miller met Vin halfway across the stage, and they rocked out together. Miller's backbeat blared the shuddering bass through the speakers.

During the bridge of the next song, McAvoy was so into the music that he stood and slammed his sticks down with more vigor than I'd ever seen.

After nearly an hour, all the guys were breathing heavily. Grant pointed his finger out into the audience, directly at me, and I stood there, stunned, wondering what he was about to do.

"This next song is a new one. When I wrote it, I was going crazy over this girl, and that has never changed. Now, I get to drive her crazy." He winked. "This is 'White Hot.'"

Oh my God, he actually winked at the crowd. He was talking about the song about us having sex to the entire room, and he'd just *winked.* My face flamed.

"God, he loves you," Cheyenne said into my ear as the intro picked up. "It's disgusting."

I laughed because there was nothing else to do. Cheyenne glanced over at me and laughed, too.

The sexual lyrics clung to me as if Grant and I were all alone, doing all the cleverly crafted innuendos he was portraying. Our eyes met across the room, and desire rushed into me. I knew he was going to be singing this song all over the country to thousands of other women, but the look on his face said the only person he was going to be thinking about was me.

The last lines of "Life Raft" echoed across the room.

In that brief moment of silence at the end of the show, I tasted life. Then, the room erupted, the crowd cheering our names and scrambling forward to try to touch us while we were still onstage. It was manic and incredible. I knew then that there was nothing else I wanted to do with my life. It was about more than the chicks and booze and notoriety.

Music was born in me, begging to be released.

It was the music.

Always the fucking music.

I placed my guitar on its stand and then followed the guys offstage.

"Damn, I'm going to miss that crowd," McAvoy said. He retrieved a joint from his pocket and was lighting up. "Smoke?"

"Bro, yes," I said, taking it from him.

"Can you believe we're going to be in New Orleans in thirty-six hours?" Miller asked in disbelief. "I know we opened for The Drift on New Year's, but this feels so much more…real."

"Yeah, it fucking does!" Vin clapped Miller on the back.

It was the most camaraderie I'd seen out of them since Vin found out that Miller and Sydney were fucking. It was surprising, considering—as far as I knew—Miller and Sydney hadn't stopped fucking the entire time she was in town on her spring break.

"We're going to be fucking famous, and we'll get so much fucking pussy. Get the fuck out of Jersey and fucking make a name for ourselves. You heard them cheering, 'ContraBand!' That's going to be in every fucking city in the nation!"

"Getting a little ahead of yourself," Miller muttered, "but I like the sentiment."

"Positive thinking, bro. You think it. It'll fucking happen."

I questioningly raised my eyebrows. "You listening to fucking New Age shit?"

Vin flexed his muscles and looked as if he might deck me for even suggesting it. He opened his mouth to throw some lame-ass comeback at me when the backstage door burst open, and the girls filtered in. One for each of us.

Cheyenne bounced in, her flaming red hair announcing her entrance before she opened her big mouth. She didn't even look at Vin. I hadn't asked what the fuck was going on between them, and I didn't fucking care as long as he stayed in this good of a mood.

Gabi and Shelby followed behind Cheyenne, both seeking out their respective guys. McAvoy immediately tugged Gabi down the hallway and into the back room. It would likely be occupied for a while. Shelby uncertainly walked up to Miller, which made me think she knew about Sydney. My fucking cousin really was the root cause of all the problems in this band.

When I turned back to the door, in the place of a princess in a cardigan stood a rocker in a leather jacket. My dog tags hung loose between her breasts. She looked fucking hot as hell. She didn't feel comfortable in her skin, but this version of my girlfriend at least showcased how much of a badass, no-nonsense chick she was.

We met halfway across the small room. She had a sad look in her eyes despite the smile on her face.

"You didn't like the show?"

She shook her head. "It was the best it's ever been."

"You going to tell me what's wrong then?"

"I'm just going to miss you."

I leaned down and kissed the breath out of her. She had no fucking idea how much I was going to miss her. But I knew this was a good thing. It would put me on the right path to make the kind of money I needed to take care of her.

But it didn't stop me from beating myself up about leaving her all alone in Princeton, knowing my dad was going to be in town. I'd sent her away on spring break because I hadn't wanted her to be here to deal with that shit. Now, I was leaving her all alone.

I'd thought he would have made his move already. *Where are you, old man?*

"Don't be sad. I'm not gone yet, Princess."

"I know. I just want to steal you away from all your adoring fans and the annoying groupies. It's a madhouse out there. I could barely get through."

"Then, let's get out of here."

"Grant, it's your last show."

She looked up at me, her big hurricane-blue eyes saying something completely different than her words. She wanted to leave with me and spend every second together until I'd board the plane in Newark. But she was too proud not let me be around all the other people I'd be leaving in my life.

She still didn't realize she was the only person who mattered.

She was my life raft.

She'd saved me from a downward spiral I'd fallen so far into that I couldn't even see light through the darkness. I wasn't going to lose her because of this.

"And you're my love. I can have a drink with strangers anytime."

Her smile was electric, practically knocking me over with its warmth.

"Okay. Slip out the back door?"

I nodded, and she walked that way as Gabi burst out of the back room, running straight toward Ari.

Up until that moment, I'd never seen the chick have anything on her face but a dopey smile. Now, her face was contorted in pain as tears ran down her cheeks, and she was hiccuping as she tried to control her breakdown.

She collapsed into Ari's arms. Ari looked up at me with a question in her eyes. I shrugged my shoulders. I didn't know what this was about.

"Shh..." Ari whispered. "What's wrong? What happened?"

Cheyenne and Shelby trotted over when they heard the cries.

I instantly felt out of place. *What the fuck was going on?*

"He...broke...up...with me," Gabi said brokenly through her tears.

I cringed.

Fuck.

Bad timing, bro.

The girls ventured into a private corner where they could talk. Gabi seemed to be on the edge of hysteria, and no matter how much they tried to talk her down, I wasn't fucking sure she would recover tonight.

With a frustrated sigh, I stomped down the hallway and into the back room. "What the fuck, man?"

McAvoy looked up at me with a joint in his mouth. He was wringing his hands in front of him, and he looked totally messed up.

"Bro," he said in acknowledgment.

In silence, I waited for him to say more. McAvoy was a man of few words, but I could tell from his body language that he was fucked up. Miller and Vin showed up a few seconds later. Vin crashed down next to McAvoy and shared his weed. Miller anxiously glanced at me.

After a few tense minutes, McAvoy puffed out a steam of smoke and sighed. "I didn't want a girlfriend on tour."

"Right. I fucking got that much."

"She shouldn't have to wait around for me."

Miller rolled his eyes. "And giving her no choice makes sense."

"Don't fucking come at me with that shit, Miller. You're fucking around with Sydney and Shelby. I at least fucking cared enough to end things before shit got worse."

I held my hand up and shook my head. "I don't give a fuck whether you date Gabi or not. But all this fucking fighting ends when we get on the fucking road. We cool?"

Vin lounged back and smirked. "I'm good, bro."

Miller shifted his eyes from Vin and back to me. "Yeah."

McAvoy nodded but remained silent.

"Good. Not my business where you're sticking it."

"That's right. Just want to get my dick wet," Vin said.

"Doesn't that happen all the time when you're jacking it in the shower?" Miller quipped.

McAvoy snorted and shifted forward on the couch.

"Bro, I get fucking pussy!" Vin cried. "I even have a new pick-up line other than 'I'm in a fucking band. Come suck my dick.'"

"This should be good," McAvoy muttered.

"So, I walk up to a chick, all sad-like, and say, 'I feel so sad.' When she asks, 'Why?' I say, 'Because my dick just died. Can I bury it in your ass?'"

All three of us groaned at the same time.

I covered my face and shook my head. *Only Vin.*

"Guys, it'll totally fucking work!"

Then, we were all laughing like idiots at Vin's horrible joke, and it felt like old times.

"Don't go," Ari whispered against my chest.

"I'll be back before you know it."

I kissed the top of her head and wrapped my arms around her.

Ari had driven us to the airport since none of the other girls were currently speaking to us, courtesy of

Gabi's meltdown on Saturday night. All our band equipment and extra stuff had been packed up and shipped down to New Orleans by the record label. So, we just had our carry-ons, which had all fit into the trunk of her BMW.

"I know. I know."

I looked down into her face and gave her a little piece of hope. "Maybe you can fly out for a weekend show."

She looked skeptical. "I have so much to do since the end of the semester is coming up. I don't know if I'll be able to get away."

"Well, we'll figure something out once the semester is over then."

"Okay," she said softly. Her eyes dropped to the floor.

"Hey, Princess." I grasped her chin in my hand and forced her to look at me. "I love you. I can't have you fucking moping while I'm gone."

"I'm not moping," she snapped. "I can miss you without moping."

Finally, I smiled. There was my spitfire.

"I believe you. Now, promise me you'll be careful."

She sighed heavily. "We've already been through this. I'm not stupid. I can remember something as important as avoiding your dad."

"I'm serious, Ari. This isn't a fucking game." My voice dropped lower as I spoke for her ears only, "My dad is a murderer. He's not going to hesitate if he figures out who you are, and I don't want you to be anywhere near him when he explodes. If you see anything that looks suspicious, call me right away, okay?"

"Okay," she agreed.

"I wish you would take my gun."

She determinedly shook her head. "No way. I don't need a gun! It's never going to come to that."

I frowned. She really had no idea what would happen if my father found out who she was. I wished I could prepare her, but there was only so much I could say. I fucking prayed there was a god out there somewhere to answer the first prayer I'd said to him in thirteen fucking years. He needed to take care of Ari. If he did, then maybe we'd start talking again.

"Grant!" Miller called. "Time to go, man."

I waved at him and then crushed Ari against me. "I love you."

"I love you, too."

"Be careful, Princess. I can't have anything happening to you."

"I'll be fine, Grant. Go become a rock star."

I smirked at her. "I already am, darlin'."

The first week wasn't that bad.

I had so much work to do for school and all the time in the world to get it done. In fact, I had so much time to do homework that I completed assignments *way* before their due date. *How had I ever spent this much time on homework?* It was truly baffling.

The second week was torture.

Even though I spoke to Grant every day on the phone, I missed him like crazy. And the worst part was, I couldn't even talk to my roommates about missing Grant without getting angry death glares. They'd all dated the other guys when Grant and I were in an argument over Christmas break, and now, Grant and I were the only ones left intact.

I couldn't fix that, and they clearly didn't want the reminder. So, I found reasons to be out of the apartment all the time. I practically lived in the library. But one afternoon, I had this strange realization. I was completely caught up on homework, and I had absolutely nothing to do and nowhere to go.

My afternoons used to be filled with band practice. My evenings had been full of rock concerts, dates, and quality time in the bedroom. Now…my days were blown wide open. I needed a hobby or something, but I'd never been that interested in anything other than school. Plus, I'd never had time to do anything with the amount of work that always piled up.

As I contemplated the various options I had—*Should I learn to play a sport, take up painting, pick up an instrument?*—I found myself on the way over to Grant's place without even realizing it. A smile touched my face as I drove down the familiar path. If he were here right now, the guys would be crowding into the garage to start band practice.

I felt a little silly, driving over there, but I didn't turn around. I still had stuff at his place, and if I was in the neighborhood anyway, then I could pick it up. Maybe I could grab a T-shirt of his to sleep in.

Oh my God, who was this girl inhabiting my body? She was so guy-crazy compared to the *me* that I knew.

To be honest, I kind of liked it. This was what it should feel like anyway—with butterflies and all that. Everything before Grant had been a joke, a cruel joke on what love was supposed to feel like. It was no wonder I had waited so long to have sex.

I didn't even blush at the thought.

My car rounded the corner, and I brightened at the sight of Grant's shiny blue truck in the driveway. I knew he missed having the freedom of his truck. Both bands were stuffed together in a tour bus driving them around to the various venues. Grant was trying to steer clear of Donovan, but it was difficult to do in a tightly confined space with zero privacy. Apparently though, there was no animosity with any of the other guys. I just thought Donovan needed to get over it.

Parking on the street in front of the house, I hopped out of the car and jogged up to the front door. I slid my key into the lock, turned the knob, and entered Grant's house. After I shut the door, I climbed the stairs up to his bedroom and sighed when I stepped inside. Despite myself, I collapsed back into his unmade bed and breathed in the smell of him.

"Oh my God," I groaned, feeling a little bit ridiculous.

I jumped out of bed and quickly located the clothes I'd left here, grabbed a black T-shirt from Grant's drawer, and then carried the bag of stuff downstairs. It would be nice to sit around at his place all afternoon and not have to worry about my roommates, but maybe it was time to confront them about this. I didn't want to have to keep avoiding my own apartment. I felt bad about Gabi's

---

breakup, but my relationship with Grant had no bearing on what had happened.

I opened the door to Grant's place, stepped outside, and screamed.

A man was standing at the bottom of the steps. He startled backward. "Sorry. I'm sorry." He held up his hands in defense.

My hands were shaking as I stared down at the man before me. Terror crept into me and was quickly sliding toward outright panic. There was a strange man on Grant's doorstep with an older yet familiar face and all too familiar brown eyes with gold ring. I swallowed hard to keep the bile from rising in my throat.

My fight-or-flight instinct was kicking in, and all the adrenaline in my body was saying to get the hell out of there as fast as I could because I was looking right at Grant's dad.

"Ca-can I help you?" I managed to get out.

He smiled what had probably once been a charming smile. "Yes, ma'am. Do you happen to know when the boys who lives here will be home?"

Oh God.

He had tracked down Grant's house. He had to know they were on tour. *Was he staking out the place to find out when he could make his move?*

Calm down. You can get through this.

"No, sir. They've been gone awhile."

"Do you have a way to get a hold of them?"

"Sorry, no," I said, quickly locking up Grant's place.

When I turned back around, he had taken a few steps toward me. I was visibly shaking at this point. I couldn't believe this was happening. It was everything Grant had warned me about. He had said his dad would show up. He had said his dad would hunt him down. Now, here I was, in the line of fire.

No one knew where I was. I hadn't told any of my roommates, nor had I spoken with Grant today. I was totally fucked.

"Excuse me. I-I have to go," I murmured.

I tried edging around him to get back to my car. His hand reached out for me, and I stumbled back a few steps in shock.

His eyes locked with mine for a split second before he spoke, "Interesting choice for a necklace."

In horror, my hand immediately went for the dog tags dangling around my neck. I was wearing Grant's dog tags—the tags that had actually belonged to his father, the military vet. Grant had worn them forever to try to remind him of the man he wanted to become—one who was the opposite of his father.

"When you talk to Grant, tell him I'm not going away. He has to come back sometime."

"I think you should leave him alone," I peeped.

He cocked his head to the side, and I saw the psychopath Grant always talked about. His father looked the worse for wear since getting out of prison. While he might be wearing a nice pair of jeans and a fresh button-up shirt, his eyes and face betrayed the man beneath the getup. I wasn't sure I would have noticed the extent of it if I didn't know what had happened.

"Is that so? Well, I'm going to have to cordially disagree with you, darlin'."

I startled at the ridiculous term of endearment I'd heard Grant say to me dozens of times. I wondered if he even knew it was something he'd picked up from his father. He'd probably never say it again if he figured it out.

"I've been waiting thirteen years to see my son. I don't mind waiting a little bit longer for him. What did you say your name was?"

I swallowed and raised my chin. "I didn't."

He laughed softly. "Fair enough. I'm Mike."

He held his hand out to me, and I stared at it. I wasn't stupid enough to touch him. I crossed my hands over my chest and tried to control the dread passing through my system.

"Okay then." He dropped his hand and then pointed his finger in my direction with a slow deadly smirk plastered on his face. "Just give him my message."

Grant's dad walked away toward a beat-up old pickup truck.

Like father, like son.

I instantly felt horrible for even thinking that. Grant was nothing like the man I'd just met. Driving a truck didn't mean they were similar.

I rushed over to my car, climbed into the driver's seat, and locked the doors. It was only then that I started to breathe normally. My heart rate was still racing, and I could feel my heartbeat in my fingertips. I tightly gripped the steering wheel in my hands to try to stop the shaking, but it wasn't really working.

I blindly reached out for my cell phone stashed at the bottom of my purse. I had to talk to Grant. I had to tell him what had happened. He had said I had to call him if I saw his dad, but I doubt he'd actually thought it would happen.

Oh shit! How could this be happening?

I dialed his number with clumsy fingers and held the phone. I desperately wanted to get away from his place, but I didn't trust myself to drive.

"Hey, Princess. I wasn't expecting to hear from you yet."

"Your dad was here."

"What?" he asked, losing his happy tone and promptly becoming serious.

"I came over to your place to pick up some clothes I'd left behind. When I was leaving, he was standing outside your door."

"Fuck!" he cried. "Fuck. Fuck. Fuck."

"I know. I know," I muttered.

"I fucking knew this was going to happen. Fuck!" There was a crash and some more cussing before the phone was muffled, and everything came out faint and distant. "Yeah. I fucking heard you! Fuck off. Don't make me fuck up your face again, asshole."

After a few more seconds, Grant returned. "Sorry about that. Fucking Donovan was in my space again. Fucker. It's hard to have a private conversation on this goddamn tour bus."

"It's okay, Grant."

"It's not fucking okay! Goddamn it. What am I going to do, Ari? I can't leave you there, all alone, to deal with this. I can't have you in danger. I'll never be able to sleep or focus or anything."

"We'll figure it out, okay?"

"What did he say? Tell me everything."

I sighed. "He was asking where you were. I tried to play it off, but I was wearing your dog tags. He recognized them and asked me to give you a message. He said he's waited thirteen years, so he'll keep waiting for you to come back. He's just...staying in the area, I guess."

"Oh, Jesus Christ! Why? Motherfucker can't take a goddamn hint. Look, Ari, I need you to stay the hell away from my place. He might have already figured out who you are, but I hope not. I'm going to...I don't know...fucking figure this out."

"Okay," I whispered.

"Princess," he murmured "I'm sorry. I'm so sorry. Are you okay?"

"Just a little shaken up. I'll be fine."

"I wish I were there right now. I wish I could ditch the tour and come back to you."

I laughed softly. "No, you don't. You love performing. You love being on tour."

"I know," he agreed easily. "But I'd still rather be there and know you're safe. I wish you'd get my gun. This proves you need it."

I didn't automatically dismiss the idea this time. "Maybe you're right, but I don't feel comfortable with it."

"Okay. Just...please stay safe—for me. I'm going to figure something out, and I'll call you back when I do."

I ended the call with Grant and suspiciously stared around at the road. I didn't feel much better about what had happened. If anything, I was more paranoid. I didn't know what Grant had in mind to help the situation, but I was shaky and uncertain as I drove away from his place. With Grant gone, I knew that there really was no protection from his father.

Fucking fuck, fuck, fuck.

Fuck.

That was the only word running through my mind after I'd gotten off the phone with Ari. I'd warned her this would happen. I'd told myself over and over that it could happen. But the reality of my dad being anywhere near my girl made my blood boil. It made me want to get on the first plane out of the next closest city and fucking find the fucker. I'd teach him a thing or two I hadn't known when I was only ten.

Miller walked into the back room where I was attempting to get shit under control. I couldn't handle the fact that there wasn't any fucking privacy, especially not when no one knew about my dad, and I didn't fucking want anyone to figure out the details.

"Bro, you okay?" Miller asked.

"Yeah. Fine," I ground out. I knew I sounded anything but fine. My hands were shaking with the unbridled anger spreading out from my chest.

"Donovan is spouting off about you and Ari being in a fight about your dad," he said softly.

"What?" I nearly screamed. "I'll fucking kill him. He doesn't know what the fuck he's talking about."

I stormed toward Miller, but he blocked my path.

"He wants a rise out of you. I didn't want you to be blindsided when you walked back out there."

"Get out of my way. I want to pummel his face in."

Miller just stared at me—completely calm and completely in control as always. "I'm not going to let you do that. You should let this shit with Donovan slide. Obviously, something else is wrong that's setting you off. Is it Ari?"

Fuck. I couldn't tell him.

"No. We're fine. I'm just…" I glanced away from him.

"Bro, I've known you nearly your whole life. I know you can't talk to McAvoy or, God forbid, Vin, and you've got shit on your chest. You should probably say it now."

I sank into the chair next to me and buried my head in my hands. "My dad got out of prison."

"What?" Miller asked in surprise.

When I glanced up at him, the look on his face showed this was the last subject he'd thought I would bring up.

"I don't know the details about that, man, but isn't that a good thing?"

I sighed heavily and let out the secret I'd been holding back from everyone but my family and Ari. "He killed my mom, and I watched him do it."

Miller's mouth dropped open.

"That's why he went to prison. He was supposed to serve twenty years, but he got out in thirteen for good behavior."

"Fuck, man." Miller staggered over to me and collapsed into the chair across from me. "Why did you never tell me?"

"I didn't tell anyone. I didn't want anyone to know…to fucking pity me. My aunt and uncle and Sydney knew. Then, I told Ari at the ski lodge."

"You should have told me. I feel like a shit friend now."

I shrugged and settled back into the seat. "I couldn't. I thought I could control it. The music helps, man, but now that he's out…"

"Have you seen or talked to him?"

I nodded. "I talked to him on the phone after Ari's birthday party and told him to leave me the fuck alone and not to contact anyone I knew, but he didn't listen. He showed up at my place while Ari was there. I don't know what the fuck to do, Miller. I have to call my uncle and get him to talk sense into my dad. I don't want him to hurt Ari."

Miller ran a hand back through his hair. "You think he's going to do something?"

"He blamed me for what had happened with my mom because I ran into the room when he was holding a gun to her. He shot her and claimed it was PTSD from the war. Then, he told me he was coming after me when he got out. What do you think?"

"You have to go to the cops, bro."

Fuck, why did everyone keep saying that?

The cops were fucking useless. They weren't going to protect Ari. They wouldn't do anything but serve a fucking restraining order that my dad could walk right through at any time. Yeah, he was an ex-con, but that didn't mean the police would do anything more to stop him.

"I'm not fucking doing that. We'll fucking figure it out without including those idiots."

"What if you don't?" he asked quietly.

I couldn't even think of that. I couldn't fucking think of something happening before I could figure out what to do. I needed to talk to my uncle and convince him to stop my dad. My uncle had seen and talked to him. He had to have some sway.

It already fucking felt like a ransom situation. I'd give my dad whatever he wanted as long as he left me and Ari alone. I couldn't stomach the thought of him finding out how important she was to me, that she was my whole fucking world. I could imagine the look in his eyes and what he'd say to me.

He would take the one thing I loved most in life because I'd taken the thing he loved most. He thought it was only my fault. So, why should I get to find love and happiness when he was left without the woman he loved?

He'd never acknowledged that it was of his own doing.

If he'd gone and gotten help for what had happened to him...

If he'd talked to my mom about the problem...

If he hadn't moved us away from all their friends and medical professionals and left us stuck in Middle of Nowhere, Tennessee...

If he had just done something...anything...

No, no responsibility from the old man.

That was asking too much.

Now, I was here, thirteen years later, trying to clean up his mess—again.

"I spoke to my uncle."

"Good," I said softly.

I'd been trying to remain calm, but my hand had been itching to call the cops all afternoon. I knew Grant didn't want me to. I also knew he didn't think logically or rationally about anything regarding his father. I didn't want to go against his wishes before he got back to me though, so I'd held off.

"What did he say?"

"He's going to get a hold of my father and try to meet up with him. I think he's starting to understand how much I want to fucking steer clear of him. My father is a determined man, but I think my uncle can talk some sense into him."

"Okay. Do you know when that's going to happen?"

"Hopefully, today or tomorrow. I think it'll get him out of Princeton for some time, so you won't have to worry."

I blew out a breath. *Thank God.*

I wanted to be strong during this, but all the horror stories Grant had told me were taking over the reasonable side of my brain. Truth was, I didn't know how to deal with the situation. I didn't want to obsess about it. *What if it ended up being nothing?* But I didn't want to blow it off either in case it was truly dire.

"You're not going to like this, Grant, but if I see him again, I'm calling the cops."

"Ari—"

"No, I don't want to hear it. You're not here. Even if you were, I wouldn't want you to get near him. I saw him. I saw the look in his eyes. I didn't understand what you were saying until that moment. I'm not going to risk anything happening."

He sighed softly. "I wasn't going to argue with you."

"What? Really?"

"Yeah. I-I talked to Miller about it."

"You told Miller?"

"Yeah."

Wow.

That was a step for Grant. He'd known Miller for a long time. He was Grant's best friend, and he'd never told Miller about it. Grant must be really stressed and worried to do something like that.

I heard noise on the other end of the line, and Grant cursed under his breath.

"Sorry, Princess. I have to go. Can't have a minute of fucking privacy on this bus. I can't wait to get back to you and have my own bed and my girl with me."

"I'm ready for that, too," I whispered throatily.

"Stay safe for me."

The line ended, and I carefully set the phone down on the table next to the Molecular Biology assignment I'd already triple-checked for accuracy.

So, here I was, stuck in the library again and terrified of Grant's dad without Grant or my friends around me. The numbers and equations on the paper blurred under my vision. I hastily moved the papers away, so I wouldn't get any unwanted tears on the assignment.

"Aribel?"

I glanced up at the voice, and with the back of my hand, I quickly brushed the tears off my face. *God, I had been a freaking leaky faucet lately.* I'd never cried before Grant.

Kristin stood in front of me.

Great.

This was just what I wanted to deal with right now— the slutty bitch who had tried to get my boyfriend to cheat on me.

"What?" I snapped.

She cringed. "Sorry. I just…are you okay?"

"Yes, I'm fine." I stood and slung my bag on my shoulder. "Just leaving."

"Okay. Yeah. All right." She shrank away from me like the sheep she was. "Um…are you sad about Grant being gone?"

"Why? So, you can somehow use that to your advantage to try to steal him away from me?" I knew I was being unnecessarily harsh, but well…she had already tried to do that, and I was in a bitch mood.

"No! No, seriously, I'm so sorry about that. You looked like you could use someone to talk to about it."

I did need someone to talk to about it, but that didn't mean I wanted Kristin.

"I'm fine," I repeated hollowly.

"Well, if you do, I finished the M-Bio assignment. We could go over it or discuss O-chem or get a drink."

I skeptically looked at her. "Are you asking me out?"

Kristin burst out laughing. "Oh my God! It totally sounded like that. I'm seriously such a dude. I legit just wanted to apologize and get to know you better. This is going to sound way bitchy, but you're a lot cooler than I thought you were."

"Yeah…that does."

"You're right. Never mind." Kristin shouldered her bag and started walking away.

What the hell? It wasn't like I had anyone else to do anything with.

"Kristin? Hey, wait up."

She stopped and looked at me in confusion.

"A drink might be nice."

Hanging out with Kristin was…*weird*.

It was the only word I could use to describe it. We had so many classes together, so there was an unlimited amount of things to discuss. Not to mention, she had been a big time ContraBand groupie, so she knew all the guys and had been to all of their shows. But I also didn't like her, and spending time with her made me feel like a traitor to my good nature.

It wasn't that she was mean or bitchy or rude. She just reminded me too much of the horrible things she had done in the past. Then, I felt as if I was using her because all my other friends had fallen apart after Gabi's breakup.

Realistically, I should have confronted them about this by now, but I'd kept making excuses for their bullshit. Eventually, I'd have to figure it out—sooner rather than later since the end of the semester was approaching.

About a week and a half later, I had gotten home from class, exhausted after a crazy lab. Kristin had asked me to hang out, and I'd bluffed and said I was busy. It had been nearly a month without Grant, and I terribly missed him. I didn't want to have to pretend to be happy with Kristin. I had planned to stay in, write up the lab results from that afternoon, and crash.

Cheyenne had a different idea.

"You've been hanging out with that bitch, Kristin, instead of us?" she asked as soon as I'd walked into the apartment.

"Hey to you, too." I shrugged out of my cardigan and glanced around to see where Gabi and Shelby were lurking, but it looked as if we were alone.

"What's going on, Ari?"

"What's going on with *me*?" I asked incredulously. "I've been getting death stares from all three of you since the band left. You've made it pretty clear that I wasn't really welcome to hang around."

"What?" she nearly shrieked. "None of that is true."

"Oh, really? I had to take the guys to the airport by myself in my tiny little car because none of you wanted to see them. When I got back, none of you would even talk to me! So, don't try to blame this on me."

"Before, when you weren't home, we knew you were with Grant, and that was cute. Now, he's gone, and you're still never home. Plus, you walk around like a zombie, studying three times as hard as the old Aribel. Admittedly, it was hard to be around you in the beginning because you love him so much, and we're all a bit heartbroken. But now, we're worried!"

I stared at Cheyenne in stunned silence. *Was I really like that?* I didn't want to stop to think about it, but I had been doing those things. I hadn't thought about what it probably looked like from the outside.

"I miss him," I said finally.

"We know. We can tell. Everyone can tell."

My eyes shifted away from Cheyenne. I was embarrassed.

Great. Now, I was this poor sad girl, pining over her boyfriend.

Cheyenne gently put her hand on my shoulder. "He's your first real boyfriend, who you care about, and now, you're doing the long-distance thing. That can't be easy. If we shut you out, it wasn't intentional."

"Well, I don't want to be a zombie."

"I suppose you're a bit too much of a sarcastic bitch to be a zombie."

"Oh, thanks." I rolled my eyes.

Cheyenne laughed and shook her head. "Well, at least we're talking again." She grabbed something out of the kitchen. "Oh! I meant to give you this." She placed a piece of paper in my hands. "Why didn't you tell me Grant's dad was in town?"

"What?" My head snapped up to hers.

"Yeah. He stopped by, looking for you. I told him you were out, so he gave me his number."

My mouth dropped open. "He did...what?"

Cheyenne uncertainly looked at me. "Should I not have gotten his number?"

"Uh…no. You're fine," I forced myself to say. I swallowed back bile and tried to check my racing pulse. This couldn't be happening.

"Well, cool. You're pretty lucky if that's what Grant is going to look like when he's older."

I stared at her in disbelief. *How did she not see how crazy he was?* "Thanks…I guess."

"Welcome! Let's hang out soon. I want to hear about all the phone sex you're having."

"Cheyenne!"

She just giggled maniacally and walked away. I couldn't even muster up embarrassment at her jokes. I was too terrified over the fact that somehow Grant's dad had tracked me down to my apartment.

How could he even have even done that? He didn't even know my name.

Oh my God, was he really coming after me?

All Grant's fears were coming true.

I didn't hesitate this time. Grant didn't want me to speak to the cops, but I wasn't going to wait around and hope nothing happened. I had to take action, and I had to take it now for my own sanity.

It wasn't really an emergency, so I opted out of dialing 911, and I called the local police department.

"Princeton Police, how can—"

"Yes, hi," I interrupted before the person could finish the spiel. "My name is Aribel Graham. I'm a student at the university. My boyfriend's father was recently let out of prison and is now stalking me. I believe he is dangerous, and I wanted to find out what I could do to get him to leave me alone."

"Okay. Is this an emergency? Do we need to send someone over to your house?"

"No. He's not here currently."

"Are you safe at the moment?"

"Yes," I answered. "I need to find out how to get him to leave me alone."

"Hold one minute, and let me connect you to an officer."

I waited for a solid ten minutes before a man got on the phone.

"Princeton Police."

I repeated everything to him in a rush. I was anxious to get this figured out.

"How exactly has he stalked you?"

"I was at my boyfriend's house, and he showed up while I was there. Then, without knowing who I am, he showed up at my apartment today while my roommate was home and left his phone number."

"Has he tried to harm you in any way?"

"Well…no."

"Have you tried to reach out to him to tell him to leave you alone?"

"No, but I told him to leave my boyfriend alone."

"Has he threatened you?"

I sighed. "No! He hasn't threatened me or attacked me or anything. He got out of prison after being in for thirteen years, and he is now trying to get a hold of my boyfriend. He keeps showing up and calling, and I don't want it to keep happening."

"I'm sorry, ma'am, but unfortunately, this seems to be a civil situation between a father and son. As long as he hasn't threatened you or harmed you in any way, then we have no grounds to take this case forward. I would recommend speaking with him and trying to figure out what it is he wants and why he keeps showing up. If you're not comfortable with that, then I suggest ignoring him. Please feel free to give us a call or have your boyfriend give us a call if you feel threatened."

When I got off the phone with the police, I nearly threw it across the room in frustration. Grant was right again. The police were no use in this situation. And if something horrible did happen with his dad, then the police would be too late.

Most nights, the only time I wasn't thinking about Ari and my dad would be those blissful sixty minutes when we were onstage. It was what made this tour worthwhile.

Other than the fact that I couldn't handle the shit I needed to deal with at home, sitting on a tour bus with Donovan Jenkins was the worst part about this situation. I couldn't fucking believe I'd ever been friends with the guy. Maybe I'd been into knowing someone kind of famous or some shit, but he was a total douche and not just to me. I supposed he had a reason to act like a jackass to me, but he was that way with everybody.

The other guys in The Drift referred to his shit attitude as PMS, but I'd never met a chick who constantly bitched like this. Apparently, I was the only one who called him out on his fucking attitude. Fame had gotten to his head, and his ego was an enormous inflated balloon flying off into space.

From listening to the guys in The Drift, I'd put bits and pieces together about him. They had all come from a poor suburb of D.C. A single mother had raised him and his three older sisters. Donovan was the one who had pushed them to get the band together, to become successful. Once they were signed and left D.C., Donovan turned into a total fuck-up.

I knew I was missing something about his past that had triggered that reaction, but I hadn't figured out what it was. Until I did, I couldn't fucking hurt him.

"Get out of the way," Donovan said, bumping into my shoulder on his way to the backstage dressing room.

We were playing a show somewhere in backwoods West Virginia tonight, and I didn't have the energy to put up with his bullshit.

"Fuck off, Donovan."

He flipped me off. "I'll save the fucking for your girlfriend's pretty ass."

I lost it. I was too pissed off about everything else, and we were living in close quarters, too close for me to handle this shit right now. I launched myself at Donovan. Grabbing him by the neck, I twisted him around and then slammed him down onto the floor.

"Don't fucking talk about Ari, you piece of shit," I growled.

"Get off of me, man!"

Miller and McAvoy came running. They hauled me off of Donovan while Vin laughed hysterically, and the guys from Donovan's band tried not to laugh.

"You're going to be so fucking over!" he said as he stood back up.

"Save your fucking breath. You might think your ass is hot shit, but it's still just shit."

Donovan shrugged and dusted off his pants. "I'm the only one over here doing anything of value anyway. I don't have to listen to this shit."

He turned around and walked into the dressing room. The door slammed in our faces, and I glared at it.

Prick!

"Do you have to pick a fight with him all the time?" Miller asked.

"He fucking ran into me!"

Ridley and Trevor from The Drift wandered over and nodded at me.

"He deserved it," Ridley said.

We fist-bumped.

"It's nice to see someone who won't take his shit," Trevor said.

"What the fuck? How do you guys put up with him? Was he always this way?"

Trevor and Ridley shared a look.

Ridley was the leaner of the two, but he was tall and straight as a board. He even towered over me. Trevor was a stockier build, but he was a chick favorite. It had something to do with the gauges in his ears, his fauxhawk, and the intense tattoos covering both arms, his chest, and back. He was even more inked up than McAvoy.

"We don't really talk about it," Trevor said.

I was intrigued. "So?"

Ridley shrugged. "It's not a big deal, but Donovan goes berserk over it. So, don't bring it up."

"All right," I promised halfheartedly.

"He freaks over this girl he dated at home," Trevor said. "They dated forever, but one day, when we went back out on tour, they split."

"That's the understatement of the century. They had a catastrophic breakup, one for the ages."

"All this bullshit over a girl?" McAvoy asked in disbelief.

I'd have said the same thing a couple of months ago. McAvoy, having just broken up with his girlfriend over touring, couldn't understand what they were saying. If Ari had broken up with me because of this tour, I'd never be the same. It didn't make me feel sympathetic toward Donovan's douche-bag behavior, but it did help me understand him a bit better.

"You guys don't know Courtney," Ridley said in response. "It was a fucking disaster."

As we got ready for the show, I considered what the guys had told me. I wasn't sure I liked having anything in common with Donovan fucking Jenkins. He was a tool. But I knew I'd be a goddamn mess without Ari.

"Bro, who knew there were so many hot chicks in West Virginia?" Vin asked, scanning the crowd from our viewpoint backstage.

I shrugged. I'd gotten used to singing Ari's songs to a sea of girls who could never measure up to her. The crowd would go crazy for "Life Raft" since it was the only song they really knew of our music, but "White Hot" seemed to be the next best thing.

I wasn't surprised. Everyone liked to sing about sex. I just wished I were getting some.

In fact, it was hard to fucking believe that I was the *only* fucking person on our bus not getting any—not that I didn't have offers every night. Some of the girls who had thrown themselves at me were drop-dead gorgeous. I'd have given up a dozen chicks from home to bang one of these groupies. But I'd never give up Ari.

So, my dick stayed in my pants, except when I found time to masturbate. And on a tour bus with eight other dudes, that was pretty slim.

Our show went off without a hitch. It was nice to see more and more people knowing the words to our songs. Maybe what Hollis had told us was actually working. Once we had a real studio album, we'd be an overnight success. But until it happened, I wasn't ready to believe him. I wanted it. I wanted it pretty fucking bad.

I wanted to be able to make something of myself, to prove that I was good enough and talented enough for someone like Ari, who was so smart, beautiful, and wealthy. It didn't matter that I knew she didn't care about that shit. I did. I cared.

"Killed it out there tonight," Ridley said as he passed us backstage after the show.

"Thanks, man."

"We have a night here in a real fucking hotel before we have to leave again tomorrow. You want to go out and party with us?"

I knew how hard The Drift partied, and for once, the thought of a soft bed beckoned to me more than some booze and watching my friends get some ass.

"I'm gonna pass."

We fist-bumped.

"Just going to crash tonight."

When I got back into the hotel room, I bolted the lock just in case and then called up Ari. She had told me that my dad had tried to reach out to her again sometime last week, but there had been no contact since then.

I always called her every night to hear her voice and make sure she was okay. But tonight, all I could think about was her wet pussy and the feel of it sliding around my dick.

"Hey, Princess," I murmured into the phone.

"Grant, I miss you."

"I miss you, too."

"How was the show?"

"Good as always. Singing about sex with you to people all over the country makes me want to come home and fuck you."

She laughed throatily. "I wouldn't mind if you did that."

"What would you want me to do?" I asked.

"Um…have sex with me?"

It was my turn to laugh. "I know. I mean, if I were there right now, tell me *exactly* what you'd want me to do."

I'd tried to initiate phone sex in the past to no avail. She would get too embarrassed, and I wasn't there to smile and coax the slutty nature out of her. Just hearing her mention sex made my dick throb.

"I…I don't know, Grant. Kiss me."

Well, that was further than I'd gotten before.

"Where?" I encouraged.

"Oh my God, Cheyenne asked me about phone sex earlier. I can't believe you're trying this."

"Humor me, Princess. Cheyenne clearly knows the benefits. Now, I want you to go into your room, shut the door, turn off all the lights, and lie in bed."

I waited a minute until she hesitantly told me that she had done it.

"Now, I'm not just kissing you. I'm running my stubbly jaw down the inside of your legs, kissing a soft trail downward. My hands are gripping the inside of your thighs. I'm squeezing your soft muscles and opening your legs before me, so I can see that soft wet pussy."

She whimpered at my words. "Grant…"

"Feel what I did to you," I encouraged.

I was sure as hell feeling it. I'd slipped my jeans and boxers on the floor. My dick was in my hand, and I was stroking it upward. Her whimper alone could almost make me pretend she was here, doing this for me.

"Are you wet?"

After a short pause, she answered, "Yes."

"God, that's hot. Are you swirling it around your clit? Imagining me doing it?"

She sighed heavily into the phone, and I pumped faster.

"I'm…I'm imagining you using your tongue. You're so good at that."

"Licking and sucking on you. Pressing my fingers up inside you. Curling my fingers against you until you're bucking underneath me."

"Yes," she purred.

She still sounded hesitant, but I fucking wasn't.

"Tell me what you want."

"You, um…let me finish before hovering over me and rubbing yourself against me."

"Oh God," I groaned, leaning over the bed.

I could just imagine it now—her touching herself in the dark, thinking about me sliding my dick across the opening to her pussy. I picked up the pace as the image flooded my mind.

"Then, you don't hold back. You just shove into me. Take me."

"I sure fucking do. I pump into you over and over again. Hard and rough just like you like it."

"Mmm…" she moaned.

I was getting close to orgasm already at the sound of her voice and the skill of my hand. *If only she were here to finish me off...*

"You flip me over," she said quietly.

"So, I can fuck you from behind," I said in admiration.

"My face is...is buried in the pillows."

"Ass up in the air as I drive into you. I feel you tightening around my cock."

"And then I..." She trailed off.

"Oh God, Ari. *Come.* Say come."

She made some soft mewling sounds that sounded as if she was close, and I could barely hold on.

"Come," she finally said. "You make me come."

Hot cum squirted out of me as I did just that.

Fuck!

It ran down my hand as I emptied myself at the sound of her voice. It was so sexy, hearing her talk to me like that. My whole body shook as I imagined her coming with me. I fucking hoped she was getting off on the other line.

When I finally finished, I lay back in the bed, spent and dying to feel her beside me. "I wish you were here for this," I told her.

"You'll be home soon, and I'll let you try all of that."

"It's a date."

Finals approached almost without warning.

One minute, I was writing out bio labs, working out equations for calculus, and trying to figure out how to boost my O-chem grade, and the next, I was frantically cramming for finals.

I'd been spending more time with the girls lately. Gabi finally seemed to be recovering. Though, sometimes, I would still see her wistfully look at my phone when a text came in from Grant. But the girls were supportive, and it was nice to have them back. But we'd barely had any time to spend together since finals started. We were all running around like chickens with our heads cut off.

I barely even had time to plan for my trip back to Boston after the semester. I was very happy the trip would coincide with ContraBand's tour stop in the city. Grant would even have a whole day off after the show, so we could spend time together. For me, that meant taking the plunge and introducing him to my parents.

Grant was pretty freaked out about it, but he seemed to be weighing that against finally getting to see me again, and he found it to be an acceptable trade. I was way more scared about the upcoming introductions. I knew my parents. I knew my brother. I already knew what they would think about Grant. Dismissing him as a phase was the nicest thing that could happen.

But I decided not to care.

I knew Grant wasn't a phase. I knew I wanted a future with him. Even though the music industry was cruel, touring would keep us apart, and a million girls were throwing themselves at him, I thought we could make it.

That thought warmed me throughout my last final, and I handed in my test to Professor Williamson with a smile on my face. If I hadn't aced it, I would be shocked.

"Thank you, Miss Graham," he said, taking the paper out of my hand. "It's nice to see a student take the initiative in my class."

"My pleasure. Would you by any chance need any help this summer with lab work? I should be in town. I would love to be of any assistance."

"Hmm." He stroked his beard as he contemplated what I'd asked. "Yes, I might have something. Come back by before the summer session starts, and we'll work out the details."

"Yes, sir. Thank you."

I was euphoric. All my hard work had paid off. I was going to get to do some real lab work over the summer, which would only help my graduate school or medical school applications. I hadn't decided between the two.

It felt great to be done, and I pulled out my phone to call my brother as I walked out of the building and to my car.

"Aribel," Aaron said briskly.

"Hey!" I said. "How is work?"

There was a short pause.

"Fine. You sound happy."

"I finished finals. It feels good to be done for the semester." I popped open the door to my car and sank into the driver's seat.

"Am I talking to my sister? Don't you usually mope when school gets out?"

"I've turned over a new leaf."

"A new leaf, huh?" He sounded unconvinced.

"Yeah. Actually, that's why I called. I'm going to a concert when I get back into town this weekend. Do you want to go with me?"

"What are we talking? Cello performance? Symphony?" he asked, sounding distracted.

"Um…it's a rock concert." I started up the car and drove back to my place.

"A what? You're going to a rock concert? Who is playing?"

"The Drift. They're this pretty popular band right now."

"I know who The Drift is, Aribel. I didn't think you even liked that kind of music."

"I do. Plus, well…I want you to meet my boyfriend. Mom and Dad told you I was bringing him home with me, right?"

Aaron sighed. "Yeah, they told me. Also, Henry told me this guy is kind of crazy and yelled at you when he met the guy?"

"Ugh, why are you even listening to Henry? I told him I don't have any interest in him. It's like an arranged marriage, Aaron. It's weird."

"I'm just looking out for you. Henry is a good guy. We've been hanging out more since Christmas."

"Great. Then, *you* date him."

Aaron laughed. I could practically see him shaking his head at me.

"So, a rock concert to meet your boyfriend, huh? I guess I could swing that. It'll be good for me to see him before Mom and Dad. That way, we can figure out how to reduce the damage. I've already heard Dad say the word *phase* a couple of times in relation to the new boyfriend."

I rolled my eyes. *Of course.* "Thanks, Aaron. You're the best."

"This should be interesting."

I laughed and agreed as I pulled into my parking spot. I slid the car into park, and then my laughter died out.

There, standing outside of my building, was Grant's dad. He was leaning against the side of the stairwell, clearly waiting…for me. I swallowed hard and tried to think about what the policeman had said on the phone. Maybe I needed to talk to Grant's dad and *tell* him to leave me alone—and also have my phone with 911 up and ready to make the call at any point.

"Aaron, I have to go." I tried to keep my voice level. "I got back to my place. I'll see you when I get home."

I hung up and then readied the phone with 911. My pulse quickened as I slowly eased out of the car. I couldn't believe I was doing this. I couldn't fucking believe he was here.

God! Couldn't he get the picture that I didn't want to get involved, and Grant didn't want to talk to him?

No, clearly not.

I took a deep breath in and out. He needed to be told. That was what the officer had said.

I closed the distance between us on shaky legs. "Hello, Mr. McDermott."

"Aribel Graham," he said.

"What are you doing, staking out my apartment?"

"I'm not staking out your apartment, darlin'. I gave you plenty of time to contact me. You did get the phone number from your friend Cheyenne, didn't you?"

"I did."

"Now, I'm simply following up on that conversation since I never heard back from you."

"Did it never occur to you that I didn't *want* to speak with you?"

I would be civil. I could be civil. This was possible. I wouldn't stand before this man, terrified and shaking, like before. I would tell him the truth and then make him leave, or I'd call the cops again.

"I considered that, but this is too important to me. I don't generally take no for an answer."

He smiled devilishly at me, and I cringed away from it.

"I'm trying to talk to my son, and since he won't answer you and you're dating him, I thought we could have a chat."

"A chat," I said hollowly.

"Yes. A chat where I explain I need to see my son, and then you convince him to do that."

"I won't do that." I crossed my arms over my chest, still tightly holding the phone in my hand. "Grant doesn't want to have anything to do with you. I don't want to either! You should leave both of us alone. Let him live his life without you. He's done fine so far."

Grant's dad dangerously narrowed his eyes. "Well, I didn't ask for your opinion on the matter. If he cares for you, then he'll listen to you."

My face paled. "You can't use me to get to Grant. I *know* what happened that day, what you've done. The last thing he wants is to confront a very messy past. So, take it from someone who knows him, he'll never want to see you again."

"You don't know the half of what happened or what I've been through. And Grant can't escape his past any more than I can. While he might be gallivanting around the country with his band, he has to come home sometime. It would be easier for everyone if you agreed to get him to speak with me."

I saw red. I couldn't believe he was trying to convince me to do this. "No! I'm not going to do anything for you, and you don't deserve anything from him, not after what you put him through."

"What I put him through?" he bellowed. "You have no idea what you're talking about. He sent me to prison."

"With all due respect," I said, slinking up the first step toward my place, "you killed his mother in front of him. You sent yourself to prison."

"So, this is my son's opinion of me?" He sounded dejected yet furious.

His eyes were murderous, and it made me take another step away from him.

"You've given him no reason to see otherwise, and stalking my apartment isn't really helping."

Grant's dad nodded. But I couldn't tell what he was thinking, if he was even considering my words. Then, without another word, he left.

I stared after him in confusion. *All of that, and he had just left?* It didn't make sense. *What did he want from Grant?* The only thing I could guess that wasn't sinister was some type of closure. *But then, why would he say Grant had sent him to prison?*

There were too many questions, and my brain was running away with me. His dad could have hurt me if he had wanted to, and nothing had happened. That didn't necessarily mean he wouldn't hurt Grant if given the option. I'd seen the look in his father's eyes. I'd seen the anger bubbled up under the surface at the mention of what had happened that day.

I knew the last thing Grant wanted to do was meet with his father, and I didn't want to play into his hands by convincing Grant otherwise. But it might take Grant talking to him to get him to leave Grant alone. He was determined, and if I knew anything about McDermott persistence, then Grant would find no peace from his father anytime soon.

35   GRANT

Aribel.

I'd finally get to see my girl. It didn't matter to me that I'd also have to go through the likely painful encounter of meeting her judgmental parents. In fact, I was the one who had pushed her to tell them about me in the first place. Though telling them about me and officially meeting them was a different story.

But it would be worth it as long as I was finally with her again.

"Grant's getting his dick wet tonight." Trevor cracked up on the bus as we pulled into Boston.

"Fucking finally," Ridley joked.

"I can't wait to fucking meet this chick who has you so whipped," Nic said.

Vin snorted. "Just wait. She's this tiny little innocent blonde. You'd never peg her as a fucking groupie."

McAvoy smacked him upside the head. "That's because she's not, dipshit."

"That's fucking right she's not," I growled possessively.

Next to Nic, Joey leaned back and crossed his arms. "How did you end up with a little innocent thing in Jersey when you have so many options on the road?"

"I wouldn't say Ari is a sweet, innocent thing anymore," Miller said, struggling to keep a straight face.

"Oh, fuck off, guys!"

They all laughed, and it felt nice for once to relax with the bands, knowing I'd be getting some ass tonight.

Then, Donovan walked in. "What's so funny?"

"We're talking about Grant's girlfriend. She's coming to the show tonight," Ridley filled him in.

Donovan arched an eyebrow at me. "Is she bringing another guy again? She seems to have a new one at every show."

"Don't make me punch your fucking face again."

Donovan smiled at me and held his hands up. "I was trying to clarify the facts here, *bro*."

"Come on, D, we're having some fun," Trevor piped up. "Have a beer and chill out with us. We have a full day off after this to get fucked and fucked up."

Donovan looked over at me for a second. It was in that moment I realized what had fucking happened. Donovan had been such a punk-ass bitch lately that even his own bandmates preferred to hang out with me and my bros. Donovan and I had done nothing but argue these last six weeks, and now, he wasn't even fucking welcome to fucking chill with us.

I lifted my shoulder in affirmation, and Donovan pretended not to notice. *Of course he would.*

"Sure, man," he said. He slapped hands with Trevor, who passed him a beer, and then he slid into a seat.

Just like that, all the animosity of the past couple of months dwindled between us, and as long as Donovan would stop acting like a motherfucker about Ari, then we could stay this way.

An hour later, the crew was already busy putting our set together, and we were doing the sound check. Once everything seemed ready to go, I made sure to reserve two front-row tickets for Aribel as well as backstage passes for her after our show.

By the time the show was about to begin, I couldn't keep from fucking bouncing with energy.

Vin punched me on the arm. "Dude, fucking chill out. If I'd known you'd start acting like a fucking freak, I never would have given you Ari that night."

I raised my eyebrows. "Is that what you think happened? You *gave* her to me?"

He shrugged. "Steered you in her fucking direction. I'm the man."

"You're such a douche bag."

"Yeah," he agreed. "But you fuckers are happy or some shit. In the long run, no harm, no foul."

No harm, no foul?

He was fucking lucky there had been no damage done. I'd just fucked some random chick I probably would have fucked if I were sober.

"Ready?" Miller asked, sidling up next to us.

"As ready as we'll ever be, bro!" Vin cried.

"She didn't bring the girls with her, did she?" McAvoy asked.

He leaned forward to try to get a glimpse of the audience. I wasn't sure if he was asking because he missed Gabi and wanted to see her or if he was asking because he was afraid to see her again.

"Nah. It's just Ari."

He nodded his head and crossed his arms. "Cool."

The lights flickered, and then the room went black. That was our cue.

We wandered onstage and received cheers from the audience. I slung my guitar over my head as the lights rose.

I walked right up to the microphone, yanked it off the stand, and said words that had never been truer, "Boston, it is so fucking good to see you tonight!"

The crowd went wild. Despite the sold-out show and thousands of people cheering for us, my eyes went straight to the front row, looking at the pair of enormous blue eyes staring up at me from the most beautiful face I'd ever seen.

Ari.

Her smile was radiant, and she only had eyes for me. It took everything in me not to vault off the stage, capture her lips in a searing kiss, and cart her ass off with me.

"We come from a tiny little town off the Jersey Shore."

There were more cheers.

"And this is our first time ever playing in Boston, so send us some love. This is 'Hemorrhage.'"

Then, I poured all my love for Ari into the guitar. Even though I was singing about getting the fuck out of Jersey, all I really wanted in that moment was to return home with her.

My memory didn't hold a candle to the magnificence that was Grant McDermott. It was a hazy outline, a foggy sketch to the masterpiece.

From my spot in the front row, he towered over me, clad in tight-fit dark jeans and a V-cut red T-shirt that made me want to drool. He always wore dark colors, so seeing him in a delicious red made him absolutely edible. His hair was a little longer and wildly finger-combed. All I could think about was running my fingers through it as I kissed him until he was breathless. His dark eyes kept shifting back to me, and I warmed everywhere. In those brief moments, I could imagine us completely alone—just me and Grant.

His eyes were like molten lava, burning away my clothes and seeing through to my heated body. I'd never felt such desire for someone before. Watching him perform usually made me appreciate him more, but I was flat-out turned on.

And standing next to my brother while my boyfriend eye-fucked me from the stage was a little uncomfortable—especially when Aaron leaned over.

He whispered to me, "The lead singer looks like he's going to pull you onstage and do something obscene."

I bit my lip, trying not to get excited at the prospect. I should have been horrified. The old Aribel would have been horrified. I could only find a mild embarrassment that my brother had noticed.

I probably should have told Aaron that I was dating the lead singer of the opening band, but I'd wanted to judge his reaction. When we'd shown up, he had been confused because I didn't have another guy in tow, but I'd explained we were going to meet him after the opener. It was sneaky on my part, but I couldn't help it.

When Grant had announced they were from the shore, Aaron had leaned over and told me he thought that was cool. Apparently, he had spent some time on the shore during his four years at Princeton. We had overlapped during his last year at school because we were only three years apart, but I couldn't remember him mentioning the shore.

I sang through the list of songs that ContraBand performed, and then "White Hot" came on.

"You sure seem to like their music," Aaron mused.

I tried not to blush as Grant sang out the sexual lyrics to a sea of people. His eyes found mine, and he licked his lips in between verses. The image seared into my mind. I found I couldn't tear myself away.

Aaron bobbed his head to the music. "I really like this one. Great lyrics."

Now, I really *was* blushing.

"White Hot" ended, and McAvoy started up the drumbeat for "Life Raft." The cheers intensified tenfold.

The lights dimmed, and a spotlight shown on Grant. He held the microphone up to his mouth as if it were life or death.

Then, his sweet voice came through the speakers as he said, "This song goes out to the love of my life."

A chorus of, "Aw," went up through the crowd as Vin and Miller brought the opening chords to meet McAvoy.

I felt like jelly, and I was completely rooted to the spot. Grant had called me the love of his life to an entire audience. Aaron was saying something in my ear, but I couldn't even hear what it was over the sound of Grant's smooth voice.

God, he was such a perfect jackass. I hated that he was on tour. I hated that he had to be away from me. Despite the fact that we were opposites, we loved each other so much.

"Aribel?" Aaron said, waving his hand in front of my face.

"Oh. What?" I snapped out of my trance.

"This song sounds really familiar. I feel like a friend from school recently sent it to me. Are they from Princeton?"

I glanced between my brother and the band. "Yeah, they are."

"Have you seen them before?"

I nodded cautiously. "Yes." Then, I took a deep breath and gave in. I pointed up at Grant with a smile. "That's my boyfriend."

Aaron stared between me and Grant and then back. His mouth slightly hung open. His eyebrows were scrunched up in confusion. "You're dating the lead singer?"

"Yeah."

"Oh, Aribel," he said, shaking his head. "You're totally fucked."

I heavily breathed out.

Shit!

That was not the reaction I had hoped for. Maybe it was what I had expected, and that was the reason I hadn't told Aaron in the first place. But I hadn't wanted to believe I was in as much of a hole as I was going to be with my parents. If that was the first thing Aaron had said though…he was probably right.

Grant finished out the last few lyrics of "Life Raft." I applauded with the crowd, but the elation from moments earlier was replaced with fear.

How would my parents react when they met Grant? What would they say when they found out he was in a rock band? How completely fucked was I?

I didn't want it to matter. I was a strong woman who could make my own choices. Over Christmas break, I had realized how truly alone I felt in the world my parents had created, and that was only due to the changes that came with Grant being in my life. But my parents' opinion still mattered to me.

I wanted them to like him for who he was. I hated the fact that they were going to judge him before they ever got to know the Grant I had fallen in love with.

With a resigned sigh, I wove Aaron out of the auditorium, through the theater lobby, and to the entrance to the backstage. I flashed our backstage passes, and then we entered the chaotic world behind the scenes. The crew was frantically switching out equipment from ContraBand to The Drift. A small line of fans were still standing in front of the remaining Drift members, who were taking pictures and signing autographs.

But I didn't spot Grant.

I ushered us through the crowd and almost made it to the dressing rooms before a staff member stopped us. Then, Donovan Jenkins appeared out of thin air. It was as if he had a fucking radar for my presence.

"Ari," he said. He nodded his head at me and gave me a devious smirk. "So glad you could show up again."

"Donovan, do you know where Grant is?" I asked impatiently.

"Somewhere around here, I'm sure. And who is this?" he asked, pointing out Aaron. "I feel like I won a bet or something. You're here with another guy. It's almost too perfect."

I sighed. *Asshole.* "Donovan, this is my brother, Aaron. Aaron, this is the lead singer of The Drift. We wonder how he's talented when he's such an asshole, too. Don't worry. Common reaction."

Donovan gave me a disbelieving look and then shook Aaron's hand. "What's up, man?"

Aaron nodded at him, completely unfazed that he was meeting a celebrity. We were definitely related.

Then, Grant rounded the corner, and my eyes were only for him.

"Donovan, you near my girl again?" Grant asked.

He smirked. "Just meeting her brother."

Grant staggered a half step, and then he quickly recovered. He continued to swagger down toward us. He had toweled off after the show and then thrown on his leather jacket. His hair was still damp from sweat.

In that moment, I didn't care who was watching—not Donovan, not my brother, not anyone.

I rushed forward and threw my arms around Grant's shoulders, knocking our bodies together as we collided. His arms wrapped around my waist and tightly tugged me against him. He breathed in my hair and sent shivers down my spine as he kissed my neck.

"I missed you so much," I whispered.

"I missed you, too, Princess."

And then, he kissed me.

It was like breathing again for the first time. This was what I had always been missing. That depressing ache in my chest lifted. All I could feel was a desperate longing for this moment to never end.

"Ahem," my brother coughed into his hand.

"Sorry," I murmured, reluctantly pulling back from Grant.

"Aaron, this is my boyfriend, Grant. Grant, my brother, Aaron."

"Nice to meet you, man," Grant said. He extended his hand toward Aaron, who was too polite not to shake it.

As soon as he dropped his hand, Aaron pointed his finger at Grant and narrowed his eyes. "I couldn't figure it out before, but now, I remember how I know you."

"Oh, yeah?" Grant asked hesitantly.

"You're Grant McDermott?"

Grant questioningly glanced at me, but I shrugged. I didn't know how Aaron could know Grant. This was the first I'd ever heard of it even though I'd never told Aaron who I was exactly dating.

"Yeah, this is Grant."

Aaron shook his head in disgust. "Aribel, you have no idea what you're getting into. You absolutely cannot date this guy."

Who the fuck did this guy think he was?

No one could fucking tell Ari that she couldn't date me. I didn't care that he was her brother. He couldn't fucking dictate who she dated. *And how the fuck did he even know me?* Sure, my name was somewhat known in Princeton but not outside of that. Something wasn't adding up.

"Aaron," Ari groaned.

"Oh, this is good," Donovan muttered. "I'll get the popcorn."

I shoved Donovan out of the way and straight into Ridley and Trevor as they came out of the dressing room. "Get him out of here."

Donovan opened his mouth to say something, but Ridley shook his head. "Not tonight, man. We still have a show."

Ridley and Trevor half-dragged Donovan away from me, and I was thankful for that. I didn't need a reason to unleash the pent-up fury.

"Come on, Aribel," Aaron said, latching on to her arm. "Let's get out of here."

"Are you kidding me right now?" She yanked her arm out of his grasp. "I'm not leaving. I thought you'd be the reasonable one in the family."

"Well, you clearly know nothing about this guy."

"How do *you* know anything about me?" I finally asked.

He ignored my question and kept looking at Ari. "He's scamming you. He will sleep with anyone who walks by."

Aribel sighed heavily. "That's just his reputation, Aaron."

"People get reputations for a reason."

"Sure they do," I said. "I got it because I fucked anyone who was hot, but that was before Ari."

"Right," he said disbelievingly.

He grabbed on to Ari again, and she leaned back toward me.

"Seriously, Aaron. Since when did you become so judgmental? You don't even know Grant."

"I don't need to. I heard enough stories at Princeton to know what happened. He even admitted it."

Oh. The pieces were falling into place.

Aaron must have gone to Princeton, and so he'd heard about me. He was a couple of years older than Ari. Maybe he was even my age. If he knew my reputation, then he was probably worried I'd fuck up his little sister. Maybe he was right, but I did love her, so that changed things.

"Yeah. I'm not denying the kind of person I was. But I'm not that way with Ari. So, it doesn't matter who I was."

"It might not matter to *you.*"

"It shouldn't matter to anyone," Ari said. "Grant and I are together, and we're happy."

"How do you know he hasn't slept with a million different girls on this stupid tour?"

"I don't," she answered. Then, she glanced up at me. "But I trust him. If he wanted to sleep with other people, then he wouldn't be with me. He wouldn't put up with my shit."

I laughed. "Sounds about fucking right."

Aaron wasn't hearing a fucking word we were saying.

What did I have to do to get it through his head?

It had fucking surprised everyone that I wasn't banging every girl who threw herself at me. Hell, it still surprised me.

But I loved Ari. In the end, she was worth more to me than some cheap pussy ever would be.

"Look, Ari, either he believes me or not. I'm not going to stand here and try to get him to fucking listen."

"I know. I know," she mumbled. "Give me a minute."

She grabbed Aaron's arm and yanked him away from me. She sounded as if she was bitching him out. From being on the receiving end of that, I knew it wasn't a pleasant experience.

I ran a hand back through my messy hair in frustration. This was not how I'd wanted to start my Boston trip. I'd thought it would be more of Ari and I being alone in my hotel, fucking all night until she couldn't walk in the morning—not dealing with her fucking moronic brother who didn't know shit about our relationship.

I heard the stage crew calling for The Drift to get ready to go onstage, and I stepped out of the way. Trevor and I fist-bumped as he passed with Donovan, Nic, and Joey in tow.

Ridley ambled out a second later. He clapped me on the back. "Hey, man. Everything all right with your girl? Tried to save you from Donovan's stupidity."

"Thanks for that. Meeting her brother for the first time, and he thinks I'm fucking every chick on this tour." I shrugged.

Ridley laughed. "Dude, let me talk to him. I'll be the first to tell him you're a one-woman show. I was fucking shocked that you didn't even touch that chick in Atlanta. Tall, blonde, and throwing money at you?"

"Bad taste. That chick had crazy written all over her."

"She also wanted to be fucked pretty desperately."

"Someone else took care of her," I said.

"Ridley!" Trevor shouted from the front. "Get the fuck over here, man. We're about to go on."

"Good luck with her brother!" he said as he jogged backward toward the stage. "I want to meet your girl though. Heard too much about her."

"Yeah, all right. Maybe after she's better rested."

Ridley cracked up. "You're going to run her into the ground."

"That's the idea."

Aribel returned a few minutes later, looking defeated and frustrated. I wanted to kiss the worry off of her face. In fact, I wanted to kiss every inch of her body. Taste, lick, and touch a road map of her lush figure. Mostly, I wanted to fuck her senseless, and seeing her standing before me—even in jeans, a blue-and-white striped shirt, and my leather jacket—was making me ache for her.

Who was I fucking kidding? I'd been aching for her every day since I'd left.

She threw her hands up. "He's an idiot."

"What happened?"

She shrugged. "I don't know. We argued. He thinks I'm young and naive. I know he's trying to protect me, but I don't need to be protected from you. I'm old enough to make my own choices."

"So, what? Did he just split?"

"Yeah, I guess." She sounded totally dejected.

I wasn't used to that from Ari. She was usually so confident about all her choices. Then, she pushed her shoulders back, and a look of defiance crossed her face. There was my girl.

"We'll see him tomorrow at dinner with my family. He'd better be on good behavior."

"He'll come around," I said. Though I wasn't sure. Her family seemed to be a tough egg to crack. And I didn't have experience dealing with family—period.

She looked doubtful. "I hope so."

I reached for her hand and pulled her to me. "There is a positive to his absence though, Princess."

Her blue eyes found mine, and she gave me a coy smile. "What would that be?"

"I get my girl all to myself."

Hours later, after we were spent, exhausted, and had thoroughly made up for lost time, we slipped back into our clothes and joined the guys at a local bar. Ari flashed her fake ID to the bouncer who barely looked at it, and then we pushed through the crowd to get to the back corner. The two bands sat in a circle, drinking heavily. There were at least two or three girls for every guy.

Ari stiffened next to me, and I followed her gaze. McAvoy had his arm around a brunette groupie. I thought her name was Amanda or Mandy or something like that. She'd followed us to the last couple of shows and had attached herself to McAvoy, who seemed to like having a constant to fuck on tour.

Ari averted her eyes. I could tell she wished she hadn't seen that. From what I'd gathered, the girls were pretty beat up about us being gone, and Gabi was the worst of them all. Ari didn't want to have to report back that McAvoy had replaced her already.

Miller saved me from saying something stupid by standing and giving Ari a hug.

"Good to see you, Aribel."

She looked relieved and sat down next to him. "Hey."

I crashed down into the seat next to Ari and introduced her to the rest of The Drift. I knew she had seen them before, but no introductions had been made.

Ridley vigorously shook her hand. "Good to finally meet you. McDermott won't shut the fuck up about you."

"Oh," she said with a giant smile on her face. "Nice to meet you, too."

"Hey, baby," a girl said, sliding onto my lap and planting a kiss on my cheek. "It's good to see you out with the guys again."

Aribel glared at the girl. "Who the hell are you?"

"Don't worry, honey. There's enough of him to go around."

I stood, depositing the girl on the floor. I had no patience for her antics. She was hot and had been throwing herself at me since New Year's. I was fucking tired of it. She knew she had no fucking shot, and she was acting this way to try to piss off Ari.

"Jaci, go blow Vin or something."

She scrambled to her feet, straightening her tiny skirt out. "What the fuck, Grant?"

"Nothing has ever happened with us Jaci. Nothing is ever going to happen with us. If you didn't notice, my girlfriend is here," I said, pointing at Ari. "Get some fucking manners."

"Will she be at the next show? Because I'm free." She winked at me.

"Are girls normally this brazen?" Ari asked in shock.

Miller shrugged. "With Grant."

"Whatever, Jaci. You know I'm not fucking interested. Wouldn't you rather take it up the ass with Vin again instead of acting so fucking desperate around me?"

Her cheeks colored. I didn't feel bad calling her out about it. Maybe I was finally getting through.

"Fine," she grumbled and then stomped toward Vin.

His face lit up at her approach, and then they were exiting the building.

I shook my head and sank back down. With her ridiculous demonstration out of the way, I slung my arm over Ari's shoulders and tried to enjoy the rest of the evening. It was damn good, having my girl here with me. It felt right.

It was the piece that had been missing on this tour. But I knew she would never follow us around like these sluts. She was too smart and independent for that, and I wouldn't fucking change that for the world. It was what had made me fall in love with her.

On nights like this, with her nestled in my arms after hours of sex while surrounded by my friends, it started to sound like the dream.

But tomorrow, I knew that reality would return with all its nightmares.

Grant and I stood outside of my parents' house. He couldn't stop staring at the massive building, and I couldn't blame him. It was an enormous six-bedroom brick creation that had been built in the early 1800s. My parents had purchased it when I was three, and it had undergone more historical upkeep and renovations over the years than the White House.

"This is where you grew up?" Grant asked.

"Um, yeah. Home sweet home."

"Fuck."

I nodded. I couldn't imagine what this was like for him. He'd come from a broken home, his parents had been lost to him at ten years old, he'd grown up and worked at his uncle's pizza place on the shore…and now, he was seeing this. It made me feel self-conscious, which was a feeling I certainly wasn't used to.

"Come on. Let's go inside."

I'd ditched my leather jacket in favor of a pale blue sundress and ballet flats. I'd even been sure to pull a straightener through my hair, which was well past my shoulders at this point.

Grant looked presentable but still like…Grant. He didn't have a lot of clothing choices on tour and even fewer opportunities to iron his clothes, not that I suspected he did it at home either. He was in dark-wash jeans and a plain black T-shirt. His hair was still unbelievably messy but in a way that made me want to walk him back to the hotel and give it a reason for being messy. I could tell his nerves had set in, making my confident boyfriend ill at ease.

We were a match set.

I brought Grant in through the front door even though I typically entered through the garage door. The house opened up into an impressive two-story foyer and a large winding staircase. My father's office was off to the left, so I immediately walked Grant in the opposite direction.

"Aribel," my mother said. She greeted us in the formal living room, looking like a Stepford wife in an A-line dress, perfect pumps, and pearls. Her blonde hair was coifed and stunning.

I'd always been told that I looked like my mother, but I was as stubborn as my father, so I frequently felt like that resemblance was lacking.

"Mom." I smiled softly. There were no warm hugs in my family. "This is my boyfriend, Grant."

She reached her slender hand out and shook his once, almost as if she were afraid his germs would rub off on her. "Pleased to meet you."

"You, too," Grant said.

Then, we all stood there in awkward silence. My mother, the ultimate hostess, made us uncomfortably stand there as if it were the most natural thing for her to do.

"Mother!" I snapped. "Dinner? Dad? Aaron? Don't we have plans?"

She blinked. "Yes, of course. I'll go speak with your father. Why don't you show your friend around?"

My friend.

Great, Mom.

"Come on, Grant." I tugged him away from my mother and into the kitchen. I sighed when we entered the bustling room. "Sorry about that."

"Went better than I'd expected."

I warily looked at him. "Really?"

"Sure. She just kind of ignored me. She didn't, you know…outright hate me."

"Oh, Grant." My arms wrapped around his neck, and I tightly held him to me.

This wasn't the way it should be. My parents really should be more open-minded. I knew it had taken me a while to get to know Grant and accept the type of person he was. *But shouldn't my parents respect my good judgment?*

It wasn't as if I was a bad kid. I had even seen Aaron with a different girl than his girlfriend when we had gone out together. I would *never* have done that, and I never would be with someone like Grant if he were still sleeping around while being with me. And I didn't think I was too stupid to know the difference.

"It's all right, Princess. I'm glad to be here with you. I was the one who pushed you to tell them who I was in the first place. You said it would be difficult, and I haven't fucking forgotten." He softly kissed me on the lips. "If I get you out of the deal, then I can get through one evening with your parents."

"Why, that might be the most romantic thing you've ever said," I joked.

He wove our fingers together and gave me a look that made my insides squirm. "I can be romantic later."

I feigned indifference, but Grant ignited a fire with a single smile.

"Let's look at the rest of the house before you start ripping my clothes off."

"Is that an option?"

"No!"

He chuckled and then proceeded to follow me around the house. His eyes were as big as saucers through most of the downstairs.

I opened a sliding double door, and he peeked inside.

"A library? Really? No wonder you're obsessed with the one at school."

I laughed. "This was my favorite room growing up."

"I'm not surprised," he said with a smirk. "I didn't even realize people actually *owned* libraries. Just thought it was Disney's way of making women have even higher expectations of men."

"Did you just make a *Beauty and the Beast* reference?"

He shrugged. "You'd never guess now, based on her slutty cowgirl getup, but Sydney used to be a princess with dresses and fake plastic heels included."

"You're right. I can't imagine that."

I eased the door closed, and then we walked up the stairs to the second floor.

Grant wrapped an arm around my waist and leaned in close. His breath breezed against my neck, and I shivered.

"So," he said, "where's your room?"

I cleared my throat and then pointed at the door at the end of the hall. He took my hand and did all the directing. Opening the door, we entered into the midst of my childhood.

The walls were still pale pink with white sheer curtains hanging in front of the windows. I had all white furniture and a plush white-covered queen-sized bed with pastel pink throw pillows. My mother had offered to redecorate for me while I was in high school, but at the time, I hadn't thought there was anything wrong with it. This had perfectly fit my personality.

Now...I was actually embarrassed to show my boyfriend.

Grant closed the door behind me. He slowly walked forward to me, backing me up toward my bed. My heart thumped in my chest, and heat radiated out of my body. I couldn't believe the way he was looking at me...as if he were going to eat me alive. And I was going to let him.

His hand trailed from my neck to my shoulder and then lightly to my waist. "What would your father say if he knew I was thinking of fucking you in your bedroom?"

"He, uh..." I mumbled incoherently.

His hand slid to my ass and then hoisted a leg up around his hip. My body pressed back into the bed as he leaned forward into me. I could feel my heartbeat in my core, begging him to follow through on his promises.

"Hmm...Princess?" he murmured against my neck.

His lips were sending goose bumps down my whole body. His tongue flicked out and caught the sensitive skin. Without thinking, I dug my fingers into his back, urging him onward.

I knew this was dangerous. I knew we could be caught at any minute. But it was a huge house. We weren't needed at dinner right this second. Maybe...maybe I could break the rules just this once.

"I don't care what he'd think. D-do it." My voice wavered, but I hoped that my eyes held confidence.

Grant pulled back to stare in my eyes, which gave me away. I was nervous, unbelievably nervous. But at the same time...I so desperately wanted to sleep with Grant right now, to defy my parents in this way. I wanted to take control of my own life and not have to feel the constant weight of their expectations.

"Do it," I repeated stronger.

I reached for his shirt collar to drag his lips back down to mine, but he stepped away from me. He visibly adjusted himself in front of me. I could see the outline of his erection in his jeans. I reached out to run my hand down it, but he pulled back.

My face reddened at the rejection.

"That was one of the hottest fucking things you've ever done, Princess."

"And you turned me down," I said glumly.

He smiled that heart-stopping smile. "You know I love you when I turn you down."

"How?" I asked, hating that I sounded small. My body was traitorous in its desire.

"Because I love you so much that I want to make the right impression. I want to be good enough for you. I want your parents to like me." He tucked a loose lock of hair behind my ear. "Something tells me sleeping with their daughter in her bedroom might not help matters."

"It might help something," I said, leaning toward him and planting another kiss on his lips.

His hands landed on my ass. "Restraint is not my forte. You're playing dirty."

"You like it."

My hand traveled down his front and toward his jeans just as the door burst open.

As the door swung inward, Aribel and I sprang apart as if we'd been electroshocked. Aaron stepped into the room.

He looked between us in silence for a moment before shaking his head. "Dinner is ready."

Then, he turned and left.

Aribel sagged against me. "Oh my God. I can't believe he saw that."

"Could have been worse."

"You keep saying that."

"Still true." And it was. We could have been fucking when her brother walked in. It wouldn't have been the *most* compromising position I'd ever been in but close.

She nodded. "Okay. Time to meet my father. Are you ready?"

Was I? Fuck no!

Her mother and brother already seemed to despise me. I wasn't sure that I was ready to take on the man of the house. But I'd do it. Apparently, I'd do fucking anything for Ari.

So, I followed her down the huge-ass staircase to the first floor. The place was a fucking mansion. I'd never seen a house this big, let alone stepped foot in one. It showed me again that Ari and I were worlds apart. The only place we found our middle ground was when we were alone.

I'd never thought much about my future. I'd figured if the booze didn't kill me, then my reckless behavior would win out one day. The motorcycle accident was proof of that. But being here with Ari changed everything. She changed everything.

She made me think maybe middle ground was possible.

Ari walked into the dining room first. Her father was an imposing man in a crisp black suit. He was talking to her mother, but when he saw her, he broke off his conversation.

"Baby girl," he said, pulling her into a hug.

"Hey, Daddy."

I held my arms loosely at my sides and waited to be introduced. Aribel pulled back and then stiffened.

"What is he doing here?" she demanded.

My eyes shifted from Ari and her father to the person standing behind them—Henry.

That motherfucker.

I glared at him, but he only had eyes for Ari. This had gone from having potential to being potentially fucking disastrous. With the look in Henry's eye, it was leaning more toward completely fucking catastrophic.

"Aribel," her mother said disapprovingly.

"I thought this was a family dinner."

"It is," her father said.

"Then, what is Henry doing here?"

"He's here because I asked him to be."

Ari rolled her eyes. "Well then, you can ask him to leave."

"I'm not imposing, am I?" Henry asked.

He was playing the victim, and I could already see that it would work.

"Of course not," her mother crooned. "Aribel is happy to have you here as a family friend. Aren't you, Aribel?"

"No," she said, looking Henry straight in the eyes.

I saw this going south from real far off, so I slowly reached forward and took her hand.

Who cared if Henry was here?

He wasn't with my girl. We were about to show them that it didn't matter that he was fucking here. I'd beat the shit out of this douche bag before letting him near Ari again.

Her eyes met mine, and I saw she was fighting to remain calm. I tried my best to let her know it was all right—even though it wasn't fucking all right for her parents to pull this shit on her.

She nodded understandingly and then took a step toward me. "Dad, this is my boyfriend, Grant."

I reached my hand out to her father, and we shook. It was a challenging hard handshake, but I gave it right back. I wasn't fucking afraid, and I wasn't fucking backing down.

"Mr. Graham, it's nice to meet you, sir," I said, dropping back into my military upbringing.

"Grant," he acknowledged me.

I could tell from his stare that he wanted me to feel about two feet tall, but I was used to intimidation factors from my old man. At least this guy wasn't going to come after me with a gun.

I hoped.

"Well then, let's all sit down at the table." Ari's mother rounded us up and deposited us into our assigned seats.

Her father was at the head of the table with her mother across from him. Henry sat at his right, and Aaron was on his left. That left Ari and me sitting across from each other. I moved to take the seat next to Henry, so she wouldn't have to be near him, but her mother shoved her toward the seat as if it were life and death. I tried to remain calm. It wouldn't do any good to blow up now. So, I took the seat next to Aaron.

Wait staff appeared almost immediately with food and drinks. It felt more as if I were at a fucking restaurant than at a family dinner. At my aunt and uncle's, dinner was a loud, messy affair with friends over all the time, scooping out lasagna onto paper plates and circling around the TV.

Being here was like a fucking cage. It made me understand Ari a little more, and I also wondered how the fuck she had turned out so normal.

"So, Grant," her father said after dinner was served, "what exactly do you do?"

Everyone's eyes shifted to me.

"I'm in a band."

"Right. But what do you *do*?"

I stared back at him, wondering if this was a fucking trick question. "I play guitar and sing lead vocals."

"Uh-huh. So, you don't have a job then?"

Ari's hand came down on the table and rattled her drink. "Didn't you hear him? He says he plays in a band."

"Do people consider that a real job?"

I ground my teeth together. I would not fucking explode. "Yes. I'm signed with Pacific Entertainment. They're a major record label. We're on tour with The Drift, a popular rock band."

"And that pays?"

"Yes."

It was easier to agree than to go into the details of how advances worked.

That seemed to momentarily satisfy him because his attention shifted to Henry. He asked him super specific banking questions that were clearly directed only to Henry.

Great. I fucking understood Henry was a fucking hotshot douche-bag banker.

He'd graduated from fucking Harvard. I'd come to realize that people who went to Harvard all had one fucking thing in common. They made sure everyone fucking knew they had gone to Harvard.

Conversation was going on all around me, yet I didn't seem to be included in anything. Ari was turning red with anger. My blood was boiling at the whole exchange. This wasn't how you fucking treated people. Just because I wasn't in line to become a CEO of a bank didn't mean I wasn't good enough for his daughter.

"Mother," Ari snapped. "I'm sure you're dying to get to know Grant better, aren't you? He's only here for one night before he has to go back out on tour."

"Oh. Of course. Grant, how did you and Aribel meet?"

We exchanged a glance. It wasn't exactly a family-friendly conversation.

I figured I'd fucking paraphrase. "Her roommates liked my band, so they got her to come to one of my shows. We hit it off from there."

"Fascinating," her mother said dryly.

"Okay. I can't hold it in any longer," Aaron said in frustration. "Did you sleep with Mary Beth Hensen?"

"Aaron! Oh my God!" Aribel cried.

"Let him answer the question," Aaron said.

I shrugged my shoulders. *How the fuck was I supposed to know if I'd slept with a chick? How many times had I met Kristin before I remembered who she was?* Five or six, and I only remembered it because she was the cause of my fight with Aribel. I was horrible with names and faces.

"I don't know."

"How could you not know?" Henry asked.

"Stay out of this," Ari growled. "Grant, ignore them. They have no right to interrogate you."

"Seriously? You can't remember if you slept with her? It was my best friend's girlfriend."

Aribel smacked her forehead with her hand and sighed dramatically. "So fucking ridiculous."

"Language!" her mother cried.

"This is like a circus. Fuck," I mumbled. "I don't know if I slept with your friend's chick. If that's what you're holding over my head, then there's not much I can fucking do for you. I never forced anyone to have sex with me. So, she must have been willing."

The table went silent, but all eyes were on me.

Great.

I must have fucked up and pulled some social faux pas, but no one was freaking out that Aaron had brought up me having sex with some other chick in the first place.

"Aribel," her father said. Disapproval rang clear in his voice.

I couldn't stand for it. They couldn't talk to her or look at her like that.

"Hey!" I cried. "You can't be disappointed with her. She's brilliant, beautiful, strong, hard-working, and unbelievably confident. Look down on me for whatever bullshit you've thought up in your head. I'm poor with no college education and no *real* job. I'm everything you wanted to keep away from her, but you can blame me for that. You can't fucking look down on her—not her, never her. She's spotless, pristine, and she's the best goddamn thing that's ever happened to me."

I stood up from the table and tossed my napkin down.

"You'll have to excuse me. I've suddenly lost my appetite."

In horror, I watched Grant walk out of the dining room through the back door and outside. *How had it all gone so horribly wrong so fast?*

"Good Lord, Aribel," my mother said. "What kind of person did you bring into our home?"

"This will not do," my father said.

I closed my eyes for two seconds and tried to calm down.

Grant and I might have had our problems in the past, but we'd worked through them. We had figured out how to have a real relationship despite our differences. With him on tour, we had tried to trust each other, work through the issues with his dad, my parents, our friends, and so far, we had come out ahead. There was no way I was going to stand by and let me family insult him for their prejudice.

"I cannot believe you all treated my boyfriend like that." My voice came out steady as I slowly rose to my feet. "None of you know him. None of you have any *clue* of the kind of person he is!"

"Your brother and Henry were both very clear about the kind of person he is," my father said.

"Neither of them know him!" I cried. "You're all going off of a stupid prejudice, and I'm over it. I'm done."

I left the table and walked toward the door.

Henry tried to stop me. "Aribel, wait. Be reasonable," he said.

"Don't touch me!" I yelled at him.

"How can you go after him? He yelled at you at the concert. It was completely unwarranted. Aaron tells me he's slept with half of Princeton. He's on tour and probably sleeping with a different girl in every city. And now, he made a fool of himself in front of everyone."

"So, this is what you think of him? This is what you all think of my judgment?" I asked, crossing my arms.

"We want what's best for you, honey," my mother said.

"I don't want you getting caught up with someone who is going to take advantage of you," Aaron explained.

"Is that so?" I asked, feeling my anger bubbling up.

My father looked me square in the eyes. He didn't have to say anything to me in that moment. I knew that he agreed with them.

"You want what's best for me? And you think the best for me is…Henry?" I asked.

No one answered directly, but I knew. Henry even smiled as if he believed I was finally in on the secret. From the beginning, I'd known that my family was trying to pit us together.

"Well, that truly shows you how shitty *your* judge of character is! Henry has hounded me to see me when I've told him I wanted to be left alone. He got me drunk after New Year's and tried to take advantage of me, and then he did so again in my hotel room in New York City on my birthday. He's an asshole, who is just trying to get an in with me so that he can get another promotion in the company. Think about the person you're trying to set me up with when you're pushing my boyfriend away."

With that, I turned and left.

Henry didn't follow.

No one followed.

I found Grant a few minutes later. He had walked out across the patio, through the garden, and into the outdoor pool area. He was leaning against a wooden pillar and staring off into the still water.

"Hey," I said softly. I came over to him and immediately wrapped my arms around his waist. "I'm so sorry about my parents."

He circled my waist and kissed the top of my head, but he didn't say anything. I didn't even know what he was thinking. *Was he regretting his decision to come here?* I wouldn't blame him. My parents had been truly awful.

"Grant?"

"You shouldn't apologize, Princess. I tried to hold it in, but I fucking blew up anyway. I'm sorry that I embarrassed you."

I sighed. He was sorry because he thought I was embarrassed.

"Oh, Grant, no. I'm not ashamed of you." I pulled back to look at his face. "I'm ashamed of them."

His eyebrows scrunched together. "I know I'm not like Henry."

"I'm glad. Henry's a fucking prick, and I told them as much before I walked out."

"You know what I don't fucking understand?" he said, running a hand back through his hair. "Why would they even fucking invite me here? Was it just to fucking humiliate me? Well, congratulations! It worked."

I consolingly ran my hand down his arm. "They're stupid. I should have known better. I desperately wanted them to meet you and love you like I do. It took me a while to get to know the real you, but I know you are not the villain they are painting you as."

"Aren't I? I have the fucked-up past. I slept around. Those things they said about me weren't a lie. I can't take care of you. I can't even fucking take care of myself right now, Ari."

"I don't care about those things! Do you know how many guys I've brought home to meet my parents? None. Not one," I told him fiercely. "But I brought you."

We stared at each other in a pregnant silence before he finally looked away.

Footsteps behind us drew our attention. Aaron was walking straight toward us. I groaned.

Great. What the hell could he have to say?

"Aribel," he said in greeting as he approached.

"What do you want, Aaron?"

"To speak with you."

"Obviously."

"And to apologize."

My eyebrows rose. "What?"

"I won't say that I approve of you dating this guy," he said, looking at Grant.

Grant just shrugged.

"But if Henry acted the way you claimed, then he's no better. In fact, I've acted nearly as bad in the past. We all have stories. We all have pasts."

"And Mom and Dad?" I asked.

Aaron shrugged. "They asked Henry to leave after you walked out."

"They asked him to leave?" My eyes bulged. "Are you sure they're the same people?"

"Pretty sure. I can't believe Henry did those things. We would never have kept bringing him around if we'd known he was like that, but it's the same reason I don't trust Grant," he said casually as if it didn't matter. "Anyway, I don't think we'll all easily come around to this, Aribel, but I have to say that I approve of you finally standing up to Mom and Dad. I would never have guessed it would be over a guy, but if you're doing it, knowing full well how they would react, then he must be important to you."

"He is," I told him confidently.

"I can see that. Maybe you should come back inside and talk to Mom and Dad one more time. I think they'll see that eventually, too."

I shook my head. "I'd rather not."

Grant and I exchanged a look, and he nodded his head in agreement.

"Suit yourself." Then, my brother did the unthinkable.

He stretched his hand out, and Grant put his hand in Aaron's and shook it firmly.

"Nice show, man."

Grant gave him a long hard look before answering, "Thanks."

Just like that, it was as if some kind of truce had been drawn. I didn't have my parents' approval. I didn't have Aaron's approval. But the worst was over.

"So, your brother sort of came around," Grant said sometime later as I drove him back to the hotel where the tour bus was parked.

My eyes widened, and I slowly shook my head. "I must have really shocked them when I told them about what Henry had done."

He entwined our fingers, brought my hand to his lips, and kissed it. "Come with me," he said, changing the subject.

"I've heard that before."

His eyes crinkled with delight. "You'll hear it again, too, darlin'. I mean, come on the rest of the tour with me. You're done with classes. I want you with me."

The way he'd said *darlin'* jolted me and reminded me of the very thing I'd been avoiding thinking or talking about—his father. I hadn't told Grant about his father approaching me. I'd been waiting this whole time for the right moment to tell him in person, but it hadn't come out. Between finally being back together and my parents, the weekend had been packed. But soon, he would be leaving again. He needed to know.

"Ari?" he asked, squeezing my hand. "I was joking. I mean, I do want you to be on tour with us, but I don't want you to freak out."

"No, I'm not. There's just something we need to talk about."

He stiffened. "Haven't we had enough heavy conversation today?"

"I know. But…I've wanted to tell you this. I didn't know how." I pulled into the parking lot of the hotel and parked the car. I popped my door and got out of the Mercedes I'd borrowed from my parents.

Grant came around the car and took my hand. "Come on. We'll talk inside."

"No, let's stay out here."

No one was outside right now, and I wanted the space to be able to tell him this.

"This doesn't sound good, Princess."

I turned and faced him with my hands splayed in front of me. "I talked to your dad."

Grant froze. "You did *what?*"

"And I called the cops."

"What?"

"I know," I gasped out. "I know. You were right. They said there was nothing they could do unless I had been threatened or harmed in some way."

"I fucking told you they were worthless. But how the hell could you keep this from me?"

I'd known this was coming. "Let me explain to you what happened. Your dad came to my house and left his phone number with Cheyenne when I wasn't home. I never contacted him back, but then after finals, right before I flew up here, he showed up at my place."

"Fuck, Ari! He showed up at your apartment?"

"He wanted me to convince you to talk to him."

"I'm not fucking doing that!"

I threw my hands up. "I told him I wouldn't convince you, that he had no right to talk to you."

"Let me guess. He insisted?"

"Yes. I just"—I sighed heavily—"I worry he's never going to stop trying to get in contact with you. I don't want to play into his hands, Grant. But maybe if you saw him and heard him out, then you could tell him that you never want to see him again, and this nightmare could be over."

"That is never going to happen," he growled. "I'm not fucking stupid enough to think if I hear him out once, then he won't try to kill me...or you. And he already knows about you, Ari. I can't keep you safe. I know I was joking before, but come on tour with me."

I shook my head. I wanted that, but I wasn't dependent on my boyfriend. And we weren't ready in our relationship to spend every minute of every day together. "You know I can't."

"I need to keep you safe."

"He didn't try to hurt me or threaten me or anything. He seemed kind of crazy but not like he'd hurt me."

"That's how he wanted to appear. You're dealing with a trained ex-military criminal."

"I know, Grant. I just want things to go back to normal. I don't want to live in fear that he's going to come after me...or you." An unbidden tear slid down my cheek.

"Oh, Ari," he sighed. He cupped my cheeks in his hands and swiped the tear away with his thumb. "We're going to figure this out." He gently kissed me on the lips. "I can't have you in danger. If I have to confront him and all my demons to make sure you're safe, then I'll do it. I'll do it for you."

Two weeks later, I saw the light at the end of the tunnel.

Our last tour stop was in D.C. The Drift was closing out their tour in the city where they had grown up, and that meant we got in two days early, so they could visit with family and friends. I was kind of wishing that we could get this over with, so I could get back to Ari and deal with this shit with my dad. But The Drift wasn't staying in D.C. after the tour, so they'd booked in some time in the schedule to stay in town.

The guys and I spent our first day wandering around downtown. Miller had been there once for a school trip, but none of the rest of us had ever been here. Seeing all the monuments and shit was pretty cool, but I was too anxious to really enjoy it. I opted out of day-two plans and worked on the new song that had hit me since I last saw Ari.

I was still messing with the guitar chords when they returned.

"Grant! Let's fucking party!" Vin cried, launching himself into the hotel room and crashing down on the bed. "Drift said there are some kick-ass places a couple of blocks down. Let's go pick up some chicks."

"It's almost perfect," I muttered through the pick in my mouth.

"You've been working on that all day," Miller observed.

"Bro, we'll have plenty of time for working on our fucking music when we're in the studio. This is our last night before our last show on our first ever tour! Let's get fucking wasted!" Vin encouraged.

I slid the pick back between my fingers and started strumming along. Halfway through, I stopped and slapped my hands over the strings. "What's it missing?"

McAvoy laughed. "Drums."

"A backbeat," Miller added. "The lyrics."

"A fucking recording studio, motherfuckers!" Vin cried.

"Maybe," I said uncertainly.

"Figure it out later. Let's go drink!" Vin said.

"Go without me. I'll meet up with you guys as soon as I figure this thing out. It's been bugging the shit out of me all fucking day."

With the combined effort of Miller and McAvoy, they finally got Vin to vacate the hotel room, leaving me all alone with my cherry red baby and the notebook full of lyrics.

I spent another forty-five minutes trying to figure out the flaw in the chords before putting the guitar aside in frustration. The music had helped me not to obsess about my dad and Ari at least for a bit. But I needed to get out of this place.

Maybe a drink or two would do me some good.

I followed the guys' directions down to the local pub. I recognized The Drift's security detail standing out front. *Who knew if that was because there were supposed to be crowds or because they wanted to look important?* I wouldn't put anything past Donovan, who had been acting whack all week.

When I strode up to the entrance, the first thing I noticed was the smoking-hot chick talking to one of the guys out front. She was so hot that I did a double take. I whistled softly under my breath as I took in her features. Her ass cheeks were barely concealed in high-waist cutoff shorts. Her large chest was visible in the skintight shirt she wore. She was tall and leggy with dark brown hair that fell halfway down her back.

I was so busy checking her out that I didn't even realize she was arguing with the doorman.

"I'm here every weekend! What do you mean I can't go inside?" she snapped.

She planted her hands on her hips, and in no hurry to get inside, I admired her hourglass figure.

"Sorry. You're not on the list."

"I don't understand! There is no list! This place is fucking empty."

"Closed event tonight."

"Well, let me see your goddamn list, and I'll write my fucking name on it!" she yelled.

"Doesn't work like that. If you'll please step aside, Mr. McDermott is on the list."

I jolted at the sound of my name. I nodded at him and sympathetically took in the hot chick.

Tough break.

When she swiveled around, her mossy-green eyes glared at me, and then her eyes widened. They traveled up and down my body like a million girls had done. I got some small measure of satisfaction from knowing I could bang this super fucking hot girl if I wanted.

"How come he's on the fucking list?" she asked.

"Because he's with the band. Now, move out of the way," he said, crossing his arms and puffing out his chest. "Or I'll have to remove you myself."

"Give it a try, fucker."

She didn't move an inch, and I watched this chick stare down a six-foot-four bodyguard security detail as if it were the most natural thing to do on her Friday night.

Fucking hot!

"Look, it's no big deal. We're not that picky about the list."

"But—"

I held up my hand and interrupted whatever he was going to say. "Come on. Just put her down as a plus-one for me." I threw my arm over her shoulders and gave the guy a big toothy smile. "No harm, no foul."

"Mr. McDermott, I'm under strict orders."

255

"And you're following them," I told him. "Come on, babe."

Without a backward glance, I marched the girl straight through the door and into the dimly lit shithole.

What the fuck? Why had the guys in The Drift claimed that this place was kick-ass? It looked like a run-down hole in the wall.

"Thanks for that," she murmured.

"Anytime."

I removed my arm from around her shoulders. She was hot, but claiming her as a plus-one was all a ruse to get her inside. There was no way I would actually tap that. I had a hot blonde, who loved me, waiting for me when I got back to Princeton next week.

"So…you're with the band?"

"Yeah." I nodded.

"That's cool," she said. "Girls dig guys in bands."

I smirked. "Yeah, I've noticed that."

She stared at me for a second in assessment. "You probably play guitar. Callous fingers."

"I do," I said, surprised that she had noticed something so small.

"Nice. Girls get hot for a musician," she said with a completely straight face, not in the leering way I normally associated with groupies who wanted to get in my pants.

"Good thing I play an instrument then, huh?"

She nodded. "Good thing. So, McDermott, do you have a first name?"

"Grant."

"I'm Courtney."

"Well, Courtney, if you're into dudes in bands, let me introduce you to my brothers."

I couldn't believe I was giving up this chick to someone else. I would never have done this before. She was way too hot to be slumming it at this dive bar. But I ignored the radar going off in my head that if she was this hot and single, then she must be batshit crazy. Really, anyone could handle some crazy for a chick like this.

We ran into Miller first. He raised his eyebrows at me when he saw Courtney. Yeah, she was fucking sexy as well. And I clearly needed to get rid of her.

"Courtney, this is Miller. She's a local."

"Nice to meet you," Miller said as he shook her hand.

"You guys seen anything but this shithole suburb? Everyone likes the tourist crap."

She and Miller talked about the different monuments he had visited this afternoon while I grabbed us beers from the bar. When I returned, drinks in hand, Vin and McAvoy were chatting up Courtney as well.

She accepted the drink I handed her and took a long swig. "Thanks."

At that moment, the chick McAvoy had been fucking on tour bounded up to him. She whispered into his ear, and then he guided her toward the bathroom. Vin was looking up at Courtney as if she were the last fucking drop of water in the whole world. Unfortunately, I had a feeling douche-bag game wasn't going to work on her since she actually seemed relatively normal, so that mostly left Miller.

"Let's find a seat," I said.

I gestured to the sitting area where I could see Ridley and Trevor smoking with a few groupies. We walked over there when Ridley caught sight of me.

He jumped to his feet. "Court, baby!"

She squealed and ran into his arms. "Rid! What the fuck are you doing here?"

Trevor stood just as quickly and practically grabbed her out of Ridley's arms. "Shit! It's been for-fucking-ever since I've seen your fine ass."

She giggled. Her green eyes were shining, and then everything hit her all at once. "Oh fuck. Guys…"

Her eyes went out to the rest of the bar, almost fearfully. She seemed to be searching for someone. I was missing something.

"So, you guys all know each other," I mused.

"Um, yeah," Courtney said. Her long hair covered half of her face, and she tucked the hair behind her ear. "I really didn't know. I haven't been keeping up with the tour schedule. No wonder the bouncer wouldn't let me in and said I wasn't on the list."

"Bouncer?" Ridley asked. "He fucking set up a bouncer to keep you out?"

"I thought it was suspicious that he would choose this place," Trevor said.

"All right. Someone going to explain to me what's going on?" I asked.

Courtney looked down at the ground and then glanced off past my shoulder. Her eyes widened a fraction, and I turned around to see Donovan walking toward us. He looked murderous for someone who looked like he'd just been fucked by each chick on his arm.

Then, it clicked. God, I was fucking horrible with names. "Courtney," I muttered, turning to face her. "*The* Courtney. You're Donovan's ex-girlfriend?"

"She is." Donovan stood imposingly next to me.

I could feel the tension rolling off of him from where I stood in the middle of his staring contest with Courtney.

"And she can get the fuck out of here."

Courtney crossed her arms over her chest. "You don't own the place, Donovan."

He cringed slightly at the way she'd said his name. "Actually, tonight, I kind of do since I rented it out."

She shook her head in disgust. Her lips curled up, and I thought she was going to snap back at him.

"Whatever. I don't want to be near you anyway." She hugged Ridley and Trevor. "Good seeing you guys. Tell Nic and Joey I said hey. If you're here for any longer— well, you know where I live."

Then, she turned and walked away.

All of that for nothing.

Something in me felt for her in that moment. I didn't know what pussy part of my body was making me walk after her, but I did. I should just let her walk her hot ass out of the bar. Donovan and I were finally on okay terms. Bringing Courtney into the mix was a surefire way to get him to hate me again, yet for some unknown fucking reason, I couldn't let her leave like that.

"Hey," I said, catching up to her.

She smiled briefly but continued walking toward the door. "I didn't know The Drift was going to be here. But thanks for getting me in tonight even though it ended up not being worth it."

"Donovan's a dick, but that doesn't mean you should leave," I found myself saying.

She stopped in her tracks, patted my cheek twice, and then smirked. "That's sweet, but I'm not going to fuck you."

I cracked a smile. "Don't worry. I've no plans to fuck you either."

Honestly, I wasn't interested in her in that way at all. Old Grant would have already fucked her but not the man I was with Ari.

"But if you want to hang out with dudes in a band who aren't as douchey as Donovan, then you should come to our show tomorrow night. We're ContraBand."

"You sing that 'Life Raft' song?"

"Yeah, that's us."

She sighed heavily. "I don't think that's a good idea. Anyway, I have to work." She smiled forlornly. "You're cute, Grant. But boys in bands are trouble. Find yourself a girl not jaded by them, and then don't fuck it up." Courtney sighed and then was gone.

What she didn't know was, I had already found that girl. And I would never wreck her life like Donovan had wrecked Courtney's.

I bounced back and forth on the balls of my feet as I stood in front of the backstage entrance.

"Calm down," Cheyenne said. She firmly placed her hand on my shoulder to try to get me to stop.

It was totally not like me. But neither was road-tripping it down to Washington D.C. with my roommates to surprise Grant at ContraBand's last show.

Convincing them all to come with me had been a bit of a feat. Cheyenne had been in, but Shelby and Gabi had both seemed hesitant about it. I understood Gabi since it had only been two months since the breakup. However, Shelby and Miller hadn't ever been anything official. They had been talking and sleeping together for a couple of months, and then when he'd gone on tour, they weren't.

Eventually, everyone had piled into Cheyenne's SUV, and we had made our way to D.C. We'd purchased crappy cheap tickets in the back of the auditorium. It was probably the farthest I'd ever stood away from Grant during a show, except maybe at New Year's in New York City. But we didn't want to risk the guys seeing us. We knew all the lyrics anyway, and the acoustics were good, even in the back of the theater.

Finally, we were flagged through backstage with a group of fans. I reveled in the carefully controlled chaos that I used to despise. Granted, these venues were much better organized than the League or the Poconos music festival.

Cheyenne took control and marched us through the crowd of people. I saw Grant first. He was laughing at something Vin was saying, and my heart skipped a beat at the sight of him. He was so gorgeous. It had only been two weeks since I saw him in Boston, but I was looking forward to taking him home with me this time.

I dodged a few groupies as I rushed Grant and circled his waist.

"Whoa!" he said, reaching for my hands to peel me off of him. Then, he seemed to realize who I was. "Ari? Oh my fucking God! What are you doing here?"

"I wanted to surprise you! I couldn't wait for you to get home."

"This is the best fucking surprise."

His lips were on mine, and suddenly, the world dropped off. My head tilted back, my eyes closed, and I let Grant sweep me away.

"How did you get here?" he murmured against my lips.

"The girls drove down with me." I pointed to them standing off to the side.

Cheyenne was somehow already flirting with Trevor, which didn't surprise me. He was absolutely her type. Gabi and Shelby were standing together, whispering. They both looked uncertain about how to move forward now that they were here.

"Can't believe you got them all to come with you."

"Is that Cheyenne?" Vin asked.

I gave him a once-over. "You don't stand a chance."

"I've already been in that, babe. No one else is going to fucking tap that."

"Sure."

Vin glared at me and marched straight over to Cheyenne. I had a feeling they'd be sleeping together before they even left the building. Cheyenne was nonchalant about her relationship with Vin, but I knew she liked him despite how much of an asshole he was. She'd kept claiming that he was different with her, but by the way they were arguing already, I wasn't sure I believed her.

"Well, that was easier than I'd thought," I said.

"You planned to piss him off to get him and Cheyenne together?"

"They like angry sex. Trust me. I hear all about it." I cringed. "Seriously, I can't *unhear* these things."

"Try living with him."

"No, thanks."

Miller and McAvoy walked in at that moment.

"Ari," McAvoy said, giving me the nod.

"What's up?" Miller said. "Didn't know you'd be here."

"Last-minute decision, and I brought you boys presents—kind of."

They looked at Grant in confusion.

"Gabi and Shelby are here, too."

Miller's smile grew, but McAvoy paled.

"Fuck!" he mumbled.

"You should probably talk to Amanda," Miller said softly.

I recoiled at the name of the girl he had been sleeping with when I was in Boston. *Was that girl still around?* Gabi would self-destruct if she found out.

"Too late," McAvoy said.

The girl sauntered across the room, heading straight toward us. McAvoy ran a hand back through his longish hair. He seriously looked torn-up about what was about to go down, but I felt no sympathy for him. He'd broken Gabi's heart, so he could fuck chicks on tour, and now, he was.

As soon as she reached us, he grabbed her arm and pulled her aside. I could see Gabi assessing what was going on.

"That's not good," I said.

"No," Grant agreed.

Everything happened so quickly.

The Amanda girl yelled at him. All I caught was, "Motherfucker," before she clawed her fingernails down his cheek to the point of drawing blood. She kicked and hit him so suddenly that all McAvoy did was stand there and took her crazy.

263

Security appeared a few seconds too late and hauled her, kicking and screaming, out of the venue. Gabi rushed over, concerned, and after she helped to stop the bleeding, the two of them disappeared.

When I looked around for Shelby, I realized she and Miller were also missing. Cheyenne and Vin left a minute later, arguing with each other, which seemed to be their version of foreplay. Then, it was just Grant and me among a sea of people.

We were the only ones actually dating...and apparently, we were the only ones not alone, trying to get it on right now.

"That was some crazy shit," a brunette girl said, walking straight toward us.

Grant smiled at her as if he knew her and gave her a hug. "You made it!"

My eyebrows rose as I got my first real look at the girl. *Oh God!* She was...gorgeous. There was no way around it. She could probably be a Victoria's Secret model with her mile-long legs and in-your-face chest. I tried not to be envious of her looks and trust that there was a reasonable explanation for Grant being excited that she was here.

"I missed the show, but I thought I'd stop by to say hey anyway. I was pissed off last night, and I wasn't really being fair when I blew you off."

My cheeks heated. That sure sounded suspicious. "Um...what?" I snapped.

Her gaze landed on me and then shifted back to Grant.

"Oh, Courtney, this is Ari, my girlfriend." He grabbed my hand and pulled me closer.

She laughed. "So, you've already found the girl I see."

"She's the one."

"Well, it's nice to meet you, Ari." She stuck her hand out, and I shook it, feeling uncertain.

"You, too. I think? How exactly do you know each other?"

"Courtney used to date Donovan."

I wrinkled my nose. "Ew."

She nodded, her head tilting back as she laughed at my reaction. "Yeah. I feel you. Biggest mistake of my life. You think you know somebody and then…it all just falls apart."

I bit my lip. "Well, if it's any consolation, he's a douche bag."

She burst out laughing again. "Some consolation, I suppose. Grant seems like a nice guy though. Hold on to him tight. Any guy who introduces his girlfriend to other girls while he's on tour has to be a keeper. Trust me."

She gave me a knowing look. I wanted to blurt out and ask her what had happened with her and Donovan, but I managed some semblance of restraint.

"Anyway, I guess I should see if Rid or Trev are around. Good to see you again, Grant."

When she was gone, I turned back to Grant. "You invited *that* girl to your show?"

"I wanted to hook her up with one of the guys. She's had it rough after Donovan. I was being helpful."

"That's not really comforting."

He smirked and drew me into him. "I'll comfort you tonight and every single day after I take you home with me."

Being back in my own house, in my own bed, was nothing short of a miracle. Being in my own house, in my own bed, with Ari was even better than that.

I ran my hands down her flat stomach, tracing the soft curves of her body. She moaned at the lightest of touches. I had her body tuned so that my slightest touch would send shivers down her spine. My mouth closed over her erect nipple, and she arched into me. A flush covered her skin, causing her cheeks to be rosy with lust. I moved my hand back up her torso to pinch the other nipple between my fingers.

"Oh!" she sighed.

She still wasn't very vocal in bed. One *oh* from her went a long way. My dick twitched at the thought of her arousal, which I could practically smell as I readied her for me.

I kissed my way back up to her mouth, pressing my chest against her sensitive tits. She greedily kissed me with none of the hesitation I had expected from her six months ago. It was so fucking hot how much she wanted me and how well she responded to my touch. The nature of the kiss made my already hard dick almost painful.

I fucking needed her body. She was my drug of choice, and like an addict, I couldn't resist.

"God, Grant," she said, shifting underneath me and rubbing her pelvis against my cock that was practically springing out of my boxers.

"I want you, Princess." I pressed against her more firmly, and another moan escaped her lips. "Let me make you feel like a queen."

She assented by running her hand down my abs, and then she proceeded to circle my dick and squeeze gently. My whole body jolted at the touch. She slipped her hand into my boxers and then grasped me firmly. After a few strokes up and down, it was pretty fucking clear that I didn't need a whole hell of a lot of foreplay.

I needed to fuck the shit out of her. There was so much I wanted to do in that moment. I wanted to make her take it out and jack me off just to see the earnest with which she would try to make me come. God, I wanted to fuck her mouth and watch her swallow my cum.

Rough. I wanted it rough.

I wanted it every which way I could get it from her, but right now, my body was dying to take her mercilessly.

I quickly stripped out of my boxers and then repositioned myself between her legs. My hands splayed out on her soft creamy inner thighs. I lightly smacked them, and her eyes flew open in surprise, but she didn't protest. Little pink marks to match her cheeks blossomed on her skin before I covered them with my hands and spread her open for me as far as she would go.

She peeped in protest, and I let up some but not much. My fingers traveled down between her legs, rubbing circles against her clit and then delving into her wetness.

Fucking hell. I'd done my job.

"I love you, Princess, but I'm about to fuck you like I don't."

She laughed and gave me the best look in history. *Sure, Grant, try it.*

I plunged into her in one swift motion, taking her fucking pussy and claiming it as I'd been doing since the day I took her virginity in December. Bending forward, I wrapped my arms around her waist and thrust deep into her. Our lips joined, our bodies lay flush together, and we remained connected more than I'd ever had with anyone else in my life.

Her walls tightened around me, and I lifted her off the mattress and onto my lap. I bounced her up and down on my dick. The new angle pushed me deeper into her. Her nails dug into my back, and she was whimpering softly.

Then, the whimpers turned into moans, and the moans turned into her coming on top of my dick.

"Fuck, Ari!" I cried.

Her body was tipping me over the edge, and I couldn't stop it. She was so fucking tight that I had no control. I came hard and fast inside her.

At the end, I was left breathless and sated—at least for the moment. We both collapsed back onto the bed with a thin sheen of sweat coating our bodies, and physical exhaustion took over as I held her in my arms. She rolled closer to me, resting her head on my shoulder. My eyes closed, and I kissed her on the top of her head. Then, I just lay there and reveled in the euphoria of the moment.

The next thing I knew, I was waking up to the sound of someone banging on the door downstairs. Ari was still safely tucked in my arms. I kissed her shoulder before checking the time.

Three p.m.

Christ, we'd fucking passed out from a sex coma for three hours. *How the fuck had the time slipped by so fast?*

I groggily stumbled out of bed and threw on a pair of basketball shorts and a T-shirt. Running a hand through my messy hair, which I seriously needed to get cut now that I was back in town, I walked down the stairs and to the front door.

The banging started up again. I yawned, barely able to keep my eyes open after waking up from my nap. Sleeping in my bed here was so much better than on a horrible tour bus or a hotel room.

"Coming!" I called as I approached the door.

I unbolted the lock and swung the door inward. My body went still just as my heart rate skyrocketed. My palms were clammy, my throat closed up, and my stomach flipped. There wasn't enough oxygen in the house…in the world.

Despite years of training myself for this moment, I still felt horribly sick and terrified as I stood there, staring at the man who had ruined my life.

My dad.

A murderer.

My mother's murderer.

The man who had told me that once he was out of jail, he was coming to get me.

To kill me.

Now, here he was.

"Hello, Grant."

I reacted immediately.

I'd told myself over and over again that when this time came, I would be ready. I wouldn't be a frightened ten-year-old kid anymore. I would be calm and collected and do what needed to be done.

I bolted for the side table next to the garage door and yanked open the first drawer. Before he even reacted, I had my 9mm loaded.

I swung around and leveled the gun at his chest. "Hey, Dad."

Aribel

"Grant?" I whispered softly as I woke up.

I stretched out my body and yawned. *Man, how long had I been out?* I checked the time and groaned. We'd lost the whole afternoon, not that I was complaining. Sex with Grant had been awesome. My body was already sore from our escapades...or *sexcapades*, as Cheyenne liked to call them.

I heard voices downstairs and figured he must have gone to talk to Vin or work on his music.

Reaching over the side of the bed, I found my clothes, slipped into my yoga pants and an oversized T-shirt, and then padded out of the room.

"Grant!" I called again, jogging down the stairs.

I froze when I caught sight of what was going on at the bottom of the stairs. Grant and his father were in the middle of a standoff. The door was wide open, and Grant was holding his gun out in front of him, pointing it straight at his father.

Time stood still. I swayed in place. This couldn't be happening.

"Ari, go back into the room," Grant said, strangely calm.

"What do you think you're doing?" I asked.

Fear prickled through every nerve ending in my body. Grant was holding a gun. If he fired that weapon, then I knew, deep down inside, that I would never find him again. He would bury the Grant I knew and loved so far inside of himself that I was afraid even I couldn't save him.

"Taking care of business."

"Grant, put the gun down!"

"You should listen to her, son," Mike said.

"I won't make the mistake of waiting for you to kill me, too."

He was so deadly calm and serious that it almost completely unnerved me. *How could he be so confident while pointing that gun at his father's chest? How could Grant have let it come to this?*

"Grant," I murmured, taking a few more steps toward him. "You are better than this. Just think…if you pull that trigger, you'll become everything you have worked so hard not to be. And you'll have to live with that for the rest of your life."

"I'll do what I have to do."

"You don't have to. You barely survived the last time something traumatic happened to you. Do you think you could survive killing your own father? No matter what he has done to you, no matter how much you suffered, shooting him doesn't bring her back."

"I know that," he cried. His hands were shaking softly, but he hadn't torn his eyes away from his dad the whole time I'd spoken to him.

"Do you? Then, give me the gun," I whispered.

Tears were stinging my eyes as I stepped forward toward him. My throat was stuck as if it were stuffed with cotton balls. Here it was, all my fears coming to fruition. I'd thought that I was enough to push back his demons. But with his father standing at his door, all the good that had happened in his life disappeared. Grant was locked inside his head, trapped with the fears of his childhood.

"I'll give you the gun when he leaves and agrees to never come back," Grant said flatly.

"Is that what you want?" his dad asked.

"I'm not sure what else a gun pointed at your chest could mean."

Mike took a step forward, and Grant fired a shot that whizzed past his father's right ear and out the front door.

"Grant!" I screamed. "What the fuck? Oh my God!"

"Next time, I won't give you a warning shot."

"Are you out of your mind?" Ari cried. "You can't fire that fucking gun at another human being! You could have killed him."

"He entered my home without my permission, and I feared for my life. It's self-defense."

I shook my head in shock. He had fired a shot. He had shot at his own father. My mind was whirring around at five million miles a minute. I couldn't process this. I was shutting down when I needed to be alive and alert for this. I couldn't let him go through with this.

"Grant, please!" I pleaded. "He'll leave. He's going to leave now and not come back. Just please…don't shoot any more." Adrenaline was kicking in, but my body was compensating for my fear with unshed tears and a racing heartbeat. I turned to Grant's father. "Tell him you'll leave."

"I just came to talk," Mike said.

Grant shook his head. "I have no interest in talking."

Mike lifted his foot to walk toward Grant. I saw Grant getting trigger-happy, and I realized I couldn't let this happen, no matter what.

Without another thought, I threw myself in between them. Grant's arm jerked, and the bullet that had been meant for his father rushed out of the gun. I screamed, and then everything happened in slow motion. My heart skipped a beat in that split second when my eyes met Grant's. And then, I was shoved out of the way. I landed roughly on my hip, and my hands barely caught my fall. I heard a loud *thunk* and saw the bullet buried into the wall.

My body shook as I stared at the small bullet hole. I didn't know if I had been standing in the way of that bullet and Mike had saved me from being shot, or if when Grant's arm had jerked, the bullet had been thrown off course. Either way, all I knew was that Grant had fired his weapon, and I could have been injured.

I could have been killed.

"Ari," Grant murmured, all the emotion flooding back into his voice.

Our eyes met across the short distance between us. The anguish that had been plaguing him since he was a kid resurfaced with full force. He was the guy all over again who had poured his soul out to me at the ski lodge, who hadn't been afraid to show me his favorite place at the beach where he would think about everything that had happened to him, and who had placed his heart in my hands despite his fear of giving it away.

Grant's hand went slack, and I watched as Mike easily disarmed him, popped out the magazine, and actually disassembled the weapon as if it were the easiest, most natural thing he'd ever done in his life.

"I wasn't going to shoot you," Grant said automatically. He rushed over and collapsed onto the ground next to me, pulling me into his arms. "I'd never hurt you. Oh God, I never want to hurt you."

"It's okay. I know. I know." I tightly wrapped my arms around him. It didn't matter that I was the one who had been shot at. I found myself comforting him. My hand slid up and down his back, and I kissed his cheek. I couldn't hide the fact that I was trembling.

"Fuck." His dad sighed heavily and then ran his hand down his face. "I never expected it to come to this. I should have told you on the phone why I wanted to see you in person. Christ, I should have told you as soon as I got out of jail. I should have told you even sooner than that."

I could tell Grant hated himself right now for what had almost happened. He didn't want to hear what his dad had to say. He never had.

"Tell him what?" I prodded.

"I'm sorry. I'm so sorry for everything." His dad fell to his knees before his son. "I wanted to tell you in person. I wanted to apologize for what had happened. That's what I told Randy, but we never expected this. Grant, you have to know that I never meant to hurt her—your mother. I loved her so much…like you love Ari. And I shouldn't have blamed you. You were just a kid, and I was supposed to be the parent. I was supposed to be the adult."

Tears welled in his eyes, and I could hardly hold in my own at his admission.

Finally…finally, Grant turned his head and looked at his father. There was a mix of shock and revulsion and hope and pain on his face. He had never thought that he would ever hear these words.

"I know I did unspeakable things. I know that you have no reason to forgive me, and I don't deserve your forgiveness. But all I want…all I've ever wanted, once I got help, is to make things right…to reach my son again. You're all I have left."

"I don't know how I can believe the words coming out of your mouth," Grant said harshly.

"I understand. And I know things aren't going to make sense right away with us. We've been living different lives. We're separated by thirteen years and blood on my hands. But I loved your mother with all my heart. I've been tormented by her death for just as long as you. I want us to be able to reconcile."

Grant slowly stood from the ground and carefully helped me up next to him. He wrapped an arm around my shoulder, tightly holding me in place as if to make sure I was still there and safe. "I don't want to reconcile anything with you. I don't want a relationship with you. You were the one person in my entire life I have tried so hard not to become. So, you're fucking right. You don't deserve my forgiveness."

"Grant, please," Mike said, standing and reaching out for him.

Grant took a step back, dragging me with him. "Don't touch me. Don't come near me. You came here to talk to me. I listened to what you had to say. That's all you asked for, and frankly, it's more than I should have been forced to put up with. Now, get the fuck out of my house."

Mike sighed. "You're right. But I want us to know each other again…sometime…when you're ready." He nodded at us both. "Ari, I'm sorry you were brought into this. Please…take care of my son."

I swallowed hard as he left the house, and I closed the door behind him, leaving us in stone-cold silence with a bullet hole in the wall, a disassembled gun on the ground, and my boyfriend's heart in tatters.

Everything rushed to me at once.

I'd pulled a gun on my father.

I'd almost shot Ari.

My father had apologized.

I'd almost shot Ari.

No matter what else had happened in the span of the last half an hour, that reality seemed to hit me the hardest. I could have killed my girlfriend, the love of my fucking life, just like my father had killed my mother.

I was a monster.

I was a fucking monster.

As soon as the door closed behind my dad, I dropped painfully onto my knees and buried my head in my hands. A sob tried to rack my body, but I pushed it deep down inside of me. In a matter of minutes, my dad had cracked open the black hole where I'd stored thirteen years of depression, anger, pain, and endless and bottomless eternal grief.

I fucking hated him. I hated everything he stood for. I hated that we were even related. I hated that he could come here and lie to my face. I hated that it still affected me.

My fist connected with the ground over and over again until I was spent, and my knuckles were throbbing. *How could this have fucking happened?*

"Grant," Ari whispered behind me.

Fuck! Fucking fuck!

I jumped to my feet and pulled her trembling body into my arms. "I'm sorry. I'm so fucking sorry. I never want to hurt you, not ever, Ari."

"It's okay, Grant. I'm fine. I'm not hurt."

"It's not fucking okay. I should never have pulled that trigger."

"I can agree with that." Her hands came up to cup my face. "But are *you* okay?"

I couldn't meet her eyes that were filled with love and concern. *How could she even look at me like that?* I could have killed her. I escaped her gaze by burying my face into her neck.

"I don't deserve you, Princess."

"Why don't you let me be the judge of that?"

"I dragged you into this, into all of this. I've put your life at risk time and time again. I can't keep fucking putting you in harm's way. And I clearly can't protect you. I only make things fucking worse."

"You listen to me, Grant McDermott," she said fiercely. She grabbed my chin in her hand and forced me to make eye contact with her. "You've never forced me to do *anything.* I love you. That doesn't mean only when it's easy or not complicated. It means all the time, no matter what. I'm standing right here, and I'm not leaving your side."

"I almost fucking shot you!"

"But you didn't! And you're never, *ever* going to pick up a fucking gun like that again. Do you realize that if you had shot him...or me...you would never be the same?" Tears sprang to her eyes, but she refused to look away.

It was fucking horrible, watching her cry. I wanted to make it all go away, but I was the one who had caused her pain.

"How could I ever find the man that I love after that? I can't lose you, Grant."

Her words stole my breath away. There was nothing I could do or say to make up for the pain in her voice. My whole world was crumbling, and I'd almost completely obliterated it.

She swallowed hard and tried to regain control. "I think we should go talk to your uncle."

"What? Why?"

"Because your dad mentioned that he had talked to Randy. Maybe he'll have some answers for you."

I shook my head. "There are no answers about my dad. He's gone. And I don't want him in my life."

Ari pursed her lips in annoyance. "He went through an awful lot of trouble to find you and speak with you for him to disappear again. I think at least some of what he said sounded…genuine."

"Wait…you actually believe the bullshit he was spouting?"

"Why would he spend so much time trying to find you otherwise? He had a chance to hurt you, Grant. He had the gun out of your hand, and what did he do?"

She stared at me, waiting for an answer.

An answer I didn't want to deliver.

He'd disarmed me, taken the gun apart, and discarded it. He'd had no interest in it. I'd been so fucked up and worried about Ari that I hadn't given my dad's actions a second thought. He could have put a bullet in my head without missing a beat. My last thought would have been about Ari's safety.

But he hadn't.

I shook off the feeling of confusion that followed the realization. Just because he hadn't taken the opportunity didn't mean he didn't want to hurt me in some other way, like taking the things I loved away from me.

"I don't trust him."

"And you don't have to," she said. "I know you're hurting about this, and you have been for a while, but I was almost shot today because he showed up. I think, if anything, *I* deserve answers about your father. Don't you think you owe me that much, Grant?"

How could I deny her anything after what had happened?

Her pleading hurricane-blue eyes fucking destroyed me.

Yes, Princess. I owe you everything.

279

We arrived at my uncle's restaurant after a silent tense drive down the shore. By the time I hopped out of my truck, which Ari had forced me to let her drive, I felt totally fucked up. My body ached. My chest physically hurt. I had a splitting headache.

Rock-bottom was like a ton of bricks on my chest. No matter how hard I'd tried to push them off and breathe again, I was crushed further under the assault.

I followed numbly behind Ari into the restaurant. It was late, and they were closing up shop. The hostess didn't know or recognize me, but I walked past her without a response to her questions anyway. Ari smiled politely and gave an explanation as I continued to the kitchen. I heard her patter of feet against the floor as she caught up to me.

"Are you ready?" she whispered, reaching out for my hand.

"These are your answers, Princess."

She sighed and looked away. I knew she was irritated that I didn't want to know more about my dad, but I was just happy he was gone. I wished it were a certainty that he'd never come back. However, I couldn't trust that.

"Grant! Aribel! What a surprise!" Uncle Randy cried when he saw us in the doorway.

He came forward and wrapped Ari in a hug. When he turned to me to do the same, he saw the hard expression on my face and gave pause.

"What? What's wrong? What happened?"

"Grant's dad paid us a visit," Ari said.

Randy sighed. "He actually showed up?"

"You knew about that?" I spat.

"Can we maybe go somewhere and talk?" Ari interrupted.

"Yeah. Yeah, sure. Let me leave someone else in charge of closing up. We can go out on the deck."

Anger boiled in my fucking veins. *Had my uncle known what was fucking happening and not told me? Could all this have been prevented if I'd just had all the information?*

He ran around, finishing up some last-minute duties and instructing another manager to close down for the night. Then, he walked us out to the back deck and sat us down where Ari and I'd had our first date.

It was empty and dark on my beach. It called to me in that moment. I'd gone down there time and time again to think about what had happened the night my father had become a murderer. I'd drowned my sorrows into that beach long before I'd turned to booze and women and adrenaline rushes, long before Ari had entered my life and turned it into *our* beach.

"So, tell me what happened," my uncle said.

Aribel glanced over at me, and when I didn't say anything, she launched into the story as she had witnessed it. My uncle's eyes widened as the story turned more and more fantastical.

"You shot a gun, Grant?" my uncle asked disapprovingly.

"I wasn't going to wait for him to shoot first."

"But he didn't draw a gun," Aribel said. "He actually dismantled your gun and tossed it when he had the chance. I don't think he was there to hurt you at all."

"My father doesn't always work with physical pain."

"I'm sorry, but I'm going to have to side with Aribel on this," my uncle said.

"You know what he did to me!" I said, standing from my chair.

"Grant, sit down," Ari said.

She tugged on my arm until I complied and then laced our fingers together for support.

"I know what happened that night. And I also know what happened the thirteen years after that with both you and your father. You only have one side of the story because you refused to learn anything else about what had happened."

I shrugged. "I still don't want to know."

"But I do!" Ari said. "You promised."

And I had. I would promise her the world for the pain I'd fucking put her through. She shouldn't have had to deal with my father showing up, unannounced, at her place, stalking her, and she certainly shouldn't have had to deal with me almost shooting her.

"Fine."

"While your father was in prison, he didn't sit in there and fester. He was released on parole for good behavior. He'd completely passed the psych exam they'd put him through. He had gone through years of therapy for PTSD, frequently seeing a specialist in military psychiatry, and worked with doctors to medicate the problems he was having. When he got out of jail, he was set up in a halfway house in between here and Princeton. He's been working part-time as a mechanic, and he has weekly checkups with his parole officer."

My uncle levelly looked at me. "I realize none of this can bring your mother back…my sister back, but he is trying to make things right. And the thing he regrets the most…is that he missed you growing up, that he doesn't know you, Grant."

"How can you believe what he's said? He could have made all of that up," I said.

"He's not making it up. I've seen the psych papers, the medical records, his release paperwork. He brought them to me from his parole officer last week."

"Why didn't you say anything?" Ari asked. "I mean…you know how Grant feels about all of this. Don't you think you should have prepared him?"

"He said he had to be the one to make this work, that he wanted to make amends. He wanted you to trust him again. He wanted to be worthy of your love…if you could ever care for him like that again. I did try to tell him that you wouldn't be receptive, but I don't think he understood. Still, I recognized that if I were in the same situation as him, I would want to be the one to explain to Sydney."

I shook my head. "I don't know what to think about all that," I said finally.

"Well, sleep on it," my uncle said. He seemed to recognize that I wasn't going to suddenly agree with everything he'd said. "You don't have to make any decisions about Mike tonight. It sounds as if it's been a traumatic long evening. Why don't I get you a pizza and some drinks? You kids can spend some time here and then come stay the night at our home when you're done. We can talk more then, if you want, or in the morning."

"Whatever," I said, pushing back my chair again.

I didn't need pizza or a drink to fix my problems. I needed to get away from here. I turned away from my uncle and Ari, hopped down the stairs to the sandy beach, and started out toward the waterfront.

I'd just found out that while I'd been at home, tormented and brooding about my father, he'd been in jail getting top-notch treatment. While I'd wanted him to be in jail forever for murdering my mother, he'd gotten out on good behavior. While I had worried about him hurting me or Ari since he got out of jail, he had been schmoozing with my uncle and swapping stories behind my back. He didn't deserve any of it.

None of this seemed okay with me.

With a heavy sigh, I watched Grant bolt toward the beach. Frankly, this had gone better than I had expected. I was sure he felt betrayed by the fact that his uncle had known some of what was going on and hadn't told him. It wasn't fair to Grant to have been left in the dark.

But the good news was, it actually sounded like his father was on the right path. It seemed he had legitimately dedicated himself to getting help and bettering himself, so when he'd gotten out, he could have a real shot at getting to see Grant again. It confirmed what I'd already guessed when I saw his father break down in front of him. Mike had meant every word of that speech.

"I didn't mean to upset him like this in front of you," Randy said.

"It's okay. He just needs time. And he's right in being upset because you were keeping things from him."

"I didn't want to, believe me. I wanted to tell him so many times. I probably should have."

"Yes, you should have." I ran my hand back through my hair. "I'm going to go talk to him. Thank you for telling us everything."

Randy smiled sadly. "He's lucky to have you, Aribel."

I remembered the sound of the gunshot, the sickening tear of plaster, and the way my body had rocked to the ground. I shuddered. I was holding it together for Grant out of necessity because Randy was right. Grant was lucky he had me. Anyone else might have already fallen apart.

My feet mechanically carried me down the stairs and out to the beach. Grant had his shoes off. His feet were buried in the sand, and water lapped at his ankles. His eyes were set on the horizon. He didn't move at my approach, but by the set of his shoulders, I knew that he was aware I was nearby.

"You think I should forgive him?" Grant said finally after a few minutes.

"No."

"But you believe them—my dad and uncle—you believe they're telling the truth."

"I think they have good intentions, and I'm a pretty good judge of character," I told him.

He brought his hands out in front of him and was studying them as if they held the answer to his question. "What do I do, Ari? I can't fucking pretend like nothing happened."

"No one is asking you to."

"Aren't they?" he asked, turning his head to look at me. "By wanting me to talk to him, aren't they asking me to forget about the blood on his hands?"

"No. You can't pretend as if nothing happened. That's not possible. What you have to find is acceptance. You know what happened. He knows what happened. You can't change the past, but you're being given an opportunity here." My throat tightened, and I barely managed to choke out the last line, "A second chance."

"What if I don't want a second chance?"

"That's a decision you have to make, I guess. But look down the road—five, ten, twenty years—will you regret never getting to know your father?"

I waited for him to answer. The sound of the waves crashing onto the shore was the only music for our moment.

"If even an infinitesimally small part of you considers that could be the case, then I believe you have your answer."

Grant stuffed both of his hands in his pockets and swished his feet around in the water.

"And what if everything you think you know about him is a lie? What if he's really put all this effort into changing for the better, and you let the opportunity to get to know a changed man slip by? It's been a long time since you've seen him. If you can change as much as you have in the past six months with me, it's not inconceivable to think he's changed in thirteen years."

"Okay, I get it. I get it."

He held his hand out, and I gently placed mine in his. He walked out of the water toward me. His mouth dropped down onto mine as if he were trying to make sure I was still real. It was hypnotizing and could easily sidetrack our conversation.

"So, what are you going to do?" I asked after breaking away from him.

His eyes left mine as he contemplated my question. "Kiss you."

And he did.

It was full of love and fear and desire. The kiss said how much he appreciated me, and it said so much more than that. He wrapped our hands behind my back, crushing me against him. We could stand here all night, locked in this endless dance, but I knew he was stalling.

Finally, I breathlessly pulled away from him.

"Grant," I murmured.

"I don't know, Princess. I know I should say that I'll talk to him, but I can't say that right now. I held a gun and pointed it at his chest today, and it felt right, natural." He rested his forehead against mine and closed his eyes. "I won't know if I'll be able to move past that unless I talk to him, but a part of me doesn't want to see him as anything but a villain."

I didn't say anything. I couldn't fix this. I couldn't put it back together. No matter how hard I tried, no amount of pushing or prodding would get Grant to change his mind. He needed to see it in himself that this was something good for him.

It wouldn't happen tonight and probably not tomorrow or the day after either but maybe one day. And that was good enough for me right now.

The sound of footsteps trudging through the sand from the direction of the restaurant drew my attention. The light from the deck silhouetted the figure in the darkness, and I didn't recognize who it was until she was practically on top of us.

"There you fuckers are!" Sydney said.

"Syd," Grant said, cracking his first smile of the evening. "What the fuck are you wearing?"

That was a valid question. She was in hot-pink string bikini bottoms and a sheer crop top over a black bra. Her dark hair was long and wild and free in a way I could never, ever pull off.

"I came from a pool party with some guys from high school."

"Do I even want to know?"

"How many guys I blew?" she asked, giggling. "No, probably not."

Sometimes, I swore, Sydney said these kinds of things for shock factor.

"Dad said *y'all* were down here and sent me to check on you," she said, slipping into some kind of fake twang at the use of the Southern word.

Grant cringed at the reminder of his uncle, and I reached for his hand to comfort him.

"Fuck. What's going on? What did I miss?" she asked.

I looked at Grant to see if it was okay to tell her, but he launched right into the whole story from start to finish. Sydney's mouth dropped open about halfway through, and it was one of the few times I'd ever seen her actually look shocked. Normally, she just looked pouty in a sexual way or smug or seductive. It was as if she was always trying to appear a certain way. I had no clue if that was natural for her. I'd never been a relentless flirt...or a whore—a title that she didn't even seem to mind.

"Fuck, cuz," Sydney said. "You're such a badass! But a total fucking idiot. Don't try to shoot Ari again. I kind of like her."

Grant laughed softly. "Don't worry. I kind of like her, too."

"So…are you going to talk to him then? Because…I don't think I've ever met my uncle."

Grant looked uncomfortable and glanced away. "I don't know."

"Well, if you decide to do it, I'll go with you, if you want." Sydney suddenly got very serious for the first time since I'd met her. "I know how beat up you are about this, but you have people here who love you. I love you. Aribel loves you. Your family and the guys love you. We'll be here through this…if you let us."

Grant wrapped his other arm around Sydney's shoulder and squeezed. "Thanks. I don't know what the fuck I'd be doing right now without you two."

Sydney laughed. "You'd be acting like even more of an idiot—obviously."

"Obviously," Grant agreed.

Then, the three of us stood around, staring out at the black ocean set against the night sky and the spattering of stars overhead. There, in that moment, I felt something blooming in Grant, something I was sure he hadn't felt in a long time. I could feel it wrapping itself around us all, knitting us together.

Hope.

Light filtered in through the blinds, casting a hazy morning glow on the room. I yawned and pulled Ari harder against my chest. My eyes peeled open, and I stared around the room in confusion—pullout couch, scratchy plaid sheets, musty homey office cluttered with paperwork. I'd forgotten that Ari and I had ended up staying at my uncle's place instead of returning home.

The weight of the day before crashed down on me all over again, and I felt suspended in this fucking limbo. If I woke up, I'd have to face the fact that my father was out of prison, had received treatment, and was now trying to live a decent life...trying to live a life with me in it. If I went back to sleep, I could forgo having to deal with everything and continue on as before.

Just a few more minutes.

A few more fucking blissful minutes with my girl, alive and well, tucked in my arms. Nothing needed to change.

"Grant," Ari whispered softly, turning over to look at me. She placed her hand on my cheek and smiled something special just for me. Her blonde hair fanned out around her face with a halo around her head from the incoming light. She really looked like a princess.

"Yeah, darlin'?"

"I love you."

My heart constricted. I'd never fucking loved anyone as I loved Ari. No one had even come close. She was it for me—the be all, end all. And it was terrifying and fucking wonderful to look into her eyes and see the same thing reflected back at me.

"I love you, too."

"I wanted to say...I'm glad that you didn't try to shut me out yesterday," she whispered. "It used to be that way, you know? So, I'm happy that we were able to be together…that you didn't have to go through this alone."

I kissed the tip of her nose and squeezed her against me. "Me, too, Ari. Me, too."

We stayed like that for a while longer before deciding to get up. "I need to talk to my uncle again."

I'd been totally fucked up last night. While I wasn't feeling much better, some time had passed to cool my temper.

"I can come with you," she said. She trailed her hands down my palm as I got out of bed.

I kissed the soft skin of her wrist and stared down at her. "I take you with me wherever I go."

A smile lit up her face, the same smile that lit up my life.

After throwing on the shorts and T-shirt my uncle had let me borrow the night before, I trudged out of the room and into the kitchen. My aunt and uncle sat around the table with the newspaper opened and cups of coffee in front of them. I poured myself a cup, added cream and sugar, and then took the vacant seat between them.

"Good morning," Randy said.

"Good to have you in the house, honey," my aunt said.

I leaned over and kissed my aunt on the cheek. "You know, I appreciate what you guys did by taking me in when I was little. I was alone. I didn't have anywhere to go, and you were there. You raised me." I stared down at my coffee. "I just wanted to say thanks."

"You don't have to thank us," my aunt said. "We love you, Grant. We were happy to take care of you. You were never a burden."

I laughed softly. "I doubt that. I was a little shit."

"You had it tough," Randy said. "But that didn't mean we loved you any less. And we want you to know that we'll respect your decision about your father…no matter what you decide."

I took a sip of my coffee. After all the shit that had gone down yesterday, knowing people who cared about me were still out there was a good feeling. I didn't know what the fuck I was going to do about my dad, but at least people would be there if I needed them.

"I think I need some time to think about all this."

"That's understandable," my uncle said. "It's a lot to think about. Take as much time as you need. We'll be here if you need us."

We finished off our coffees in silence.

Ari and Sydney woke up and joined us sometime later. My aunt and uncle busied themselves in the kitchen, making us a big breakfast before we got on the road. Somehow, in the midst of it all, Sydney had weaseled her way into coming back to Princeton with us. I didn't even try to fight her on it. It'd be nice to have her crazy ass around even if she always caused more trouble than she was worth.

When breakfast was over, we got back on the road. My brain wouldn't shut down as I thought about the last fucked-up twenty-four hours of my life. Ari seemed particularly quiet. I was glad to have Sydney around to fill the silence with her constant chatter.

When we finally made it back to my place, I took a deep breath as I put the car in park. I hadn't realized how fucking messed up I'd been in the car, wondering if my dad would still be here. I hadn't known what I would fucking do if that were the case. But my dad wasn't here. There was no sign of him, except for the bullet hole in my living room. I was sure I was going to have to explain that to the guys, and I was *not* looking forward to that conversation.

Sydney hopped out of the truck, and instead of heading for my house, she marched straight over to the neighboring building. I shook my head when Miller answered the door with shock written all over his face. The man had his work cut out for him with that one.

I walked to my house when I realized Ari wasn't with me. "You coming?" I asked.

She chewed on her bottom lip and shook her head. Fear prickled through my nerve endings.

What the fuck? I thought we were okay. I thought everything was okay.

I knew she had been quiet on the drive over here, but I hadn't thought it was anything serious.

"What's going on, Ari? Is this about my dad? Is it about the gun?"

"Oh, Grant, no." She walked over to me and placed her hands on my chest. "I just…need to take care of some things."

"What things?"

"Things I've been neglecting. I think seeing everything that happened with your dad and being surrounded by your family who loves you *so* much…I don't know. It made me realize that maybe I'm missing something in that department, too. Need to make my own amends. You know?"

I smiled. "I think that's a good idea."

"You do?"

"Yeah, Princess. Not everyone has my fucking baggage. Your family might have treated me like shit, but they're still your family."

She sighed heavily. "That's a relief. But…there's something else."

"What?"

"I can't go on tour with you this summer with The Drift," she said in a hurry. "I'm going to accept a job working in a lab with one of my professors."

My mouth opened, and then I closed it. I knew I'd told her I wanted her to come on tour with me before, and I did want her there. But…a rock tour was no place for someone like Ari. Working in a lab was exactly the place for her.

"That's great, Ari. I didn't expect you to drop everything to come on tour with me."

"Oh."

"I want you there! I do, but you have school. You're so brilliant, babe. Someone like you needs to make something of yourself. You're going to cure cancer and fucking save the world."

"Oh, Grant," she said in that adorable way she always said my name.

"I don't want you giving up any of your dreams for me. I'm still going to be here. I was gone for two months, and we were fine. We'll make it," I told her. Then, I punctuated it with a kiss.

"You're right." She leaned in for another kiss. "Are you going to be okay if I leave right now?"

"I'm fine. I'm not a delicate little flower," I joked. "I need to fill the guys in anyway."

She nodded, we kissed, and then she was gone. I watched her drive away in her BMW. My chest fucking ached as I watched her leave. I wanted her here. She was as much my life raft now as the day when I had written that song about her all those months ago.

Then, it hit me—what I'd been missing in my new song all along.

I dashed into the house, grabbed my notepad, and scribbled down the lyrics and melody that had been evading me all during the tour. Everything crystallized, and by the time rehearsal came around, I had our new song polished and ready to go.

A couple of hours later, I walked into the garage to find Miller, McAvoy, Vin, and Sydney waiting for me with giant fucking smiles on their faces. "What did I miss?"

"Just got off the phone with Hollis," Miller said. "We start recording in L.A. in a month."

My eyes bulged. "What? A month! Shit! That's...fuck!"

"Yeah, it's the shit!" Vin cried.

"He wants all our new material, none of the stuff that's on our EP, except for 'Life Raft.'"

"All new?" McAvoy asked warily. "Do we have enough new shit for an album?"

"We have to make it work," Miller said.

I slapped the papers down on the table in front of them, looked around the room at my brothers, and said, "Well then, let's get to work."

The coward in me went to talk to my professor before calling my parents. I wanted to have good news for them once I finally got them on the phone. I'd been putting off speaking with them since they had met Grant almost three weeks ago.

The silence between us had been unnerving. I'd never been lovey-dovey with my parents, but we had always been kind of close. I'd check in with them. They'd check in with me. I hadn't realized how empty it all felt until I walked into Grant's uncle's kitchen to see a loving family sitting over coffee in the morning.

I missed my parents.

I missed Aaron.

Maybe they wouldn't come around right away, but maybe they would one day.

"I can't wait to start," I told my professor a short while later.

He was enthusiastic to have free help for the summer. I was excited to get into some real lab work. It would boost my resume and possibly open doors later on down the road. At this point, the possibilities seemed endless.

"Thank you for stopping by, Miss Graham. I'll see you in the lab Monday at eight a.m."

"Sounds great. Thank you again!" I said before walking out of the office.

On Monday, I'd start training with the project he was working on and all the procedures and tests I'd be running all summer. I stuffed my copy of the university summer internship paperwork, which guaranteed I'd get class credit for my work, in my bag and exited the chemistry building.

Stopping at a bench on the mostly empty campus, I pulled out my cell phone, pushed down all the fears that had clouded my mind the last two days, and called my father. After five or six rings, I was sure he wasn't going to answer.

Then, the line picked up, and my father's deep baritone came through the line, "Hello, Aribel."

"Hi, Dad," I whispered.

He gave me no indication as to what he was thinking, so I dived in, "How are you and Mom and Aaron?"

"We're fine, Aribel. Is there a reason you called?"

Ah. There it was—the reason I was so blunt. *Like father, like daughter.*

"I've had a rough couple of days and wanted to talk to my dad. Is that not acceptable anymore?"

"Did you break up with your boyfriend?"

"No. In fact, we're better than ever. When are you going to get over that? I was calling because I was with his family and realized how much they loved and cared for each other. It made me miss you guys. I want things to get back to normal, but I can't tolerate you being so derogatory toward Grant."

After a short pause, my father responded, "Okay. Tell me about him because the man I met is not fit for my daughter."

I sighed. "He's sweet, Daddy. He cares about me. Ever since we've been together, he's wanted to better himself—not just for me, but also for himself. He had a job at a recording studio, but then a big label signed his band, and he's been on tour. I don't know what you want me to say. He makes me *feel.* Do you know what I mean? That I feel alive?"

"It sounds like childish frivolity to me."

All I wanted to do was bang my head against the bench. *How could I get through to him?*

"Before Grant, I wasn't happy, Dad. I dated guys who I didn't care about because I thought they were the kind of people I was supposed to date. They were the people you'd raised me to find worth in. When Grant pursued me, I couldn't see past his flaws. Rock band? Bad. No college?

Worse. Thought he could get someone like me without even trying? Laughable."

I smiled at the memories and how much I'd changed.

"Then, I got to know Grant. I got to see how fiercely he loves his family and protects his friends, how eager he is to succeed, and how much he was trying to get to know *me*—not the me who drives a BMW and has a CEO for a father. You'd raised me to see the good in people, Dad, but you didn't mean people like Grant. You didn't mean someone who could corrupt your baby…who couldn't take care of me. That's your problem, not mine."

"What are you trying to say, Aribel?"

"I'm saying that I don't need to be taken of. I'm a smart, independent woman. You raised me to be that way, and now, you seem frustrated when I've chosen my own path. I don't want the people you've been introducing me to. I want Grant, and all I'm asking is for you to give him a chance. I don't expect things to change overnight, but he's not who you think he is."

My father sighed. I could practically see him pressing two fingers to his temple and leaning forward at his desk.

"You know I want you to be happy, Aribel. I want someone who is worthy of the strong woman your mother and I raised you to be."

"He is. Grant is." I sounded breathless. "Plus, I've been doing good things with my life, so it's not as if he's changed who I am. I got straight As in my classes this semester, and my organic chemistry professor offered me an internship position, working in his lab for the summer."

"Now, that is what I like to hear. When do you start?"

"Monday. It's unpaid, but it's a foot in the door."

"It's all about who you know and how hard you work."

"You're right," I agreed easily. Then, I immediately switched back to the original subject. "So, about Grant…"

He sighed heavily again. "I don't want to create a wedge between us."

"Then, don't let it," I urged.

"Okay, fine. Your mother and I will discuss it, and we'll find a time to come down and have a proper meeting with the young man. Is his band still touring? When would be convenient?"

"Oh my God!" I cried. I'd never expected my dad to agree. It wasn't a statement that said he was okay with me dating Grant, but it was a step in the right direction. "No. No, he's not on tour right now. Anytime is good. I can double-check with him, but whenever you're free should be fine."

We chatted for a few minutes after that before he had to get off the phone to get back to work. I knew that everything wasn't fixed. I knew that my father still likely saw this whole thing as a phase, something I'd get over. But I knew better. Eventually, he'd see it, too.

I'd made it halfway back to Grant's house when I received an incoming call from him. "Hey! I'm on my way back to you."

"You'll never guess what happened!"

"What?" I asked.

"Hollis called at the beginning of rehearsal. Within the month, we're leaving for L.A. to record our debut studio album!"

"Grant, that's amazing! Congratulations!"

"I had to call you and let you know. How did things go with your family?"

"Better than expected," I admitted. "My father is finding out when he and my mom can come down here to meet you again...try to get to know the real Grant McDermott."

"Princess, the real Grant McDermott would scare them shitless."

I cracked up. "You're ridiculous. A real charmer."

"That's fucking right. So, when are they coming to visit? We're planning another League show since we're back in town. Maybe they could come see the band? See that we're not some hooligans or whatever the fuck they probably think."

"Hooligans? Really?" I shook my head. "I'll find out when they'll be here, but hopefully, they can make a show. I think that's a great idea."

"I think you're a great idea. Hurry up and get your hot body over here, so we can celebrate."

I rushed over to Grant's house and let his tender kisses, wandering hands, and effortless lovemaking wash away the events of the last couple of days.

In his arms, I was home.

49 GRANT

Two and a half weeks later, I stared through the smudged glass window of The Coffee Bean at the mostly empty location. During the school year, the small coffee shop was jam-packed with students studying. I'd brought Ari here once when I was first pursuing her. I could see our booth from where I was standing.

A girl jostled me out of the way as she reached for the door. "*Excuse* me," she said in a way that made her sound like a rude bitch.

"Sure thing," I said sarcastically.

All I had to do was go inside.

Open the door.

Walk one foot in front of the other.

Sit down.

It was that simple yet that difficult.

Why had I agreed to do this?

All the confidence and fucking swagger in the world couldn't make me feel any better about the situation. But I couldn't go back now. It had been my decision after all. Everyone else might have agreed that it was in my best interest as they nudged me in the direction, but ultimately, I'd made the choice.

Taking a deep breath and reminding myself that I wasn't a fucking pussy, I opened the door to The Coffee Bean and walked toward a booth in the back of the shop where my dad was seated. When I reached the table, my father's head tilted up and looked at me.

"Grant," he said, surprised, as if he hadn't believed I'd actually show.

I plopped my ass down in the seat across from him, crossed my arms, and slouched backward. No fucking way was I letting my guard down through this exchange. I still didn't trust him. "Let's get this over with. I've got other shit to do."

The surprise on his face evaporated. No fucking lovey-dovey moments for me. I couldn't forget who this was just because we were having one conversation. I was willing to hear him out, but I didn't have to make it easy for him.

"Right. What are your plans?" he asked.

"Does it matter?"

"Just curious about your life, Grant."

"And you have a lot of time to make up for."

He clenched his jaw. "I do. You're right." His whole face slackened, and he took a shuddering breath. "I have a lot more to make up for than time, too. I...I want you to know that I am *so* sorry about everything that happened." He swallowed, his Adam's apple bobbing in his throat. "That night with your mother should never have happened. I take full responsibility for my actions, but it should never have happened. You were way too young to witness something so traumatizing."

I turned my head away from his words. They hit so close to home. It was the exact thing I'd been pushing away my entire life. They were the same words Ari had said to me the night she had found out what happened.

"I loved her so much, Grant. She was too young to die. She should have been here to raise you." My father covered his eyes with his hand and took a deep breath. "I'm sorry. God, I can't even get this all out. I want to apologize the right way. I know I don't know what you went through afterward, but I know that I was depressed beyond belief. I was so guilt-ridden. I contemplated killing myself. It felt easier than dealing with the pain."

"Really?" I asked, surprised despite myself.

"Yes. It was rock-bottom for me. It's what made me decide to go to therapy. After what I'd done, I knew I couldn't leave you all alone without either parent. So, I want you to know I'll be here, trying to make it up to you, for as long as you'll let me."

"Yeah," I said, reeling slightly from the stark apology. "So, what exactly is this? What do you want from me?"

"What do I want from you? Grant, I'm your father. I want to get to know you. Is that so hard to believe?"

It actually was. *How could the person who had said and done such horrible things think one heartfelt apology and getting to know me would change anything?* That wasn't fucking reality.

Then, Ari's words from the first day when I'd seen my dad nagged at me.

"If you can change as much as you have in the past six months with me, it's not inconceivable to think he's changed in thirteen years."

Fine, Ari. Fine.

"It is hard for me to believe. The last time we spoke before you went to prison, you said you were going to get me for what I did to you," I finally said.

"I...I never said that," he said. His eyes suddenly looked confused and unfocused.

"Yes, you did. I've been thinking about that moment every day for thirteen years. I didn't suddenly make up what you said."

My father shook his head and closed his eyes. "I don't...I don't remember saying anything like that. Is that what made you think I was going to harm you when I came to your house?"

I nodded. I couldn't believe what he was saying. *He couldn't remember threatening my life?*

"My God," he said, covering his mouth. "I've spent the last thirteen years trying to do everything I can to better myself and get out to see you, and you've spent them thinking I was going to kill you at the first opportunity."

"What was I supposed to think?" I asked. Suddenly, I was more frustrated than ever. All this time, I'd had to deal with the guilt and pain on my own. Now, my father was saying that all of it was fucking pointless. "You never tried to contact me. You never apologized or tried to explain."

"You're right. I am guilty of that."

And he looked guilty—his head hung low to his chest, his mouth drawn, his shoulders sagged.

"I wrote you letters in prison. But I couldn't send them. For a long time, I thought I wasn't good enough to be a father for you. Randy was taking care of you. You deserved the best, but I was too messed up to be that for you. Hell, I'm still not anywhere close. But it made me try harder. My therapist said I should send them to you once I'd made sufficient progress, but by then, it felt...too late. It wasn't until I knew I was getting released early that I managed some semblance of hope for the first time."

I turned my face away from my father and stared out through the coffee shop window. Because of everything I'd endured, I hated to think anything he was saying made sense. But in his words, I recognized how much he despised himself, and I heard the hope just as easily.

"So, where do we go from here?" I finally asked.

"Honestly, it is completely up to you. My therapist suggested I leave the ball in your court. You know I want to get to know you, and I know we won't suddenly become father and son again overnight. I'd be happy to come and have coffee with you here when you have some spare time."

"That's it? Just coffee?"

"I do have a small request if you're up for it."

I narrowed my eyes. *Here it was.* "What?"

"This might sound crazy for you, but I'd really like you to come to therapy with me sometime."

"Therapy?" I asked incredulously. I didn't need fucking therapy. I didn't need to talk to some quack about my problems. Just because it supposedly worked for my dad didn't mean it would work for me.

He barked a short laugh. "That was my exact reaction when it was first suggested to me."

I glared back at him. That was not what I'd wanted to hear.

"I want us to get to know each other. I want us to be able to remember the past, confront the past, and also move on from the past. I can't fix our problems though. I'm no professional, and our issues are too deeply ingrained in both of us." He shrugged his shoulders. "Once I finally admitted I needed help, I found help. You might find it, too. My therapist was the one who pushed me to reach out to you in the first place."

"I don't *need* help," I muttered.

"Grant, you saw something terribly traumatic because of what I did. I think you know you should go."

My father sat back in his chair and waited. He didn't say anything else. He just looked at me. It was pretty clear to anyone around that we were related—same facial shape, same dark hair, same brown eyes.

If only there were something else between us that was similar…then maybe we could reconnect.

Did I even want to search for that something?

Was there a thread that inherently connected us somehow?

Despite all the years apart, the jail time, the gun I'd pulled on him, I knew the look he was giving me was one of disappointment…and I hated disappointing him. It was ingrained in me.

Fuck! No! I was not going to fucking therapy. *So fucking stupid.*

"I can't do therapy."

"Okay, Grant," he said, resigned. "Well, I'm glad that we're talking again. That's a step."

It was.

I stared down at my hands and tried not to think about all the emotions rushing at me head-on. I was sitting here, talking with my father. He had apologized for what had happened. He still loved me and wanted to get to know me.

The reason I was sitting here right now was because some part of me knew that if I hadn't at least tried, I'd regret it. One day, my dad would be dead—just like my mom. One day, he wouldn't come back into my life. He'd be gone forever. *Then, what?*

Then, I would be fucked for the rest of my life—again. *No mother, no father.* And as much as I loved the rest of my family, my brothers, Ari, it would be different. I had this man's blood. He was the only parent I had left. I didn't live for regrets.

I sighed heavily. I couldn't believe I was doing this. "Okay."

"Okay?" he asked.

"I'll try it out—on one condition."

His face lit up. "Anything! Of course."

"You try my therapy."

His eyebrows rose questioningly. "What do you mean?"

"The one thing that always had my back, that always listened, that always made everything better while I was all alone was my music." I glanced away from him and then back. "My band has a show this weekend…I don't know if you…you know…want to come?"

He beamed at the invitation. "I'll be there. I wouldn't miss it for the world."

"Okay. Well then, I guess we'll figure out the other stuff later."

I glanced down at the time on my cell phone. I couldn't believe nearly an hour had passed. The time had flown by. But I needed to get out of here. It was too much all at one time.

"I'm going to head out now, but, uh…I'll see you Saturday at The Ivy League."

We both stood. My father stuck his hand out at me, and I slowly placed mine in his. We shook hands. Tears welled in my father's eyes. I wanted to look away, but I couldn't. My own resolve was weakening.

"Thank you for giving me this chance, son."

"Thanks for proving that you deserve it."

"I have a surprise for you," Grant whispered in my ear as we stood backstage.

"What is it?"

His nose trailed down the soft contours of my neck, making my skin break out into goose bumps. His lips landed on my shoulder as his fingers made a line up the waist of my light-pink sundress.

"It's not a surprise if I tell you, Princess."

"It's a tiara, isn't it? You've finally realized that I need a tiara with this whole princess routine."

He laughed and nipped at my skin. "Cheeky tonight, aren't we?"

"Every night." I turned around and wrapped my arms around his neck. "So, what is it?"

"Later. It'll come in parts throughout the night."

"Parts?" My eyebrows rose. "This sounds complicated."

"Well, part of it just walked through the door," he said, pointing through the open stage door that led out into the audience.

My eyes searched through the sea of people already out there until I saw where he was pointing. My mouth dropped open and I gasped. "Are those my parents?"

"Yep."

"Oh my God! And Aaron and Sarah?"

"Yep!" he said, sounding smug.

"They said they couldn't come down for the show this weekend!" I cried.

"Aaron got a hold of me to keep it a surprise."

"That's…that's amazing. Let's go say hi."

I grabbed Grant's arm and pulled him out through the excited crowd, heading straight to my parents, who stuck out like sore thumbs and looked uncomfortable as hell, even from a distance. My mother was in a square neck dress with a cardigan wrapped around her shoulders. My father was in a very expensive-looking Tom Ford suit. At least Aaron and his girlfriend, Sarah, were dressed more casually.

I threw my arms around Aaron. "I can't believe you guys made it!"

Grant shook hands with Aaron when I moved to hug my mom and dad.

"Hey, man."

Finally, I turned back to Sarah. She giggled and stretched her left hand out. On her ring finger was an enormous rock. My mouth dropped open for a second time, and then I was squealing and jumping up and down.

"You're engaged? Oh my God, I'm so happy for you. I'm so excited. Tell me everything. How did it happen? Where did it happen?"

Grant wrapped an arm around me and squeezed. "Maybe give them a chance to answer your questions."

"You're right. Wow. Just…wow. Congratulations! Both of you."

Sarah launched into all the details about the engagement, which had happened at a romantic dinner a couple of nights ago. They had been waiting to make an announcement because they wanted to tell me in person. Grant had been the catalyst behind keeping it a secret from me. And I was surprised and thrilled. It was good to see my brother settling down with Sarah and not gallivanting off with anyone else. It would definitely do him some good.

My parents were also pleased with the news, which was no surprise to me.

"It's going to be so glamorous. A big Boston wedding!" my mother said. She looked down at the grimy barstool and upturned her nose. She carefully slid the pad of her index finger over the surface and then examined it. She shuddered. "Anyway, I've already had an engagement announcement drafted and sent to the newspaper. It's going to be the event of the season."

I laughed at my mother's behavior but nodded. "It certainly is."

The news seemed to ease the discomfort that had occurred with my family, and even though my parents looked stuffy and uncomfortable, they carried on a conversation with Grant without snubbing him. It seemed like enough progress to me.

Almost too soon, Grant was kissing the top of my head and whispering my ear, "Time to go backstage. I'll see you after the show. I love you."

"I love you, too," I said.

My hand held on to his until he was too far away, and we had to let go. He gave me a mischievous smile before disappearing in the crowd.

"Jim, I'm going to need a drink." With disdain, my mother's eyes scanned the dive bar, but it was nice to at least see her here…trying.

"Of course, Diana."

"Vodka martini. Grey Goose." Then, she seemed to think better of it. "Do you think they even have Grey Goose?"

He shrugged his shoulders, and I tried to keep from laughing hysterically.

Only my mother.

"Well, I'm going to go to my normal spot. I'll see you all after the show? We can get dinner or drinks? Talk about the wedding some more?"

"Yes, of course, dear," my mother said. "We'll go somewhere…a bit classier, I hope?"

"Sure, Mom." I wrapped my arms around my father. "Thank you for giving him a chance."

"We love you, baby girl. We trust you to make the right decisions…even if we don't always agree with them."

"Thank you," I repeated before pulling away from my family and veering through the packed crowd.

I found the girls standing at the center of the pack, only about three rows back from the stage. Not speaking to each other, Shelby and Sydney were on opposite sides of Gabi and Cheyenne. Sydney didn't seem bothered in the slightest. While she was around, Miller didn't seem to realize how much Shelby cared for him. It was such a weird juggling act that no one had expected from Miller. He had turned into this accidental player, and I wasn't looking forward to the fallout when it all blew up.

At least for now, McAvoy and Gabi were back on. I didn't know how that was going to work out with the band going to L.A. for the summer, but Gabi seemed confident enough. She already had plans to visit. Cheyenne had sworn up and down that she and Vin weren't serious, but I saw her eyes sparkle when he walked onstage. Another mystery—someone actually liked Vin. It baffled me.

My eyes cut to the left, and I saw Kristin standing in the audience with a guy at her side. She smiled at me and waved. We hadn't hung out much since school ended because she had gone home for the summer, but it looked like she was back—at least for the night.

Then, it all came down to Grant and me.

He strutted onstage to an eruption of applause, cheers, and catcalls. He looked like a god in jeans and a button-up with the first two buttons undone and the sleeves rolled up. His hair was wild. His eyes were even wilder as they searched me out in the crowd.

Our gazes locked, and then I was lost.

He only had eyes for me.

The show was as incredible as ever, maybe even better.

I'd seen them twice on tour with The Drift, but being here at home had them in their element. Everyone knew the songs, and now, the band was even more comfortable in front of huge crowds. "White Hot" still made me blush. "Life Raft" still made me swoon. I was certain I would never stop swooning at the fact that Grant had written this amazing song just for me.

"We have one last song for you tonight," Grant said into the microphone after they'd finished "Life Raft."

"One more?" Cheyenne asked. "They've played everything I know."

I shrugged. "I don't know. Maybe something new?"

Intrigued, we both looked back up at the stage.

"I've been working on this song for a long time. It was missing something for so long, but now, I think it's perfect. So, you get this exclusive, Leaguers. This one is 'Take Me with You.'"

Everyone quieted as the intro music filtered through the speakers. It was a heady melody with a soft sound like "Life Raft."

Then, Grant sang his beautiful lyrics with his hypnotic voice,

I'm an arrow,
Aiming straight for your heart.
Pierce the skin, take you in.
It's tearing me apart.

Love-struck, dumbstruck,
Can't think without you close.
Can't even dream.
Give me another dose.

So, baby, I'll take you with me
Wherever I go.
Just promise you'll take me with you
Wherever you go.

I'll take you with me
Wherever I go.
If you take me with you
Wherever you go.

The words hit me hard as if he were actually shooting an arrow at me. Grant had obviously written songs about us before, but every time it happened, it felt so deeply personal, like he was exposing so much about us to the world.

I could remember lying in bed, stretching my arm out to him, as I'd tried to get him to stay, and he'd told me just that, "*I take you with me wherever I go.*"

My heart constricted as the lyrics sank in.

No matter where we were or what we were doing, I would always hold his heart...and he would always hold mine.

The split second between the end of our new song and the burst of applause that followed was like a slice of heaven. It was that moment where I was looking at Ari and only Ari…when I saw that she really understood. She knew what the song meant—that it was for us…that when I'd record this album or go back out on tour or wherever the fuck this crazy road would take me, she would still be there through it all.

I crooked my finger at her as the crowd roared its approval. Just like that first time, her friends pushed her forward through the mob, up the stairs, and into my arms. Then, I kissed her as if it was the last thing I was ever going to do.

The cheers rose up louder, and Ari giggled against my lips. She was embarrassed, but I was lost to her.

I straightened after our kiss, waved at the audience, and then followed the guys offstage. They were already bumping fists and congratulating each other on another successful performance. It was a bit surreal to be on such a small stage again, but it was better simply because of the kick-ass audience at home.

"I can't believe you wrote that for me," Ari whispered.

"Who said it was for you?"

She gave me a don't-mess-with-me look, and I laughed.

"You're right. I wrote it for you. What can I say? You inspire me."

"I bet she fucking does!" Vin yelled from across the room.

"Hey, asshole! Butt out of our fucking conversation!" I yelled back.

"I can't help it when you leave me so wide open."

"Bet you've never heard that before."

Miller and McAvoy cracked up.

"Come on," McAvoy said, punching Vin on the arm. "Let's go find the girls. Give them some privacy."

They were exiting when Miller stopped abruptly in the doorway. "Uh, Grant? There's someone here for you."

He warily looked over at us. And that was when I saw my dad walking through the backstage entrance. I'd told the guys what had happened with my dad. I'd completely fessed up to everything even though Miller had already known from the tour, but McAvoy and Vin hadn't. It was a load off my chest. But I hadn't even told Ari that I'd invited my dad to the show.

While I *had* invited him, for some reason, I hadn't exactly expected him to show. Maybe a part of me was trying to keep myself from being let down.

"It's okay, Miller. You guys can go."

Miller nodded his head and then ushered the other guys out of the backstage area. I stared at the distance between my father and me. I was uncertain how to bridge the gap…if I even wanted to.

So, he had showed. *So what?*

"I get what you mean now," my father said finally.

"About what?" I asked.

Ari squeezed my hand for reassurance.

"Music being your therapy. You…you were incredible."

"Oh."

"Thank you," Ari said. "He meant, thank you. And he is incredible."

His eyes flickered to Ari, and they crinkled at the corners when he smiled. "Good to see you again, Ari."

"You, too, Mr. McDermott."

"I hope you still plan to keep up your end of the deal," he said, addressing me again. "After that, I think I'm starting to understand you more, and I'd love for you to understand me like that."

I swallowed back the rising panic at the thought of going to therapy with my dad. *It was just fucking talking, right?* I could handle it at least once, and if it fucking sucked, then I'd never have to do it again.

"Yeah, I'll go," I finally said.

"Great," he said, genuinely happy. "I just...wanted to come backstage and say congratulations. I see why your band was picked up. You're all very talented. I'm looking forward to seeing more of y'all in the future."

"Thanks," I murmured.

"I wish I could stay, but I think it's time for me to get back to the house. I hope the two of you have a good night. Feel free to contact me anytime, Grant."

"Sure."

"Have a nice night," Ari said softly.

"Good night."

"You, too." I nodded my head at him, and then he turned and walked out the door.

"I can't believe he came to the show!" Ari gasped when he was gone.

"Well," I said, scratching the back of my head, "I invited him."

She playfully smacked me on the arm. "You did? Why didn't you tell me?"

I shrugged. "Didn't think he'd actually show."

"I'm glad he did."

"Oh, yeah? Why?"

"Because he obviously cares for you, Grant," Ari said as if it were the most obvious thing. "It's good to see you two interacting and making progress. It's already better since you talked."

"Yeah...it really is," I admitted.

Ari threw her arms around my neck and held me close. "I'm so proud of you for doing this."

I snaked my arm around her waist and breathed in her familiar scent. I kissed her neck once more. "You know, I have one more surprise for you."

317

"You do? Don't you think my parents and the song were enough?" she asked. But her eyes were alight, and she was excited about the possibility of another surprise.

"Never enough for you."

"All right. Well?"

I took a step back, smirked at her, and then slowly unbuttoned the long-sleeved button-up I had on. Her cheeks instantly turned a rosy pink at the gesture.

"Don't you think we should go to the back room if my surprise includes you getting naked?"

I laughed. "So, you want me naked, huh? Thinking about me fucking you?"

Now, her cheeks were bright red. "Grant!"

"So, yes?"

"Fine. Yes! Okay? Satisfied?"

I arched an eyebrow. "Not yet, Princess." Then, I winked.

"You're ridiculous."

I stripped out of my shirt and tossed it on a nearby table. "As much as I want to continue giving you a strip tease backstage, *this* is my surprise."

I held my left arm up and revealed the inside of my bicep. On the sensitive skin in that space, I'd had an arrow tattooed onto my flesh. All those months ago in the library, I had doodled it into my lyrics notebook while thinking about Ari. I'd been inspired by the lyrics I had written for Ari.

I'm an arrow, Aiming straight for your heart. Pierce the skin, take you in. It's tearing me apart.

And I was inspired by Ari herself, of course.

Her fingers traced the design, her mouth agape. "Is this…is this for me?" she whispered.

"A way for me to always take you with me."

Her gaze rose to mine, and then she smiled. "I want one."

My eyes widened into saucers. "A tattoo?"

"Yes. I want to take you with me, too."

"Are you sure? You know it's permanent, right?" I joked.

"I'm well aware. I know it's…crazy. But it feels right. Let's go."

I laughed at her enthusiasm. "I don't think anyplace is open right now, Princess."

She smiled, stretched onto the tips of her toes, and kissed me. "Then, tomorrow."

"Okay," I murmured against her mouth. "Anything you want."

"Anything?"

I nodded, and then she dragged me to the back room.

We kicked the door closed behind us, and I couldn't help reveling in this beautiful woman who had utterly stolen my heart. We'd been so worried about our parents and the tour and her school and every other thing that could get in the way. But it was clear to me that we hadn't only survived. We had flourished.

And as she stripped me out of my clothing and brought her lips back to mine, I knew she was it.

There was no turning back.

"So…how much is this going to hurt?" I asked.

I was seated in the chair in the back room of the tattoo parlor, staring up at a man completely covered in tattoos from head to toe. I swallowed hard at the realization of what I was doing. It had taken me two weeks to actually find time to go, what with my parents here and then the new job.

Grant leaned back against the doorframe and smirked at me. He was loving this.

"It shouldn't be too bad," the guy said.

He was opening a package of needles in front of me. My heart rate spiked. I wasn't even afraid of needles.

Get it together!

He filled a small vial with black ink and then set it out next to the needles. Earlier, he had redrawn the arrow on Grant's arm into a daintier, smaller version for me. I'd decided to put it in the same place on my arm as Grant's. I didn't want it to be particularly visible in a normal everyday atmosphere, and I also needed it somewhere easy to cover up when I got a job. Plus, I liked the thought of both of us having the tattoo in the same place.

My eyes cut to Grant, and he laughed.

"You're going to be fine, Princess."

"If it hurts, we can take a break," the guy said reassuringly.

He adjusted my arm on the chair, placed the outline of the arrow on my skin, and got to work. I hissed at the first contact, but after a few minutes, adrenaline kicked in, and it didn't hurt too badly.

I wasn't sure how long I had been sitting there when the guy sat back and smiled. "All done."

"What? Really?" I gasped.

I was shocked that it hadn't actually taken that long. And now, it was over.

"Want to see?" he asked, producing a mirror.

He held it out in front of me, and I stared forward in shock. There, on my arm, was the cutest little arrow I'd ever seen. Grant's design was incredible.

My mouth hung open. "Oh my God."

"Is that a good *oh my God*?" Grant asked. He walked across the room and looked at it. He beamed down at me. "Ari, it looks fucking badass! Great job, man."

He bumped fists with the tattoo artist.

"Thanks."

"Hey, Princess. Say something. What are you thinking?"

I clamped my mouth shut when I realized it was still hanging open. "It's perfect."

Grant fished out his cell phone and took a picture of the tattoo before the tattoo artist slathered some ointment on it and wrapped it up to protect it. I listened to his careful instructions, Grant paid for it at the register, and then we left.

He took my right hand in his and brought it up to his lips. "How do you feel?"

"Relieved," I admitted.

"Really?"

I nodded. "I'd been putting it off, waiting for the perfect time, and now that it's completed, I'm glad. I shouldn't have waited. It feels right, having a little piece of you with me."

"Did you think when you'd met me at the League back in the fall, you'd be getting a tattoo with me?"

"Ha! Yeah, right. I thought that I would never speak to you again."

He poked me in the ribs. "But you kind of hoped that you would."

"Nope. No interest. I totally resisted the whole McDermott charm."

"Yeah. You really resisted," he drawled.

"I'm pretty sure I said no to you more times than you've ever heard it before."

"Well," he said, smirking at me, "I'd never heard it before you. So, technically, you win by default."

"One, you're such a whore, and two, I do *not* win anything by default!"

"Manwhore, Princess. I earned the title. Don't take it away from me," he said. His eyes sparkled in the afternoon sunlight.

"Sorry to break it to you, but I stole that title away from you a long time ago."

"Shh…don't let anyone hear you say that. Can't risk my reputation."

"Forgot to mention that I ran an ad in the paper about it. Sorry," I said, lifting one shoulder.

Grant grabbed me around the waist and swung me in a circle. "It's a good thing I love you, or I wouldn't put up with your smart mouth."

"You love my smart mouth," I murmured, standing on my tiptoes.

He kissed me full on the lips, drinking me in. It was like a match had been lit between us at the contact. My body ignited, and suddenly, the rest of the world slipped away. There was only here and now and this moment. Grant was everything and everywhere. Nothing else mattered. We had somehow found a perfect balance in our lives.

I never felt as if I had to give up my identity to be with Grant. It was more like we were two pieces from different worlds that managed to fit together despite the differences. My family was perfectly intact yet lacking in emotional support, which Grant not only provided to me, but also tried to bring out in my parents and brother. His family had completely fallen apart, and now, he was trying to figure out how to fit in a world where it was rebuilding. I'd been there for him through the hard times, and now, he and his father had started to go to therapy together. It had been shaky at first, but I knew in the long run, it would be worth it for him to try to have this relationship with his dad.

My fingers threaded up through his dark hair to try to bring him closer, but sooner than I could ever want, he pulled back. The look he gave me was one of complete adoration.

"What am I going to do when you leave tomorrow?" I asked softly.

ContraBand's time was up, and tomorrow, they would be leaving for Los Angeles to start recording their new album. They'd been hard at work, putting together new songs and trying to have enough new material for what Hollis wanted. I had faith that they would make it work, but the guys were a bit frantic.

"Probably masturbate a lot like I will."

I cracked up and nudged him in the ribs. "Oh my God, I can't take you anywhere."

"We both know you'll be fine, Ari. You'll be working in the lab and hanging out with the girls. Hopefully, you'll come to visit me. But even if you can't, I know we'll be okay. I'm your arrow, and you're my arrow." He touched the tattoo on his arm. "There's no one else out there for me."

"I'll come visit," I insisted.

He smirked. "You'd better."

Then, we were kissing again, and the world was right.

Neither of us knew what tomorrow would bring. All that we did know was, we would take the journey together.

THE END

Acknowledgments

Writing a book doesn't happen in a vacuum. So many people give up their time to read, edit, rewrite, brainstorm, critique, promote, and so much more to make this book a reality! I can't thank everyone enough who has been there to make this second book, which was much harder to write than the first, come to fruition.

My CPs—Jessica Carnes, Bridget Peoples, Rebecca Kimmerling!

My betas—Lori Francis and Katie Ross.

The early readers—Katie Miller, Amy McAvoy, Trish Brinkley, Jessica Sotelo.

The groupie sluts—Tammi Ahmed, Christy Baldwin, Michelle New, Christy Peckham, Stephanie Powell, Katie Stankiewicz, Reanell Tisdale, Brook T!

My fearless blogger friend who kept me on task and planned everything—Christine Estevez of Shh Mom's Reading.

My author friends—Jenn Sterling, Gail McHugh, Jamie McGuire, Jillian Dodd, Laurelin Paige, Lauren Blakely.

The best editor and formatter out there—Jovana Shirley of Unforeseen Editing.

My incredible cover designer—Najla Qamber.

Nancy, who cheered me on the whole time I was writing.

All the blogs and readers who participated in the cover reveal, release blitz, blog tour, and release party.

Any and all of you who purchased this book, wrote reviews, or told your friends. Thank you!

Of course, my friend, Ryan Williamson for comedic relief, a good deal of Vin's more ridiculous lines, and his personal experience.

As always, the love of *my* life, Joel, as well as our two puppies, Riker and Lucy.

About The Author

USA Today bestselling author K.A. Linde has written the Avoiding series, the Record series, and the Take Me series as well as her new adult standalone *Following Me.* She grew up as a military brat traveling the United States and Australia. While studying political science and philosophy at the University of Georgia, she founded the Georgia Dance Team, which she still coaches. Post-graduation, she served as the campus campaign director for the 2012 presidential campaign at the University of North Carolina at Chapel Hill.

An avid traveler, reader, and bargain hunter, K.A. lives in Athens, Georgia, with her fiancé and two puppies, Riker and Lucy.

K.A. Linde loves to hear from her readers! Feel free to contact her here:

kalinde45@gmail.com

www.kalinde.com

www.facebook.com/authorkalinde

http://www.pinterest.com/authorkalinde/

http://twitter.com/AuthorKALinde

http://instagram.com/authorkalinde